TOMB
OF THE
UNKNOWN
RACIST

TOMB
OF THE
UNKNOWN
RACIST

A NOVEL

BLANCHE McCRARY BOYD

COUNTERPOINT
Berkeley, California

Tomb of the Unknown Racist

Library of Congress Cataloging-in-Publication Data
Names: Boyd, Blanche M., 1945– author.
Title: Tomb of the unknown racist : a novel / Blanche McCrary Boyd.
Description: Berkeley, CA : Counterpoint Press, [2018]
Identifiers: LCCN 2017052537 | ISBN 9781640090675 (hardcover)
Subjects: LCSH: White supremacy movements—United States—Fiction. | United
    States—Race relations—Fiction. | Brothers and sisters—Fiction. | Family
    secrets—Fiction. | Domestic fiction.
Classification: LCC PS3552.O8775 T66 2018 | DDC 813/.54—dc23
LC record available at https://lccn.loc.gov/2017052537

Jacket designed by Nicole Caputo
Book designed by Jordan Koluch

COUNTERPOINT
2560 Ninth Street, Suite 318
Berkeley, CA 94710
www.counterpointpress.com

Printed in the United States of America
Distributed by Publishers Group West

10 9 8 7 6 5 4 3 2 1

For Leslie, James, and Julia, who gave me a new life

TOMB
OF THE
UNKNOWN
RACIST

FACTS

1. *The Silent Brotherhood, also called the Order, was a white supremacist terrorist organization reportedly destroyed by the FBI after a shootout and fire in 1984.*

2. *Robert Mathews, cofounder and leader of the Silent Brotherhood, was the only person actually killed in that confrontation. Other members were arrested.*

3. *Alan Berg was a Jewish radio shock jock in Denver who was assassinated by the Silent Brotherhood on June 18, 1984.*

4. The Turner Diaries *(1978) is an apocalyptic novel recounting a future white takeover of the world by a group called the Order. It predicts the extermination of all nonwhites, Jews, and homosexuals. William Luther Pierce, a white supremacist leader and theorist, wrote* The Turner Diaries *and its "prequel,"* Hunter, *under the pen name Andrew Macdonald. More than half a million copies of* The Turner Diaries *have been sold since its publication; it is highly valued by many white extremists, and some consider it a kind of revolutionary blueprint.*

5. *Timothy McVeigh, the ex-soldier who blew up the Alfred P. Murrah Federal Building in Oklahoma City on April 19, 1995, had pages*

of The Turner Diaries *in his car when he was arrested. These pages provided basic instructions for building a fertilizer bomb similar to the one McVeigh used.*

6. *A month after the Oklahoma City bombing, authorities discovered an unidentified leg in the rubble of the Murrah Building. The existence of this leg was not disclosed for at least another month, and it was later identified in variously contradictory ways.*

7. *A white supremacist compound continues to exist at Elohim City, Oklahoma. Timothy McVeigh phoned this compound several weeks prior to the bombing, asking to speak to a man named Andreas "Andy" Strassmeir, reportedly a German national with significant expertise in explosives; he and McVeigh had met at least once before. After the bombing, Strassmeir left the United States without being interviewed.*

8. *Kenneth Trentadue, a man who his lawyer brother believes was arrested because he looked like the sketches of John Doe #2, was said by authorities to have hanged himself in his jail cell. (John Doe #2 was the unknown man alleged to have accompanied McVeigh when he rented the Ryder truck used in the bombing.) An independent examination of Kenneth Trentadue's body revealed more than forty wounds and bruises as well as a cut throat; suicide seems an unlikely explanation.*

9. *According to the Southern Poverty Law Center, there were over one hundred armed militias in the United States by the year 2000. There are now over five hundred.*

PART I

The world is wrong. You can't put the past behind you. It's buried in you; it's turned your flesh into its own cupboard.
—Claudia Rankine, *Citizen: An American Lyric*

1

One spring evening in the year 1999 my mother and I were watching *Wheel of Fortune*, our matching rocker recliners locked into their forward positions so we could reach our fast-food burgers and fries, when a news bulletin interrupted the show: two young children had been kidnapped from a Native American reservation in New Mexico. The announcement was brief but *Wheel of Fortune* switched straight to commercial, and Momma had already guessed the puzzle: *Surrender to win*. Dark, shiny smudges marked her hamburger bun since she had painted blue eye shadow on her lips that morning. On the days I took care of her, I let her do whatever she wanted.

Later that evening, after I had arranged her in the great canopied bed with the white George Washington spread (she was wearing a cotton nightgown embossed with an image of Rudolph the Red-Nosed Reindeer) she whispered, "It was the *s* and the double *r* combination that gave it away."

"So how did you know the first word wasn't *serrated*?" *Serrated* had been my own guess.

Her dark eyes gleamed up at me, deep in their orbits. "Don't be silly, honey. That word only has two *r*'s, and there aren't enough letters." She called me "honey" whenever she couldn't remember my name.

Her hair was encased in a pair of white nylon underpants to preserve its shape. I had removed all of her makeup, including the lipstick on one eyelid. Either she had stopped with one eye because she sensed something was wrong or she simply got distracted.

Leaning back against her wedge of puffy pillows, she stared past me through the balcony's closed glass doors toward the lights of the Cooper River Bridge, glittering in the distance. Still fully clothed, I kicked off my hiking boots and settled on top of the covers on the other side of her bed so we could watch the eleven o'clock news together.

The kidnapping in New Mexico was the lead story. A brief video revealed a teary young woman identified as Ruby Redstone emerging through the doors of a hospital emergency room. She wore an ankle-length mauve skirt and a white blouse splashed with dried blood, almost like a matching decoration. Her straight black hair was pulled back, and a lemon-size patch of scalp above her forehead had been shaved and bandaged. She leaned intensely toward the camera. "I beg of you, whoever you are, let my children go unharmed!" She was riveting, although my view may have been altered by recognition. Despite her auburn skin, Asiatic eyes, and different last name, I knew immediately who she was.

"Momma," I whispered, "that's our Ruby, all grown up."

She reached over and patted my hand. "Don't be upset, honey. Don't you worry." In my mother's lovely present, distress was rarely permitted.

"I'm not upset," I lied. I hadn't seen my brother, Royce, since his daughter was a baby, but this young woman had the curve of my shoulders, her mouth resembled mine, and her hands were bewilderingly familiar. I was too stunned by our physical similarities—and her sudden reemergence in our lives—to respond.

In the early 1980s, Royce had vanished into the white supremacist underworld, sought by the FBI as a possible member of a terrorist organization called the Silent Brotherhood, or the Order. Unsuccessful in apprehending him, the FBI could not find his Vietnamese lover and their six-year-old child either, although it was assumed that Santane and Ruby were hiding *from* Royce, not *with* him. When the private detective I'd hired did not locate them either, I let the situation drop, because why would Santane have trusted me? The child, though . . . I had fretted a great deal about the child.

The one time I visited them, Royce and Santane and their baby were living peacefully in a cabin in Mendocino, California. In that phase of his life, my brother was presenting as a gentle faux Buddhist nurturing his budding family while he wrote his novel, *The Burning Chest*, using pencils on lined paper. In the evenings, their cabin was lighted with oil lamps because Royce eschewed electricity. Before I departed, he took me outside to confide, his face tight with emotion, that he had named their daughter after the old black woman who had cared for us as children. But not long after his novel was published to high critical praise, Royce suddenly abandoned Santane and Ruby and plunged headlong into the maw of white extremism. It was as if another man had been coiled inside him and sprang forth, full-blown and monstrous.

Because of his novel's critical success, Royce's conversion invited attention. In an underground newsletter, he began writing what he deemed "position papers." A canny writer at the *Village Voice* discovered them and produced a front-page piece titled "The Disintegration of Royce Burns" chronicling the rise of white extremist groups, especially the Silent Brotherhood, and my brother's possible connection. The Brotherhood had successfully counterfeited twenty-dollar bills, robbed a Brink's truck of several million dollars, and assassinated Alan Berg, a Denver radio host who had mocked and baited them. Berg, being Jewish, had been deemed a significant part of ZOG, the Zionist conspiracy they believed was secretly controlling the world. Berg was shot in his driveway while peacefully unloading his groceries.

I doubted this purported connection between my brother and the Silent Brotherhood because through his position papers I knew of their "theoretical disagreements." In "Position 4," Royce insisted that Hitler's crucial mistake was, in fact, his anti-Semitism and that Jews were an essential element of the coming white revolution. Royce, therefore, would have viewed the killing of Alan Berg as a disastrous mistake.

In 1984, the FBI successfully trapped half a dozen members of the Silent Brotherhood, including its leader, in a "safe house" on Whidbey Island in Washington State. A shoot-out took place, during which an incendiary grenade set the house ablaze. The group's founder and leader, Robert Mathews, chose to remain inside while the house burned to the ground. Most other members surrendered or were captured, and the FBI proclaimed the Silent Brotherhood effectively disabled. Then, in 1986, a full two years after the shoot-out, the FBI notified us that the remains of another body had been detected in the Brotherhood fire. My brother's identification, we were told with what might have been a whiff of pride, involved one of the earliest uses of DNA for such a purpose.

The box containing Royce's remains troubled me, of course—it's hard to believe in anyone's death without visual proof—but we buried what they sent us in a child-size coffin. Our mother, still cogent and witty at that point, had remarked, through her grief, "Well, I do remember him best when he was small." When I replied, "I guess he'll always be my little brother," she even tried to smile.

The next morning Momma and I watched the news on the TV in her condo's kitchen while she ate Cheerios with sliced bananas and milk, a ritual she had been clinging to since my childhood. National media were quickly assembling some details of Ruby Redstone's background, mainly the fact that her father had been the novelist-turned-terrorist, my own brother, Royce Burns.

According to news reports, Ruby Redstone's husband, a full-blooded Nogalu Native named Lightman Redstone, had come home from work the previous evening to find his wife unconscious and bound with silver duct tape, a strip of skull exposed from a freely bleeding wound, a hammer on the floor beside her. Their children were nowhere to be found. The car, with the child seats inside, remained in the gravel driveway.

The account that Ruby stumbled through with him and then with local and federal authorities was so outlandish it seemed convincing. White supremacists, she said, had come to her home looking for her lost father. They already knew about her mixed blood and had mocked her, but they were infuriated by the sight of the children—River, two, and Lucia, four—whose lineage, they said, had been entirely destroyed. Their leader was a tall, clean-shaven, narrowly built man who said her children were "the worst kind of mongrels, abominations, and sins against God." Ruby described how she had begged them not to take River and Lucia, who were innocent, but their leader had shouted, "No one is innocent in the land of Nod!" No, she did not know what the land of Nod was, but she thought the attack must involve some kind of blackmail plot against her father. She had never for one minute believed that her father was dead.

Even after I knew much more about what actually happened, I could not comprehend why Ruby would have wanted to bring my brother out of hiding. He was a dangerous, hate-filled man who had abandoned her. But, despite her dazzling lies, she soon dragged me out of the serene light of my mother's dementia and into the glare of dreadful public events, the kind I had so carefully learned to avoid.

2

I was standing in the guest bedroom packing a few clothes for my flight to New Mexico when my friend Estelle arrived on her lunch hour. Estelle wore her white nurse's uniform with her identification tags; she did not take off her dark glasses. Yes, of course she would manage my mother's care for me for a few days, and no, she would not answer the condo's phone unless I was calling, and yes, she would give similar orders to the other caretakers. "But, Ellen, why on earth are you rushing out there like this?"

"Tell the guards at the gatehouse that no one but the sitters can come in. Absolutely no reporters. Do your best to keep Momma inside."

She leaned against the doorjamb, removed her sunglasses, and watched me as I threw clothes into Momma's purple-flowered suitcase. "Well, I know you're upset if you're going anywhere carrying that bag."

I stopped what I was doing and tried to stare her down. "Estelle, goddamn it, she's my niece, and she looks like me. She's like some kind of weird doppelgänger."

Her gaze softened. "Well, she's twenty-four years old and half Vietnamese. But, yes, she does look a lot like you. I was startled by it."

I sat down on the bed, this one draped in an embossed Martha Washington spread, and Estelle sat down beside me, taking my favorite safari shirt out of my hands. I liked this shirt best because it had eight pockets instead of six. "Estelle, how can I possibly leave my brother's daughter in this situation? No matter who he was, or what he did . . ."

Estelle and I, both prodigal daughters who had returned to live in Charleston after being away for decades, had first met in Alcoholics Anonymous in Cambridge, Massachusetts. Although we were familiar with each other's recovery stories, we had always remained reticent on the subject of race: Estelle was African American and I was white. She knew my dead brother had been a prominent white supremacist and reportedly a terrorist, and I knew that her great-aunts had been among the heroic women who led the black women's hospital workers' strike that had paralyzed Charleston in the 1960s. But these events had occurred decades ago, and recovery in AA is personal, not political.

Estelle folded my shirt as if she were soothing it. "Why don't you take another day or two to think this through? Let the situation settle out a bit."

"I'll stay sober and go to meetings, Estelle, but here's the truth: I should have dealt with my brother's fucking disasters a long time ago. What could the AA slogan 'live and let live' possibly mean in a circumstance like this?"

After a silence, Estelle said, "If I were you, I wouldn't go near this situation until I knew a lot more."

"But I should have tried a lot harder to find his daughter when they disappeared."

Estelle and I had first been drawn together by our down-home Charlestonian cadences. Her skin was a coppery brown and I was pink with Scotch-Irish forebears, but we soon found ourselves having coffee together after AA meetings, laughing while we exaggerated our accents. In a ridiculous attempt at Gullah I once said, "I be goein ta get me summa dat choklit cek," and Estelle replied, "De choklit no good fo de skins." Otherwise, Estelle spoke what she called "power English," and my own accent had faded considerably. Still, within months of meeting, we began confessing our yawning nostalgias for the lazy rivers of the Low

Country, the smell of swaying marsh grasses, the unhurried politeness of Charleston natives. Yankees, we agreed, were born rude, and the traffic up here was just awful.

Estelle returned first; she had only been away for twenty years. She said she had always intended to go back home and start a clinic out on Johns Island, where her family lived, but as a pediatric nurse practitioner, she was surprised by the salary cut necessary to work at the Medical University in Charleston. When I returned a few months later, ostensibly to manage the care of my increasingly demented mother, Estelle was still living on her family's land. "It's fine out there. I don't like all the driving, but I do have my own little cabin. And it's good to be home. We catch shrimp and crabs right off our dock." Nevertheless, she seemed glad to spend a few nights every week at my mother's condo, whenever I needed personal time at the cottage I had rented at the beach on the Isle of Palms. Estelle let me pay her well and off the books, although only out of my mother's funds. Still, this was an ethically complex situation, augmented by our personal relationship. Yet we seemed comfortable with each other, and I think she liked my mother. I know she liked me.

After Estelle left, I finished packing, and an aide I trusted arrived carrying an overnight bag. I told Momma, who had little sense of time, that I was going to the grocery store, and then I took a cab to the airport.

From the airport I called ahead to the police station in Gallup, the town nearest to where the children had been kidnapped, and the chief, a man named Ed Blake, got on the phone. Yes, he certainly would like to have a private conversation with Royce Burns's sister.

"It can't be anybody except us," I said. "And it has to be off the record, at least for right now. Are you okay with that?" I was surprised that he agreed to those terms.

In Albuquerque, I rented a car and drove the hour eastward toward Gallup. Because of the time difference and long days, the afternoon light was still strong. I hadn't been to New Mexico in twenty years, but it had remained serenely beautiful. Not as beautiful as Charleston, maybe, but flat like Charleston, except for the mesas and mountains inscribing the horizon. The sky, larger and bluer because of the dry air, overhung a landscape of orange and ocher and streaks of purple. The colors here were crisper and brighter.

Ed Blake turned out to be a smart and surprisingly attractive man. His manner was genial, and his gray eyes, set deep in his weathered skin, appraised me with what might have been amusement. Although the sixties were long over, I still dressed as if I were on my way to a demonstration: black jeans or cargo pants, lots of pockets, boots, and dark tees with safari shirts or fishing shirts slung over them. Also, I carried a trout bag instead of a purse.

Only the badge clipped to the pocket of Blake's linen shirt revealed his official status. He wasn't even wearing a gun. I judged him to be early fifties, maybe a few years younger than me. No, he hadn't told anybody that I was coming to Gallup, although of course he would have to do that soon.

At first, he let me do the asking. He said he'd been police chief for less than a year, hired away from Bowling Green, Ohio, where his grown children still lived, although, he added gratuitously, his ex-wife did not. Before Ohio he had worked as a detective on several small-town police forces before settling down as chief in Bowling Green. In his twenties, he'd even been an FBI agent, before realizing he wanted to do something less complicated, less political. He liked Gallup, he liked New Mexico, and he thought he might stay put for a while.

I did not go near his use of the word *political*. "You were once in the FBI? A guy I went to college with became an agent, but he was a jock."

"I'm not much of a jock." He patted his small gut like it was a trusted friend. "There's an FBI branch right here in town. It was my good friend over there who convinced me I'd like it here in Gallup."

"And did your good friend fax you my brother's file this afternoon? Unofficially, of course."

His thick brows rose in acknowledgment. "That is a very shrewd guess. I met him downtown to pick it up, so there'd be no official record of it reaching my office."

I glanced around. "He faxed you mine too?"

He hesitated, then nodded.

An imitation Navaho rug covered part of the stained linoleum floor. A tacky print of a sand painting hung behind him, and a bronze copy of a Remington cowboy rested on the corner of his oak desk. Its leg had been gnawed. "You have a dog?"

"Nope, that was the last chief's puppy. A Rottweiler named Daisy."

I had always suspected there might be an FBI file on me because of my involvement with radical feminism in the 1970s—I'd gone underground with a fugitive lover and ended up in a psychiatric hospital for several weeks—yet learning that it was true and that this man had been reading the government's version of my earlier life was more than disconcerting. "Did it say I had an affair with the FBI agent too? Did he put that in his damn notes?"

When Blake didn't answer, I blunted my discomfort by recounting facts he already knew: My brother, Royce, had written a promising first novel that was still in print after more than twenty years, partly because of his notoriety and violent death, and yes, the introduction had been written by Norman Mailer. No, I did not know Norman Mailer.

"I like Mailer's work," Blake said. "And I admired your brother's novel very much, when it first came out."

These remarks seemed as odd as the one about an ex-wife, so I volunteered that our mother was senile and our sister now dead.

"You sure look a lot like Ruby Redstone."

"That's how I recognized her. And by her first name, of course."

He stared at me openly, and I let him look. I'm not as tall as my brother, but I have his quality of self-assurance, which is presence if you like me, arrogance if you do not. I thought he did. "You're quite a family."

I smiled with my eyes. "I'm the only normal one."

"Being a writer is not my idea of normal."

"Oh, please, I'm not a writer. I once put together a redneck cookbook that sold a lot of copies. You should try my mayonnaise sandwich. The crushed Doritos are the key. My big break was getting to write for that soap opera about the Confederacy, *Rise Again*. They still run it a lot on cable, so now I get to live—somewhat frugally—on royalties. But Royce was a real writer, before he lost his mind. What is your idea of normal?"

"Evelyn Roach?"

"My alias? Give me a break on that. I assure you I would have chosen a different name if I could. False identities were a lot harder to come by than anyone realizes. Could you let me have a look at my file? Sometimes I get my own chronology mixed up."

He laughed out loud, which made me like him more than I already did. "Okay, Ellen Burns, do you think you can help us with this situation? We've got a mess here, and all this press is making it worse. Since the kidnapping took place on reservation land, the FBI is in charge at the moment. But they're letting me hang around as if I have some kind of role."

"Do you think Ruby's children were kidnapped?"

"You tell me."

"Somebody hit her on the head pretty hard. And somebody tied her up."

"Yes, and Lightman Redstone insists that she could not have gotten free without his help."

"So, what's your theory, Ed Blake? Is there any possibility my brother is alive?"

He tilted his head, studying me. "I don't see how. The DNA evidence was conclusive. They claim they were confident."

"But now you're wondering too?"

"Do you think your niece will talk to you?"

"She might not even know I exist."

He broke his gaze and stood up. "Let's go find out."

We left his office and emerged into the dry, dusty street. I had a moment of disorientation because I realized I wasn't in South Carolina before we got into his unmarked car, which smelled leathery and male. A scanner and crackling radio separated us, but he immediately turned them both off.

Two press cars followed us out to the reservation through the glowing evening light. The hills were undulating and lovely, but the dry air kept making me sneeze. Only a tiny marker indicated when we entered the Nogalu reservation. Once we reached the deserted main street, most of the stores were closed or boarded up. Outside a local grocery, three children leaned against a bare wall, staring balefully at us. We entered an area of small reddish houses, some made from original sandstone, others built with cinder blocks or plywood and painted sandstone red. "Well," I said, "it's not Disneyland."

"No," he said, "it's surely not."

Three press vehicles and several unmarked cars were parked along the pocked paved road. Two TV trucks stared at the sky with round white eyes. Ed Blake explained that Ruby and Lightman were staying at his sister Loretta's house because their own home had been roped off as a crime scene.

Half a dozen men, two in dark blue uniforms with NOGALU RESERVATION police patches, guarded the door as well as the perimeter of the red dirt yard. They stared at me too, perhaps because of my resemblance to my niece.

Blake knocked, then opened the front door without waiting, and I stepped in behind him. The room was shadowy and smelled of foods I could not identify. Ruby sat on a sofa wedged tight between two elderly shawl-wrapped women. She stood up, as startled by the sight of me as I had been of her.

Again she wore a long, dark skirt and a white cotton blouse, this one unstained by blood. Her black hair looked wet, her brown-yellow skin slick with sweat or suffering. No one said anything while we stared at each other.

Ruby's face went through several changes that I could not decipher, but terror may have been one of them. "I'm your father's sister, honey. I met you once when you were a baby." I took a step forward, but she backed away, making a frightened, animal sound.

When she moved toward me, I had the awful notion she might kneel. Instead she stepped so close I could feel her body's heat. She rested her forehead gingerly in the crook of my neck, and I put my arms around her. "I came to try to help you."

She stayed still, breathing wetly into my throat. I gave Ed Blake a what-should-I-do look, because I did not want to be this vulnerable, and something terrible was happening inside my chest.

3

My brother, my brother, my brother. What can an aging lesbian out-law do if her brother is a white terrorist and he might still be alive? After Royce's death, I had been sad but relieved. Twice before he had vanished and emerged transformed. When his marriage to a Charleston debutante ended while he was still in his early twenties, he disappeared for almost three years; then he reappeared in Mendocino, embracing Santane and fatherhood and trying to write that novel. The second time he disappeared, the FBI declared him armed and dangerous, then dead. Was it possible he would reemerge again?

Over the next two days I sat with his daughter while tides of rumors rose and fell around us. The white van with the dented front fender that Ruby claimed to have seen in the driveway had been spotted in Boulder, in Reno, in Denver, in Seattle. White separatists in Montana were brought in for questioning; other racists were being questioned in Idaho and Washington State. Yet no traces of the children had materialized.

Ruby said little and ate almost nothing, drinking cup after cup of water. "I can't swallow food." She refused pain medication and even the antibiotics prescribed as a result of her wound. Nor would she drink the concoctions Lightman's mother kept offering. When Lightman introduced me to his mother, she acknowledged me with a harsh stare. Lightman said he was so exhausted at night he didn't know whether or not Ruby slept. He was a sturdy, silent man who seemed indifferent to my presence. His need to search—and perhaps his increasing doubts about his wife—drove him from the house early each morning.

There was a great deal of pressure from the press and no one else took charge, so I stepped into an authority that has always come naturally to me. I became the family's spokesperson, going out of the house several times to give short statements to a string of microphones and cameras, later trying to fend off a reporter at my hotel. "Ruby is doing as well as can be expected," I kept saying, variously. "She is praying constantly for the return of her children." I refused all questions about my brother—"My brother's dead, that's factual"—and even wrote a brief statement that Ruby agreed to read the second day, after which she contradicted me.

She spoke these words woodenly: "I ask the men who took Lucia and River to please to take good care of them and release them unharmed. I do not believe you are evil men, not in your deepest hearts. Lucia and River, your father and I love you more than anything, and we are waiting for you to come back." Then she crushed the note and began to sob. "Daddy, please come help me. I know you're listening."

Profiles of the Silent Brotherhood and other white supremacist organizations from the 1980s, among them the Aryan Republican Army, the Posse Comitatus, the National Alliance, the CSA, and a group still living in a compound in Elohim City, Oklahoma, began to appear on TV. I called Estelle several times because I knew my mother could not be kept away from the screen, but she said Momma was delighted during the moments she recognized Royce. She thought he was part of the cast of *The Young and the Restless*, a soap opera she watched daily. When my own image appeared, she waved cheerfully and greeted me, untroubled by my lack of response.

I did not know what to make of the fact that Ed Blake already owned a hardcover copy of Royce's novel, which overnight became nearly impossible to buy. The signed first edition I had brought for Ruby she left on the table and did not touch, except to turn it over once and gaze at Royce's photo, bearded, long-haired, well-muscled from outdoor living, leaning against the doorframe of their Mendocino cabin with his arms crossed, his expression quietly somber.

"Do you remember when your father looked like that?"

"Sort of." She was holding a child's coloring book in her hands and slowly tearing off the corners of random pages.

"Do you remember living with him and your mother in Mendocino, next to the big redwoods?"

"No, but I remember Rommel."

"You remember the German shepherd?"

The stack of paper triangles drifted off the sofa. "I remember when Daddy shot him."

I said, stupidly, "Royce shot Rommel?"

But Ruby said nothing more for the rest of that day.

I had dinner with Ed Blake that evening, although I did not trust his motives in befriending me. We ate at his home because, he said, reporters were stalking both of us, and he was cautious about the new long-range microphones.

Blake turned out to be a decent cook, steaks and chops and salads with strong, unpretentious seasonings. He lived in a log cabin with a ceiling of varnished cedar—"built from a kit, don't be impressed"—and showed me pictures of his daughters, who were, like him, tall, thickly made, and surprisingly good-looking.

"They look a lot like you."

"Ha. Poor kids."

"What happened to your marriage?"

"We wore it out," he said. "And she met someone else."

"You did too?"

He put the photographs back on the pine shelf. "Listen, Ellen Burns, the road to hell is paved with mistakes. Don't misinterpret me asking you to have dinner out here."

"Oh, please, I'm older than you, not to mention more jaded."

"Actually, you're two years younger. And jaded is kind of a pejorative word to use for people just because they've had real lives. I need somebody smart and knowledgeable to talk with about this situation, and there appears to be pressure on my friend at the FBI that hinders our frank communication. I think you and I might be able to help each other. Maybe it's fortuitous that you've showed up." He gestured past me toward the porch. "Let's go outside now. I need to handle the chops and take that corn off the grill."

I walked behind him and spoke into his shoulder. "We have different agendas, Ed Blake. I will admit I'm impressed by a cop who can use the word *pejorative* in a sentence. Not to mention *fortuitous*." He wore a green cotton shirt and jeans and smelled faintly of aftershave lotion.

He held open the screen door and glanced down into my eyes. "Maybe some policemen are smarter than others. We both want to find Ruby's children, don't we?"

"Of course," I said, stepping past him. "I want to help Ruby too. But I need to find out what has really happened to my brother, and my guess is you know a lot more about that situation than you're going to tell me."

He lifted the top of the grill, which rested on the red dirt yard below the porch. Growing grass seemed impossible out here. In downtown Charleston, grass was meticulously maintained. Blake was cooking with charcoal, and a cloud of pleasant aromas enveloped us. "I'll tell you what I can," he said, "if you'll be straight with me about your brother."

So, while eating pork chops the first night and porterhouse the second, he gave me new information about Royce and his friend, Joe Magnus, and I told him part of our family's history.

4

Royce, Marie, and I had been born into what seemed, in retrospect, wincingly ordinary circumstances. That is, we were white but not conscious about it yet, and we lived in a working-class neighborhood of houses built for returning WWII vets (whites only, of course). Our father, an ambitious plumber, had prospered in the postwar economy, and soon he owned a business with forty employees. We became the only house on our block with central heat, two bathrooms, and a fashionable new room called a "den." But when I was twelve, our parents suddenly bought a rundown plantation outside of Charleston called Blacklock.

Nineteen fifty-seven proved to be an unwise year to try to imitate plantation life. Our mother, permanently enthralled by the version of history presented in *Gone with the Wind*, had hoped to remodel Blacklock into an evocation of Tara. We acquired horses, but the architect made a mistake and built the stables too close to the house, so when the breeze blew in from the west, we often smelled shit. During the Civil War the original house had burned down, and during Reconstruction a white country frame with wide porches and a wonderful view of the ruined rice paddies had been raised on the old foundations. Our mother hired workmen to knock down an inside wall, and she fashioned a large, sweeping room with blond waxed floors, like a ballroom. She had our father's portrait painted and hung over the fireplace.

But the Supreme Court had recently declared segregation illegal, and trouble was already burbling outside our big white gates. In our former neighborhood, the only African Americans had been maids and work-men, but at Blacklock the nearest whites lived four miles away. The cattle that ornamented our pasture soon began to disappear, one by one.

Royce, who was five years old, did not find Blacklock at all trou-bling. Instead, he turned wild, like our housecat that disappeared into the woods, reappearing occasionally, filthy and snarling and happy. Royce was dirty like the cat, and he followed the old caretaker, John Tillman, everywhere. Together they dug up a Confederate buckle in the pasture and discovered four arrowheads near the mouth of the river.

The first winter we lived at Blacklock, our father was killed in an automobile accident. Our mother, widowed at thirty-six, now had horses that bit us, a stable that stank, vanishing cattle, and a son who kept ad-dressing the ancient caretaker as Mr. Tillman, even though she had told him repeatedly to call the old man John. She ordered floodlights installed on the lawn and began sleeping with a loaded pistol under her pillow. "These nigras will steal us blind," she said. "They're acting like those rus-tlers in cowboy movies."

Royce loved the blacksnakes that he captured with John Tillman, and he sometimes wrapped them luxuriantly around his arms or even his neck. He and John killed the dangerous kinds, the water moccasins and rattlers, and Royce nailed their skins to boards that he left beside the front door. He treasured his collection of their rattles, but I lay awake at night tormented by images of dark faces crawling through our windows to murder us. This fear of black people was new, and I missed my father with an anguish like a hole torn through me, because maybe he could have helped me understand why the Freedom Riders and civil rights marchers on TV seemed like heroes, not like troublemakers or cattle thieves or outside agitators, the way we were being instructed. I began to glimpse that I had been born on the wrong side of a dreadful historical conflict.

•

After Ed Blake and I finished dinner, we sat in armchairs outside on his porch in the near dark. Amber light streamed dimly through the window behind us. I was drinking coffee, and Blake was on his third beer. "So let me understand this. The man who was driving the car when your father was killed was actually Joe Magnus's father?"

"Yes. His name was Skip Magnus. He stayed on with the business as chief foreman."

I described Skip Magnus, a hard-bodied man swarthy with years of outdoor work. After the accident, perhaps out of guilt, he had briefly aspired to become a father figure for Royce, but Skip was not the model of maleness Momma had envisioned for her only son. She quickly enrolled Royce and my sister, Marie, in expensive private schools in Charleston, while I chose to drive many miles the other way to attend a poor white public school because that was what I thought my father would have wanted. Marie was an indifferent student, but Royce turned out to be bright and talented and ambitious. In high school, he played golf, wrote poetry, edited the literary magazine, and earned perfect scores on several national tests. Yet each summer, over our mother's fierce objections, he insisted on working as a field laborer for Skip. Skip's only son, Joe, a year older than Royce, also worked in the field. He and Royce became constant summertime companions.

I said Joe Magnus had been a husky young man with an odd, monkeyish face. He and Royce had enjoyed their unusual friendship and got into several bar fights with men who challenged my brother's long hair. Royce introduced Joe to the Rolling Stones and to smoking marijuana, Joe introduced Royce to getting blind drunk, and together they went to every venue where a black band called the Hot Nuts played.

On the morning Skip planned to have the workers hold Royce down and cut his hair, Joe forewarned him. Royce had sawed off the handle of our mother's broom and hidden it in the waistband of his pants. In the altercation that followed, Royce swung the handle and caught Skip Magnus on his temple. After two days of a brain bleed, Skip Magnus died.

"And that's just the stripped-down version," I said, sipping my lukewarm coffee.

"It just sounds so damn complicated," Ed Blake said.

I shrugged. "Most real stories are."

"So, was the accident that killed your father Skip Magnus's fault?"

"Of course not. A drunk driver hit them. But I don't know if that mattered so much to Skip, the guilt he felt."

"And did your brother intend to kill Skip Magnus?"

"Again, of course not. Royce wasn't even arrested. He was seventeen, and it was clearly self-defense. All of the men gave statements to that effect. But Joe didn't get to join the Marines the way he'd always talked about because he had to get his mother and sisters situated, and when his draft number came up, he just went straight into the army. Royce cut his hair so short he looked like a Mormon missionary. This isn't in the FBI file? I'm telling you things you don't know?"

"It's just an amazingly different version," Blake said. "The official story is that the sons, Joe Magnus and Royce Burns, were bonded by the murders of their fathers. It adds to their myth, how dangerous they were."

"They were supposed to have killed my father when they were five and six years old?"

"Well, the story runs more like this: Skip killed your father on purpose, and then the sons conspired to kill Skip."

"And then Royce got married and went off to college while Magnus went to Vietnam to train as his future racist ally?"

"The truth is always a bigger mess than its outlines, Ellen."

"Yes, and I've learned that melodrama is something to be avoided, but that idea's not doing me much good at the moment."

"No," he said, "I guess it's not."

"The rest of the story you're probably more familiar with. Royce tried to construct a stable life for himself. Momma gave him Blacklock as a wedding present, and he moved out there for a while, but it didn't work."

"How did Santane enter his life?"

"That wasn't her real name. He named her that. I think they met at a Buddhist temple in San Francisco."

There was a silence, and then Blake said, "It was BATF, the Bureau of Alcohol, Tobacco and Firearms, that originally encouraged your brother to go visit the Silent Brotherhood with Joe Magnus. Apparently they convinced Royce that it would be patriotic and that he might be able to pull Joe Magnus back from the brink. Next thing BATF knew, your brother and Magnus were thick into the Brotherhood together. So the government was at least partially responsible for the whole situation, and there was a lot of infighting about who was at fault."

"So that's why they declared my brother dead? To cover their fucking asses? Who needs outside enemies when we've got our own government?" I put my coffee cup onto the table, spilling it, and for the first time since Ruby had reappeared in my life, feared I might cry. I stood up. "Listen, I need to go back to my hotel now. I want to visit Ruby early in the morning."

"Tell me more about the old black man, John Tillman. And about his wife, Ruby." There was something personal, something needing in his voice, or maybe I was imagining it.

"Oh, Christ, read the fucking novel again. It's all in there." My voice had thickened with tears, and I hoped he wouldn't realize it, but he stood up, stepped close, and stared right down at me.

I stood too but kept my eyes fixed on the pine table, which was fake rustic like everything else he owned. When he reached for me, I stepped wordlessly into his chest. His scent was Old Spice, like our father's. He said, "And you're feeling all this right now because?"

"Because I loved the Tillmans too, goddamn it, and once upon a time I even loved my fucking brother."

And that is how I ended up in bed with Ed Blake the first time, a mistake in a situation already knotty with conflict. Less than an hour later, when I was pulling my jeans back on—I hadn't even taken off my shirt—I said, "This was so stupid. I hope it's not part of some government plot."

"Just weakness," he said, lying naked across his bed, a lodgepole pine affair with a striped wool blanket. His arm was covering his eyes, and his thick penis lay curled against his leg. "Just being a weak, careless man."

"Listen, I've ended up in bed with lots of people. Don't take it too personally."

He uncovered his eyes and gave me a long look. "You're way too smart to believe that."

5

The next morning, when I returned to the reservation, I threaded my way wordlessly through press cars and FBI agents as well as the Nogalu police, who allowed me to pass into Lightman's sister's house without incident.

For most of the morning Ruby and I sat silently side by side on the sofa in the dim living room. Several toy trucks and coloring books that I assumed belonged to Loretta's children lay scattered across the floor. A rumbling air conditioner blocked the light from one window, and the other was heavily curtained. The house smelled like cats and chili. Three old women, indistinguishable to my eye except for Lightman's mother, walked in and out of the room, eavesdropping. She glared at me but twice offered us lemonade. Although Ruby refused it, I drank mine down greedily. The next day I would try to remember to bring a supply of Cokes.

While the waiting hung thickly around us, I began to tell Ruby about her namesake. I wasn't sure how much she could hear, but I thought the sound of my voice might soothe her. Everyone likes my voice. It makes people trust me who probably shouldn't.

"Ruby and John Tillman were the caretakers on the plantation where your father and I grew up. They spoke a mixture of English and a West African language. Ruby was our housekeeper, and she was really nice to us. When your daddy was little, he followed John Tillman around like a puppy. It was John who taught him to fish and hunt and speak Gullah, and who taught him to handle snakes."

Ruby looked at me wild-eyed, and I realized she was listening. "Rattlers?"

"No, blacksnakes. Your dad loved blacksnakes."

"For practice?"

"I don't think so. He and John killed the rattlers. Your dad kept a collection of their tails in his room."

"He still has it," Ruby said.

"Ruby, why do you keep speaking as if Royce is alive? Do you have any real knowledge about that?"

She turned her face away, and I waited almost a full minute before I said, "Your dad had large, graceful hands. Maybe you remember them? Even when we were children, people noticed his hands." I extended my own hands directly in front of her, so she would have to look at them. "Yours and mine aren't the same. His hands had this special quality."

She began to mumble something that sounded like chanting. The murmur of voices from the kitchen went instantly silent, and she stopped.

"Ruby, what are you saying? Are you praying?"

She leaned in close to me, sudden fury in her face. "How did you know Rommel?"

I drew back. "I saw him when he was a puppy," I said uncertainly. "I had gone home for Christmas."

Then Ruby began to talk, her voice mumbling like a child's. They had been living in the mountains, and Santane kept a garden with squash, tomatoes, and green beans. There were chickens in a shed, and Ruby wanted to get the eggs by herself, but she was afraid of being pecked, so Santane let her wear Daddy's work gloves. A key was hidden in the cuff that opened Daddy's office, and that was where Ruby found the pictures of him wearing a suit and tie. His hair was short, and the woman beside him was holding Rommel like a baby. But how could that be? Because Rommel slept beside her on the floor every night, and he waited for her to get off the school bus every day, and he never bothered the chickens.

But when Daddy learned she had gone into his office, he burned those pictures in the kitchen sink. Santane tried to stop him because she knew too much about burning. Daddy got his rifle and pulled Ruby outside under the big pine tree where Rommel liked to lie down in the cool beds of needles, and he dug a big hole and ordered Rommel to climb down into it. Then he shot Rommel through the head. He told Ruby to quit crying and help him cover Rommel with the dirt, but she wouldn't do it. Afterward, they went back inside the house and ate egg salad sandwiches with sliced tomatoes.

Ruby looked right into my eyes now and spoke in a hoarse, grown-up voice. "He covered Rommel's eyes with his hand. He told me Rommel wouldn't understand what was happening."

From the silence in the kitchen and the women's faces crowding the doorway, I knew I was not the only one finding significance in this tale. Maybe I should have said *Ruby, have you hurt your children? Did you cover their eyes?* But I wanted to protect her as well as myself. "Royce got Rommel for a wedding present. So this must have been a second dog, a second Rommel."

"He covered Rommel's eyes with his hand, but Rommel screamed and tried to climb out of the hole."

"Avery was the woman in the pictures. Avery was his first wife. Before your mother."

"He screamed and tried to get out of the hole."

The quietness of the room must have made her realize she was saying something troubling because she retreated to the high, childlike voice. "Daddy explained it to me. That we are all just meat. Meat of the dog, meat of the human. But in the realm of the spirit, we are one."

"Ruby, do you remember how old you were when all this happened?"

"Five? Six?" She seemed to think I was the one who should know the answer.

"Honey, do you know that at first your father was working for the federal government?"

"No, he worked for the purification of the white race."

"But why did God's plan involve only the white race? Did he explain that to you?"

She reached for my hand but dropped it. "He said he was sorry, but it did."

"What did that mean about you and your mother?"

"We were his proof."

I stared down at my own hands, palms up, urgently seeking something. "Did you believe him about all of this, Ruby?"

"He told me I was his biggest sin."

"But I know how much he loved you, honey. I saw how he held you when you were a baby." I wasn't sure if I was saying this for her or for myself.

"I thought he loved me more than God."

6

Sometimes, if I want to drink again, a flutter starts inside my chest, as if a small bird is beating upward toward my throat. This wish for a drink is rarely conscious, but my breathing gets shallow and fast, and strange thoughts enter my head, as if the wires of my identity are loosening. I don't drink when this happens, or at least I haven't for many years. Instead I go to AA meetings, where my interior chaos gets eased by friendliness and order and the sturdiness of hope. I had already checked through the meeting list for the Gallup vicinity, so I knew there was a 5:30 group called "Attitude Adjustment" every day at a clubhouse on Persimmon Street.

I told Ruby I had to be somewhere important, and within an hour I was away from Royce's life and its ghastly consequences and back onto familiar ground. The famous Twelve Steps were unfurled on the wall, the slogans scattered around on placards: THINK THINK THINK, EASY DOES IT, and K.I.S.S., which I'd been told many times meant, especially for me, *Keep It Simple, Stupid*. My breathing began to loosen up.

The meeting had just started. Someone was reading out loud "How It Works," the first two pages of chapter five of the Big Book, *Alcoholics Anonymous*, the section my first sponsor made me memorize early in my sobriety. I could barely listen, but I caught this phrase: "Those who do not recover are constitutionally incapable of being honest with themselves . . ."

It wasn't simply the shock of locating Ruby again or the possibility, increasing with every second, that her young children were now dead, it wasn't the fact that I was a lesbian who without any forethought had leapt straight into bed with a man for the first time in decades. No, it was the specter of my brother, my brother, my brother.

In AA, I had found a solution for my anger and self-destructiveness, and I thought I had let go of Royce and the hatreds he promoted, just as I had let go of our molested sister and our loopy mother and our dead father and God knows how many ex-lovers. "We will not regret the past nor wish to shut the door on it" is one of the AA promises, and "We will comprehend the word *serenity*, and we will know peace." For many years that had seemed true, but from the moment I recognized Ruby on television, the door to the past had blown back open. The racism my brother and I had been taught—how deep did that training go? Was it still lodged in my unconscious? Could it be genetic? How can we know what we have inherited?

Why one person recovers in AA and another does not has remained mysterious to me, but when I first joined, I just did whatever was suggested. I didn't have a better idea then, and I still don't. From the first meeting, I loved the extremism of the program. *You don't drink alcohol at all? Or do any drugs? Not cocaine or LSD or nitrous oxide or even a little marijuana here and there?* Occasionally I wondered if AA was my own version of Royce's radicalism, but, regardless of any ironic analysis, AA saved my life. So, while swells of fury and grief rose inside me, I sat quietly in the Gallup meeting, listening carefully to other people's words, taking comfort, as always, in the steadiness of the meeting, the even-handed respect. "We come from Yale, we come from jail," Bill Wilson, the cofounder of AA wrote.

A man named Jack, just released from a treatment center, said he was attending his first meeting without medical supervision. "Welcome!" we said in unison. "Keep coming back!" A woman named Clara announced that she would be getting her son back from foster care next week. She had a year and a half clean, and she was weeping with gratitude. A Native woman caught my glance and told me with her eyes that she too was long-term sober. A man with a Celtic tattoo on his cheek was chairing, and I hoped he wouldn't call on me, but right after I'd gotten a second cup of the bitter black coffee and settled into my folding chair, he did.

"I'm Ellen, alcoholic and drug addict, visiting. Wires seem to be hanging out of my head tonight. I just need to listen."

Later, when I looked back, the young reporter who had followed me inside was no longer in sight. I waited a few more minutes to make sure she wasn't in the bathroom or lurking around, and then I raised my hand. When he called on me, I said, "Still Ellen, still alcoholic. Sorry to speak twice, but there was someone here earlier I couldn't share safely in front of. I'm Ruby Redstone's aunt, if you know who she is. In any case, I'm in Gallup because someone in my family has big trouble, and I seem to have ended up in the middle of it. I'm beginning to understand that I was always in the middle of it. I'm pretty shaky, so I could use some phone numbers after the meeting. Thanks for listening."

Next the chairperson called on a man with pocked, ruddy skin and black hair that was pulled back in a ponytail. He wore Levi's and cowboy boots and a denim shirt with the sleeves torn off. His arms displayed tattoos of Mickey Mouse, the Road Runner, and Bugs Bunny. "I'm Melvin," he said. "Alcoholic and addict. Sometimes I have trouble staying out of the past because of Vietnam. Whenever that happens, I just go look at the mountains for a while. I tell the mountains what I'm grateful for, or what I would be grateful for if I were in my right mind."

The chorus of individual stories continued to sound around me, and after a while I managed, momentarily, to forgive my brother for shooting Rommel in front of his young daughter. I wasn't there, I don't know his reasons, and judgment doesn't belong to me. And I might never know what happened the night he beat Santane (I'd learned about this from the private detective I'd hired, who had located the hospital record) or why he changed so appallingly. "Walk your own path," my AA sponsor kept telling me. "Look down at your feet. This is where you are. You are not in the past or the future. You are right here, and you only have one job: don't take a drink or a drug today, no matter what. Go to bed tonight feeling like you're a tiny part of what is good in the world. Let go of everyone else's journey. Live and let live. Keep it simple, stupid."

So I asked God or the mountains or whatever it was to take care of the children and the kidnappers and even of Royce, whether any of them were alive or not. After I left the meeting I had several phone numbers stuck in my shirt pocket, including that of the old woman whose eyes had fastened on mine.

7

My mother was videotaped by a Charleston TV station in front of the Piggly Wiggly grocery, where, after her relentless insistence, Estelle had finally taken her shopping. In one phone message, Estelle apologized and warned me. In another, Ed Blake said, "We need to talk about Joe Magnus. I'll cook you a decent steak, and I'll only drink coffee. I'm sorry about last night. I do have a little sense, even if I don't always act like it. I'll call you back at seven."

It was already after seven, and when the phone rang I didn't answer it. The room service menu offered a green chili omelet, so I ordered that, asked the concierge to have the minibar supplies removed from my room, and told the switchboard not to ring me again. I checked in briefly with Estelle, who said everything was fine.

The *Times* and the Albuquerque papers contained stories about the Silent Brotherhood, but I watched *Entertainment Tonight*, and there was my mom, impeccably made up, with her hair newly coiffed, saying, "Royce is such a wonderful boy. I am so proud of him. He finished second in the state golfing tournament, and now he is on television all the time!" When asked about "your granddaughter Ruby," she frowned and said, "Ruby didn't understand the silverware."

I laughed off and on throughout supper, a *Law & Order* rerun, and the disappearance of the minibar. When I felt safely grounded, I checked the message to hear Ed Blake say, "Can you call me at the office tomorrow?"

It was after ten o'clock, but I called him anyway. He answered on the first ring. "Chief Blake here."

"Ruby Redstone's aunt here," I said. "Back from my small fit of pique."

"I'm glad you called. I'm feeling guilty as hell."

"Me too, but it's not like we kidnapped anyone or tried to start a race war. On a scale from one to ten, it was a one. Okay, maybe a two. But listen, Ed Blake, we cannot go to that place with each other."

"I agree completely."

"Can you let it go?"

"Yes."

"Good. Did you see my mother on TV?"

"I sure did, and I hope my spaceship lands alongside hers."

Neither of us said anything for a moment, because it's hard to restore a boundary once it's breached. "I'll do dinner again," I said, "if you really think we are okay."

"I've got somebody working in my office I don't trust, otherwise we could retreat there."

"Have there been any new developments?"

I felt him hesitate. "They've found some caves under a couple of old barns about twenty miles north of town. They might have Ruby's tire tracks out there."

I could taste green chilies in my throat. "They're searching?"

"Yes."

"Can we go out there now?"

"No, Ellen. The FBI has to handle this. They know what to do. If there's anything to it, I'll call you back tonight. Or we'll go out there in the morning."

"Where is this place?"

"No way," he said. "You'll have to trust me on this one."

8

The third morning after the children's disappearance was the most difficult at Loretta's. Ruby wanted to return with Lightman to their own house, and she seemed unable to grasp that it was a crime scene. For the first time, she admitted to having a headache. She had pulled off the bandage above her temple and kept touching the angry stitches. I knew her head must hurt a lot. She seemed to have emerged from her stupor into a glittery web of denial. She wanted to go home so she could get the house ready for Lucia and River, and she wanted to buy Karo syrup, because that was their favorite, toast with butter and Karo syrup.

Lightman was still at Loretta's house when I arrived, his face engorged with rage. "I'm going to kill the men who did this. Even if they treat my son fine, I'm going to kill them! If your father had any part in this, I'll kill him too."

Ruby fumbled at the stitches, which began to ooze blood. "He'll be the one to bring them back. He'll love River. He always wanted a son instead of me, and Lucia is his granddaughter. He'll love Lucia because he loves me."

"She's losing it," I said to Lightman.

"Call a doctor if you want to," he said, "but she's crazy. She's always been crazy, just like her father. Tell her what you do, Ruby. Tell them that you pray to him at night. Do you think I don't hear you?"

"Did she pray to Royce before the kidnapping?" This seemed like an important question, but Lightman looked at me wild-eyed while Ruby sank to the floor. She tucked her head against her knees and began to rock back and forth making a keening sound.

"Were you out at the Catacombs?" he shouted down at Ruby. "Chief Blake said they found your tire tracks out there last night. They know you were there, Ruby! What were you doing out there? Goddamn it, Ruby, tell me what happened!"

She just kept rocking back and forth making that sound.

"What else did they find?"

"Nothing!" he yelled into my face, and spittle landed on my cheek. "They found nothing! It's just an old camp!" He started to make his own sound, more like bellowing.

I turned to signal one of the guards outside, but Lightman's mother stepped into the room and warned me off with her hand. She tapped Lightman on the elbow and handed him a glass with several inches of black liquid in it. He immediately stopped making the noise and drank it straight down. Then she thumped Ruby's shoulder hard. Without looking up, Ruby took the other glass the woman held out. Within half a minute, Lightman stumbled to the sofa, where he blacked out sitting up. Ruby passed out on the floor.

"What did you give them?"

She signaled me away again as she covered Ruby with a blanket. She pushed Lightman down onto his side, pulled off his boots, and covered him too.

Fiercely she turned to me and said one word: "Leave."

9

Outside, most of the press had disappeared. I understood now where the reporters had gone. "Statement later," I said to the single cameraman. I signaled the woman who had followed me to the AA meeting toward my car. She climbed right in, but I didn't start the engine. "So, who are you?"

"A stringer for the *New York Times*," she said earnestly. "I only do background and research. A reporter named Del Mead does the actual writing."

"You look like a kid." She seemed to be about Ruby's age, maybe a little older. "What are you, twenty-five?"

"Twenty-eight." She pulled the sun-clips off her glasses so I could see her eyes. She was nervous and scared. "I wasn't following you last night, Miss Burns, and I left as soon as I realized you were there."

"Call me Ellen and recite the Preamble."

"Um, 'Alcoholics Anonymous is a fellowship of men and women who' . . . shit . . . 'experience, strength, and hope' . . . Is that part of the Preamble? . . . 'Our sole purpose is to stay sober and help other alcoholics to achieve sobriety?' I know that last line's right."

"How long have you got?"

"Seven months. Wait. I have this." She pulled a green token with a 6 engraved on it out of her pocket. There was a quarter taped to one side. I hadn't seen money taped to a chip in years.

"Your sponsor's been in the program a long time, and she gave you that?"

"Public phones still cost a quarter in New Mexico. And I have a credit card. Also, a lot more change." She pulled a handful of quarters out of her handbag.

"What's your sobriety date?"

She named a date six and a half months ago.

"Don't fudge your time," I said, trying not to smile as I started the car and pulled out of the yard.

"Where are we going?"

"I don't know yet. Let's drive." I headed back toward Gallup. "It's really beautiful out here, isn't it?"

"I don't think it's all that beautiful. Then again, it's my home."

"The reservation? You don't look Indian."

"Don't say 'Indian.' Oh, I see, you're baiting me now. No, I'm from Gallup. My name is Claudia Friedman. A small group of Jews have been living in this part of New Mexico for more than a hundred years." She giggled. "Not exactly Native. We hardly even qualify as being from Gallup yet."

"Educated back East?"

"At Brown."

"And then what happened?"

"Do you always talk this way to people you don't know?"

"Pretty much. I can't seem to help it."

"I liked your cookbook," she said.

"Everybody likes my cookbook, and I can't even cook."

Soon we were laughing out loud. "This situation is so fucking *vile*," I said, which set off another round of laughing. "So here's the deal, Claudia Friedman, I'm betting you know where this place called the Catacombs is. If you don't, I can find out another way."

She tried not to look too pleased. "My boss told me I should stay at the reservation, but I'm thinking that riding with you is much better journalistic judgment."

"It certainly is."

"So, take the turnoff out to El Morro National Monument."

I did not believe there would be anything significant to see at the Catacombs because Ed Blake would have called me—I trusted him that much—but I wanted to see the place for myself. Whether or not the Catacombs had anything to do with the kidnapping, the Silent Brotherhood, if it still existed in any form, might be connected, and I wanted to tell Blake that Ruby was cracking up. I thought she should be interrogated again, along with Lightman, as soon as they were awake. And if those really were her tire tracks, they should carry her out to the Catacombs and see whether she might admit anything. I was certain now that Ruby was hiding something and that the old woman had drugged her and Lightman on purpose.

Claudia told me that the barns out at the Catacombs were part of an old ranch that had been private property when the park was first formed. For a while it had been used by some religious group that prayed 24-7, which is where the nickname came from. After that, it became a place where kids went to drink and take drugs, but she'd never heard anything about racist groups out there.

"Listen, I need a pipeline," I said. "You do too. So here's my real proposal. I'll keep you on an inside loop, but you have to hold back anything I tell you unless I say it's all right. Your people will like this arrangement. If you don't think so, don't tell them. Use that 'journalistic judgment.' And, in return, you give me whatever you can. Just don't get yourself in any trouble, but tell me whatever you can. It is a deal?"

She gave me a sad, cagey smile. "Does this mean I'm going to get an exclusive interview with Ruby Redstone?"

"I can't promise anything like that. I may not even have a voice in it."

"Okay, it's a deal," she said.

"Swear it on the grave of Bill Wilson," I said, which made us both start to snicker.

Claudia showed her press badge at the first roadblock, and I said to the cop, "Call ahead to Chief Blake. Tell him Ruby Redstone's aunt is here."

At the second roadblock, where the press had parked their cars, the police signaled us through while Claudia scrunched down in her seat. "Aren't you going to wave at your press cronies?"

"I'll do better explaining this situation later."

Ed Blake was standing in the dirt road, waiting for us, his arms folded across his chest. We were all wearing dark glasses now, which was helpful. "Hi, Chief Blake," I said as we got out of the car. "Thanks for that heads-up about telling Lightman Redstone you have Ruby's tire tracks out here. All hell broke loose at Loretta's house."

"Hello, Ellen. Hello, Claudia. I didn't know you were this enterprising. What happened at the house?" Blake looked immediately regretful that he'd asked this question in front of Claudia.

"One of the old women drugged Lightman and Ruby, and now they're both unconscious."

Claudia said, "Is that true?"

"You might want to get a doctor out there," I said to Blake, "in case she's killed them."

"No news on this, I mean it," he said to Claudia. He turned away and began talking into a walkie-talkie and a phone at the same time.

Four FBI-labeled cars and several other unmarked vehicles were scattered around, but there were no ambulances. All I could see in the distance was a run-down old ranch house and two rotting barns. Police tape extended about fifty yards around their perimeter.

"Let me speak with Miss Burns privately," Blake said to Claudia. "You get back in that car." He waited until she obeyed him. Then he took my arm and led me about ten feet away. "What happened?"

"You tell me first."

"They were questioning Lightman separately. They've begun excluding me, but I'm not sure why. That's the reason I didn't call you. They told Lightman about the tire tracks as a way of creating pressure between them, and I guess it worked. We don't know yet what the old woman gave them, but one of the guards got the EMS people out there fast. Apparently, it's just some kind of sedative. Ruby's out cold, but Lightman's not as bad. They'll be fine. Here's the real news: those are Ruby's tire tracks. It doesn't prove anything about when she was here, and, of course, the first people out here drove right over them. But forensics thinks they're less than a week old."

"No sign of anything else?"

"No sign of the children, if that's what you mean. The first people out here trampled all through those barns too, but nobody else has, as far as we can tell. There's a cave entrance hidden behind some boards, but it seems like nobody's been in there for months."

"Claudia says kids used to drink and take drugs out here."

"I heard she used to be one of them."

"Don't try to undermine her credibility with me, Blake."

"Speaking of forthrightness," he said, "why, exactly, didn't I find out about Ruby and Royce and the family dog so picturesquely named Rommel when I talked to you last night?"

"I told you before, we have different interests here. Do I get to see inside those barns and that cave?"

"No," he said. "And I can't go in right now either. They're still doing forensics and expanding the search area."

"Because?"

"I'll call you if anything happens. I've got to get back to work, and you need to get that reporter out of here."

The second time I had sex with Ed Blake was only a few hours later, and we didn't even bother to eat dinner first. I did manage to get all my clothes off this time, but again the sex was quick, rough, and wordless. Afterward, he said, "How'd you get to be so tough, Ellen Burns?"

"Too many trips around the block," I said. "Also, I'm not so tough. You know that."

"Because you cried?"

"Yes, because I cried."

"Would it be impolite to ask why?"

"Just happens sometimes."

"Will you please talk to me?"

"Could I just say I've had an intense life?" I felt his penis stir against me again, and I reached down to help it along. "It's been a lot of years since I've fucked with a real one of these."

"Is that why?"

"Nope. Fake ones are better. This stuff makes me itchy."

"I'm a country boy. Do I want to know all this?"

"Yes, you certainly do. Look at you." I sat over him and slipped him back inside me. "This is so fucking inappropriate."

He caught his breath and didn't speak.

"Tell me what it's like in there."

"Could you please shut up?"

"Tell me what it's like in there."

His words were jagged, harsh. "My spine."

I leaned over and bit his shoulder, yanked his hair hard. "I'm going to make you cry too, before I'm through. Look at you. You already can't talk."

I rode him without speaking, but a humming had started deep within in my chest. "There's a blinding place. You've got to find it. Don't you dare come yet."

The light was rising around me now. "We're going to take it all the way. Come when I tell you. It's all there. Come now. Now."

He shouted, and I was lost with him. We probably sounded like we were being murdered.

When we were back to being two middle-aged people sweating on a bed, I said, "I like a man who lets me do things to him." I was lying stretched on top of him, and I tried to roll away.

He held on to me, and I let him. "Please stop talking that way." His face was streaked with tears.

I put my wet face against his. "I'm afraid we might understand each other."

10

According to Ed Blake's new information, Joe Magnus had only been in Vietnam a few months before some loose talk about fragging his lieutenant earned him a dishonorable discharge. Magnus's racial fury took him to Montana, where a group of white survivalists were trying to make a community. They welcomed him as a hero because the lieutenant he'd threatened to kill had been African American. Magnus's hatred of Asians and Jews was also righteous, so when Magnus heard that Royce had married a Vietnamese woman and named their baby after some old black woman, he learned Royce's location in the Mendocino woods and drove down there to confront him.

Blake didn't know what had transpired in the first meeting between the two men, or in a second one that took place soon afterward. What he did know was that within a few months Royce had moved his family eastward to Montana, to a village within thirty miles of Robert Mathews and the compound that housed the Silent Brotherhood. Royce soon developed connections with both Mathews and with William Luther Pierce, author of *The Turner Diaries*, a white supremacist novel still in print and considered a blueprint for the future by many racists. This book chronicles a white revolution occurring in the twenty-first century that begins in California and leads to the subjugation of the entire world by white men. All other races—and the Jews and homosexuals—are exterminated.

"Have you read it?" Blake asked.

"Years ago," I said. "It's sort of like the *Story of O* for racists."

Showered and dressed and comfortable, we now were eating the promised porterhouse steaks, sitting in his kitchen on ladder-back chairs at his pine table, which he'd covered with a red-checked cloth. When I pointed at the tablecloth and then at the Tiffany-copy lamp made of plastic hanging over us he said, "Hey, it all came with the kit." Between us was a companionship and ease I hadn't felt with a man in a long time.

"There's nothing better than western meat," Blake said. "It's one of the best reasons to live out here."

"You know that sounds like Royce's line of thinking? If you breed cattle and dogs for specific qualities, why not people? Haven't you read his 'position papers'?"

"I skimmed them. They're in his file. And *The Turner Diaries* was required reading at the Academy."

"Were they wanting you to join the white revolution or prevent it?"

He did not react well to that remark, just sat looking at me, his fork still in midair.

"Sorry," I said.

In Royce's first "position paper," he renounced art as a deluded path and apologized for having written a counterrevolutionary novel; in the second, he described individual love as a form of impotence; and in the third, he wrote that "We must immediately begin to breed human beings for specific qualities." The fourth was perhaps the most outrageous: "Anyone who understands Darwin knows that altruism is a form of weakness, and compassion must be overcome. The control of eugenics is our destiny."

"Royce was always a seeker," I told Blake. "I suppose we both were. When I visited him in Mendocino, he told me about this medieval religious group he admired because they had walked onto their own funeral pyre."

"Your brother found that commendable?"

"It was this group called the Cathars. They were going to be extermi-nated by the Catholic Church. Royce admired them for their courage."

"You and your brother are both so extreme."

"Yes, I suppose so, but I'm not dangerous, just picturesque. But I be-lieve my brother had a strong desire to die for something he believed in."

"You're suggesting that he and Robert Mathews might both have remained in the burning building to martyr themselves?"

"I don't know what actually happened out there, but no matter which way you turn it, Royce killed Joe Magnus's father, and that karma had to play itself out somewhere."

"Karma? You really are a sixties person."

"It's just another term for 'sins of the fathers.'"

This was a weird point to start smiling, but we were both filled with endorphins from the sex. "You and your brother," Blake said. "What about ordinary reality? What about a perfectly rare steak?"

We were laughing now. "Royce should have gone to Vietnam with Joe Magnus and gotten himself killed. Then he wouldn't be trying to make us complicit in his behavior."

"We're not complicit in his behavior, Ellen."

I stopped laughing and laid my fork back onto the plate. "Then why do I feel responsible? Aren't all white people somehow complicit? If only by doing nothing about people like him?"

He grasped the salt shaker in a way that made me realize he was try-ing not to touch my hand. "This is all very interesting, Ellen, but who do you think took the children, and where are they?"

"Has it occurred to you that Royce might have them? That would ex-plain the sense that Ruby is hiding something. Because she would never admit to that. Jesus Christ, I hope that's not what happened."

"You think Ruby could have turned her children over to her father?"

"I think it's possible. And if he's still alive, Royce is capable of any-thing." My gorge rose. "It doesn't play. Because why would he leave Ruby behind?"

"You're right, it doesn't play. Stop this."

I looked at my hands, made from the same human stream as Royce's. "You're a nice man, you know that?"

"Lots of people don't think so."

"Being with you is like seeing a car wreck on the road and knowing you're going to plow into it."

He reached over and touched my fingers. "Listen, I understand what you're trying to tell me, Ellen. I see the ways you're like your brother. But Royce Burns was—or still is—an evil person, and you're not."

"You believe in evil?"

"Of course, don't you?"

"I don't know yet."

When I got back to my hotel room, the phone was already ringing. It was after 2:00 A.M., and I had given the switchboard instructions not to call my room under any circumstances except an emergency.

"Ellen, they found the children," Blake said. "They're both dead. There was another cave, a fully stocked area, and it does look like a white militia thing. The children had been shut up inside a refrigerator. No signs of suffering. They were gone when they went in, or at least unconscious."

I tried to control my breathing. "So it's possible Ruby has been telling the truth?"

"I don't know. We'll need more time to figure out what happened."

"How can I help?"

"An FBI agent named Pete Peterson is on his way to pick you up right now. He'll take you out to Loretta's house while they break the news to the Redstones. I want you to be there with them, not only for Ruby's comfort but also to give me your sense of their reaction."

"I hope a doctor is coming with us."

"Yes, Pete's picking him up first."

"And you're going straight back to the site?"

"I'm still here."

"Thank you for including me in all this, Blake. I mean it."

My brother would have considered it weakness, my grief for children I had never even met.

After we arrived at Loretta's house and Pete Peterson gave Ruby and Lightman the news about their children's deaths, Lightman had to be forcibly restrained and sedated. Ruby remained shrunken and ashen on the sofa, silent with what seemed like shock. She kept murmuring, "I knew they were safe with God, I knew they were safe with God."

I sat with Ruby all night while the house filled with friends and neighbors, and press vans and police cars began lighting up the street like a carnival. Ruby's lips kept moving, but she no longer formed discernible words. After a while she pushed Lightman away from her and fell asleep, leaning close against me on the sofa. She was still sleeping this way when, soon after dawn, several FBI agents arrived to arrest her. Her fingerprints had been found all over the door of the refrigerator.

11

A few nights later, Blake and I sat in his unmarked car outside the Santa Fe jail, waiting for a police van that would transport Ruby to a more secure facility, when he gave me a piece of information that would remain off the record for a long time. On the naked chests of her children, inside their clothes, the coroner had found handwritten slips of paper that read GOD LOVES THE CHILDREN OF NOD.

I tried to imagine Ruby writing these notes. Did she fasten them to the children's chests before or after she gave them the Benadryl? Because they had not been sedated with anything mysterious, just ordinary cold medicine from a drugstore. In Ruby's handwritten statement, she described what she called "the plan." She was supposed to meet up at the Catacombs with a woman named Mary, who would then take the three of them to see her father, and Ruby had given the children the Benadryl so they wouldn't be afraid. But after several hours of waiting, no one had showed up, and she could offer no explanation of what else had happened. She did not remember how she got back to the reservation or who had hit her and tied her up. She knew only that she had waited and waited while the children were asleep on the cots, and she opened the refrigerator and took out a child-size carton of apple juice and drank it.

"Let's talk about Nod," I said to Blake. "I'm sorry to say that I think I know what it means. According to our dead grandmother, Cain killed his brother Abel and was banished to the land of Nod, where there were no other people, so he married an ape, or maybe a bear, and that's where the dark races all come from. According to Granny, Nod was Africa. I hope you realize that versions of this theory still float around in Christian fundamentalism. It's brought to you by the same folks who, not that long ago, believed slavery was sanctioned by the Bible."

Blake studied the contents of a box of donuts. Finally, he said, "Where does Granny's theory leave the Asians and Native Americans?"

"Well, you know how fast those mud people propagate. They'll take over the world if they're not stopped." I reached over his arm and picked up the chocolate glazed. "These aren't just for you, are they?"

"You're making light of this, Ellen?"

"Of course not, I'm just trying to stand it. Listen, millions of Christians have been brought up with these views, or with watered-down varieties. You think all this stuff has gone away?"

He chose a donut with multicolored sprinkles. "I don't understand how you and your brother turned out so differently."

"I can't account for it either. But maybe Royce and I aren't so different, except for our values and politics. If you can describe his views as political rather than genocidal. Actually, I think it was television that changed me. When I saw the Freedom Riders on TV, I began to suspect that maybe I'd been born on the wrong side of a mess. It was kind of like figuring out your grandparents were Nazis. And Royce seemed to understand all of this when he wrote his novel, before he turned into a fucking monster. I just don't know what happened to him. Maybe some kind of bizarre religious experience."

Blake consumed half his donut in one bite. "Here's something I've been thinking. If Ruby's prints hadn't been on the refrigerator, her story might have worked. That place really was some kind of camp for white supremacists, and Lightman didn't have any idea that Ruby was in contact with people like that. I doubt he'd ever heard of the Brotherhood, and he believed her about the kidnapping. Of course, he did find her tied up and knocked out, which would have been pretty convincing."

"Do you really think she some drank apple juice and doesn't remember anything? Did you even find an apple juice carton? I assume there were no prints out there besides Ruby's. And we still don't know who assaulted her."

"No juice cartons, and I'm sure anybody connected with the safe house is trained to wear gloves. They probably wear gloves when they're in the shower."

"Why are we so certain Ruby did this? Her fingerprints on the refrigerator don't make anything clear. It's not like she's confessed, and other people drove all over the tire tracks. I mean, what if Nod is a real place? Could there be some kind of camp with that name? Or sometime back in the eighties?"

"I don't see how that could have happened without one of the agencies knowing about it."

"I need to understand what Ruby did or didn't do. I need it for my own sanity. What I mean is, how the fuck could something like this happen?"

"Well, you may not even get to find out."

"Because?"

"Because the FBI and BATF won't want Ruby to stand trial. They'll portray the children's deaths as a personal crime and downplay any possibility that anyone from the Silent Brotherhood or its allies might still be operating. They'll present Ruby as a nut job who killed her children, which you realize may be accurate. But I'm sure they will want to locate your brother, if there is the least possibility he's still alive. Also, they'd probably like to find Magnus, unless they're the ones running him now. Or maybe—and this is my cynical side talking—maybe some inside group has been manipulating this situation all along, for its own reasons."

"For a law enforcement officer, that's a pretty outrageous thing to say."

"I suppose it is. But I think it's what you believe."

"Then you'd better give me another donut."

"A fundamentalist donut," he said when I chose a plain one.

"Listen, Blake, for someone who might be declared incompetent to stand trial, don't you think Ruby has managed to concoct very contradictory and detailed stories? I can't decide if she's a skilled liar or a mental case or both."

"It doesn't matter, because they'll get her to plead guilty, and that will be the end of it."

"I'm getting her a lawyer. The white supremacist underground won't want publicity either, so they'll agree with the feds about that."

"I wish you wouldn't keep pointing out parallels between these people and the United States government."

"It's all just white boys to me."

"Are you joking?"

"I wish I were."

"So where does that leave you and me?"

"Stuck in the mess with everybody else. There aren't any right moves for people who get it, Blake. We might or might not have insights about what's wrong, racism, sexism, money, but we're powerless to change much of anything. That's why you've ended up as a cop in Gallup and I go to AA meetings and take care of my crazy mother."

This bitter analysis left us wordless, but I could hear Blake breathing, which soothed me.

One unmarked car waited across from us in the empty parking lot. Inside it was my young reporter friend from the meeting, Claudia Friedman. The rest of the press had been notified that Ruby was going to be moved at 10:00 A.M. tomorrow and that a press conference would be held then, but with Blake's permission I'd told Claudia the truth.

A number squawked through Blake's radio, and he said, "Okay, they're bringing her out." With the light in the car switched off, we slipped out, not even shutting our car doors, so they wouldn't make any noise. Claudia did the same.

We moved quietly over to the dimly lit back door while two police cars and a van, all with their lights off, glided into the lot.

The side door to the jail opened, and Ruby moved sluggishly through it, flanked by two matrons and one male guard. Blake had told me they would all be wearing bulletproof vests. The hood of Ruby's sweatshirt had been pulled up, her hands and feet chained.

"Ruby," I said, "Ruby," I repeated, until she finally glanced at me. Her face was shrunken, blank as a mummy's. "I'm staying. I'm still here."

12

Ed Blake and I were lying in bed in my room at the El Rancho Hotel when he volunteered the information that Santane had been living for many years in Albuquerque, only an hour and a half from the Nogalu reservation.

I sat straight up. "Jesus, Blake, why didn't you tell me this before? How can I ever start trusting you?"

He turned on his side unperturbed, perhaps because of the sex. "You know I would have told you before if I could." He studied me for several seconds before saying, "When the children first went missing, the FBI tried to convince Santane to come to the reservation to help Ruby, both to comfort her and to see if she could get her to remember more. Santane refused. It was hard to make sense of her reaction."

The next evening, when I appeared without notice outside Santane's condominium door, standing in her bland hallway, she was unhappy to see me. "I cannot help Ruby," she said, before I could even speak. Her English remained beautifully modulated, though her British accent had lessened. Behind her I could see her into living room, sparsely furnished and serene.

I didn't bother with preliminaries either. "Why didn't you come to Ruby? She's your daughter. Why didn't you come when she first said her children had been kidnapped?"

She turned wordlessly, inviting me inside.

"Ruby has a head injury," I said to her retreating back, as graceful and narrow as I remembered it. "She needs you. You're her mother. There may be a trial."

She said, without looking at me, "She murdered her children." She pronounced the word oddly, like *murther.*

"But how do you know that's what really happened?"

Santane turned to face me. She looked much the same as she had two decades ago, when I'd visited her and Royce and the infant Ruby at their cabin in Mendocino, but there was something barren in her composure now. "Either Ruby did it or she let it happen."

"Who tied her up? Who hit her in the head?"

"Perhaps she did those things to herself."

"You look so much the same," I said, although every feature of her face had sharpened, deepened, as if it were not age that would destroy her but too much definition.

"I am not the same, and it was better that your brother left us. He was a very unhappy man." This seemed an overly generous assessment of someone who had once broken her arm.

"My brother may have turned into a monster," I said, "but he was not always so."

"No, not always."

We stood there considering each other. I wondered how she saw me, dressed in a T-shirt and jeans, my fishing overshirt hanging unbuttoned, in sandals because of the heat. "Stay here," she said. "I will make tea."

Soon we were sitting in her living room drinking tea from plain white mugs with Tetley teabags. The peaceful environment, I realized, was an illusion, the result of stringency, not of ease. There were no extraneous objects, no magazines or papers, no television, and her decorations contained no human images. Her environment felt like a large, well-done hotel room. "You don't have any pictures?"

"I have pictures."

"Santane, did you know Ruby's children?"

"Their fingerprints are on the chair you're sitting in."

My hands jumped up from the arms of the black enameled chair, a lovely replica that looked like a prop for a noir movie.

Her face still had that carved quality. "I can detect their scents in this room. For many years I thought that working with so many hair products would make me less susceptible to odors, but it has not."

Gingerly, I lowered my arms. "I heard you own your own shop. That you're married and successful now."

"The Vietnamese community has been kind to me."

I wanted to say something else, but instead I said, "What did they smell like?"

She had composed this answer: "Lucia smelled like a small white flower in Vietnam. *Merry* is the closest translation. Americans would find it odorless. And River smelled like running water. But sometimes he smelled like a puppy. A small, clean puppy."

"I'm sorry for your loss."

Something flickered in her eyes. "Don't say such stupid things."

I looked down at my hands. "I'll try to remember that."

She said, "Your hands are much like Ruby's."

I kept my head down.

"Royce is dead, Ellen," she said.

I wiped my eyes on my sleeve. "I don't believe that anymore, and my guess is you don't either."

"Royce is dead, and River and Lucia are dead, and soon Ruby will be dead too. We must let them go."

I studied her face. "How can you even talk like that?"

She breathed deeply, and for a second I felt her breath inside my chest, a white-hot locus of pain.

"What do you mean, Ruby will be dead too? They won't execute her."

"You don't know Ruby," she said.

"I want to help her if I can."

"How American of you. Does Ruby want your help?"

"I'm not sure."

She sighed again, her irritation now visible. "How is she handling herself?"

"She's on suicide watch, and they won't even let me to talk to her. They're keeping her in a paper dress in a single cell with only a mattress and paper sheets. Video cameras monitor her all the time."

Something unreadable crossed her face again.

"Santane, if Ruby is responsible for what happened to her children, then why didn't she take her own life as well?"

"Because suicide is a sin."

"And murder is not?"

"Ruby wanted to become a Catholic, and in Catholicism, one cannot be forgiven for suicide, because there is no opportunity to repent."

"That sounds so crazy." I placed the mug outside its saucer onto the enameled coffee table, wishing its finish would blister. "None of you are going to tell me what's going on, are you?"

"Ellen, nothing is going on, in the sense that you mean." Then, perhaps to distract me, she said, "All right, I will visit Ruby. But I hope you will begin to let go of my daughter and the rest of us too. Royce's family has only been a source of danger, and of much pain."

"I don't think of myself as Royce's family anymore. Royce became a horrible person, and his beliefs and actions were ghastly."

"But you're his sister."

"And she's his daughter."

A strobe of anguish crossed her face. "Don't you think we know that?"

Behind her, the front door opened and a man appeared in the frame. He paused and spoke sternly to her in Vietnamese. He was smaller than Santane and looked considerably older.

She answered him at some length, then turned to me and said, "My husband, Giang, is home."

He spoke again, not acknowledging me.

"You must go," she said.

He held the door open, his expression averted. I assumed he was angry about my presence.

"Thank you for talking with me," I said as Santane escorted me to the door. "Will you ask Ruby to speak with me too?"

"I have no power over Ruby's choices."

Her husband said something harsh, and for the first time Santane looked at me as if I were not an enemy. "My husband says you should stay away from us. And if you cannot do that, please have the good sense to be afraid."

13

W hen Santane arrived to visit Ruby at the Albuquerque jail, her small husband accompanied her. He and I sat for almost an hour in a waiting room that had the sterile feel of a doctor's office. I had not desired nor been asked to be present at the meeting between Santane and Ruby, but neither did I want to sit with this man who seemed to be glowering at me. Finally, he said, in perfect English, "Americans believe in the fresh start. Today is the first day of the rest of your life."

I realized he must be joking, so I said, "Into every life a little rain must fall."

He laughed, a surprisingly pleasant sound. "Pull yourself up by your bootstraps."

"When bad things happen to good people."

"Every cloud has a silver lining."

"Make that lemonade."

"I don't understand that one," he said.

"When life give you lemons, which are sour, you're supposed to make lemonade, which is sweet. Who were you in Vietnam?"

"A restaurant owner."

"And what did you have to do to get out?"

"Be very fortunate," he said. "What did your own forebears have to do?"

"I understand your point. Three of my grandparents were part of the Scotch-Irish migration. And the fourth—who knows? Cherokee is what I wish, but English is what I suspect. In any case, they were desperate people. What now is called white trash."

"Americans have no history. It is such a convenience."

"Of course we have a history. We crushed the natives and brought in the slaves, didn't we? And you're an American citizen now too, here in the land of self-invention. History is what keeps pushing us along."

"Only four generations in this country, and already you are a dangerous family."

"My brother is dangerous. I'm just obnoxious and well-meaning."

"I suspect you are nearly as dangerous as he."

"How?" I asked, genuinely interested. "Because all white people are dangerous?"

"If you understand that, then you know it's true. But, no, that is not what I mean. You are meddling in our affairs, Miss Burns. You bring your innocence, your hope. You believe there is some larger truth you will discern." He smiled with a trace of mockery.

"It's been a long time since someone labeled me innocent."

"You radiate your innocence, Miss Burns. My wife values it in you more than she wishes to, and I believe it is what she saw in your brother. And, of course, she loves it deeply in Ruby."

"Maybe the right word is naïveté?"

"Here is the mistake you are making: You may be innocent, but your blood is not. Blood has its own demands. An acorn cannot become a pine tree, no matter how good the quality of the soil."

"So are we talking symbolically now? Is this a conversation about genetics?"

"We are having a discussion about soil, Miss Burns, and about what can grow in it. You must come to my restaurant. I would like to feed you. And bring your police chief with you. He is a decent man. This is a serious invitation. Let me know when you would like to visit."

"May I ask why you call him my police chief?"

"Don't confuse privacy with secrecy, Miss Burns."

When Santane returned, she looked tired and gravely beautiful. She spoke first to Giang in Vietnamese, and there was something sharp in the exchange. Or maybe it was just the unfamiliar sound of their language. To me Santane turned and said, "Ruby has decided to try to tell you what happened, and I will attempt to do so as well. It is a difficult decision for us. Perhaps even a risky one."

"Let the chips fall where they may," Giang said.

14

Santane would not agree to meet with me at her apartment or at her husband's restaurant, and she would not permit me to take notes on our conversation. Instead we met in an Albuquerque diner, face to face in a booth with red imitation leather seats. She put a manila envelope on the table between us but kept her hand fixed upon it.

I ordered a chocolate milkshake, and Santane ordered tea. I had not been this close to Santane physically before, and perhaps this was some of what my brother had felt: an attraction to her opacity. She was probably only a few years younger than me, ten at most, but even with my face-lift I looked older. For the first time, I wondered how she had gotten from Vietnam to America.

After the waitress left us alone, Santane said, "I'm still not sure what you want from us."

"If Royce is alive, I want to find him. I hold him responsible for what has happened. And I want to help Ruby too, if she can be helped. But, Santane, I'm not sure why you think I'm intruding. Am I putting you in danger? Could that possibly be true after all these years?"

"How do you imagine your presence is helping? We would have gotten a lawyer without your intrusion. And please don't use that technique on me, addressing me by my first name in an attempt to foster false trust between us. That was a favorite of the Bureau of Alcohol, Tobacco and Firearms. Your BATF."

"My BATF?"

"They had a Korean woman question me first, before they realized I did not speak Korean and was not reassured merely by the sight of another Asian female." She smiled without any warmth. "BATF had some very bad people in it, but they were also quite stupid."

"Were the FBI people stupid too?"

"No. They seemed to want to protect Ruby and me. They were not using us in an attempt to find Royce. Or not only using us."

The milkshake was too thick to drink, so I picked up the long spoon. "I'm an alcoholic. I've been sober for a long time, but I still have this sugar thing."

Santane blew on her tea. "Yes, and you are probably a member of Alcoholics Anonymous. I have several clients in AA. You all have a certain gaze."

I felt even more unsettled. "What do you mean?"

"Your eyes have a quality of serenity. But is it real?"

I held steady on her gaze, which was not easy. "No, it's not. Not always. I used to have an AA bumper sticker on my car that said SERENITY, but I had to take it off because of several episodes of road rage."

When she smiled again, I studied her tea-stained teeth.

"I forgot how beautiful you are," I said.

She looked away. "You look too much like Ruby for me to be comfortable. Your skin is a different hue, and you're much older, of course. And you do not have Ruby's eyes. I believe the cast of your skin is called 'olive,' is it not?"

"No, it's called 'pink'. I think of myself as a pink person now because 'white' has become too contaminated. Is that envelope for me?"

She did not hand me the envelope but began to answer my questions in surprising detail. She said she had arrived in the United States with the first wave of refugees after the fall of Saigon; the Anglican mission in San Francisco had recruited her because their diocese had received a letter praising her virtues and devotion to the faith. This letter had come from her keeper—*keeper* was the word she used—a defense contractor who had required her to accompany him to Anglican services after every time they had "intimate relations." Santane had understood, even at fifteen, that she was not sinning, and she did not hate this man, who had been kind and who prized her British-accented English, but when an abortion became necessary, it left her with a sense of ruin she could not easily overcome. She had started going to a nearby Buddhist temple where she met Royce. He was young and hungry, and his eyes were as open as windows.

She pushed the envelope across the table and said, "Who knows why anybody loves anybody?"

Back at my hotel room in Gallup, I ordered a second milkshake from room service and opened the envelope she'd given me. Two papers were inside. The first was a note scribbled in Royce's cramped handwriting, in pencil on blue-lined paper.

> *My dearest Santane,*
>
> *A writer I admire once wrote that if we could hear the grass grow and the squirrel's heart beat, we would die of the roar that lies on the other side of silence. The first time I saw you, I heard that roar. Do you understand what I am saying? How much I love you?*

The second letter had been printed on computer paper.

> *Santane,*
>
> *I'm sorry I hit you. I do regret what I said to Ruby, but, as you must know by now, you and Ruby have become a source of anguish for me. I am a white man, and the white race is being eradicated. Without large-scale resistance, there will be no more of us, only this disastrous mongrelization that Ruby embodies. Caucasians are the core of civilization, and we must seize the future now, whatever the personal costs.*

As I had speculated, a bizarre religious experience was at the root of Royce's personality change. His letter tried to describe this event in some detail because apparently he needed Santane to "understand." He explained that the second time he'd gone to the Brotherhood compound, an evangelist named Billy Valentine had been preaching. During the speaking-in-tongues part of the service, which Royce had at first found ridiculous, he had raised his arms.

And this is what happened to me. Soon after I raised my arms a current of energy began to flow down my right hand. It was as real as water pouring over my skin. Then my feet got hot, and when I opened my eyes—I hadn't known they were closed—my legs were being transformed into black and yellow lights. What looked like luminous jewels were replacing my feet and ankles, and diamond and gold snakes were wrapping my legs and rising up me. I don't remember shouting, but it seems that I did. "Ecstasy" is not the right word because there is no right word. When I awoke several hours later, I was lying on a sofa, and William Luther Pierce, who later became my friend and mentor, was waiting in an armchair beside me. "You have a great gift. I have been looking for someone like you for a long time." Because this is what I had been shouting: "I AM THE ONE. I AM THE ONE." I don't remember much about how Ruby and I got back home, but it wasn't Joe who drove us. I was still confused by what had happened, and when I carried Ruby inside I whispered, "Don't you worry, baby, I love you more than God." I assumed she was asleep. In any case, what I said to Ruby was not true. I AM THE ONE, and I have to accept my destiny.

I did not know what to make of these letters. Royce had clearly loved Santane and Ruby, and it had mattered to him to attempt to explain his transformation. But what was it that had happened? I knew from my own experience that there are strong energies not yet understood—early in my sobriety I'd had powerful encounters with a shaman in Peru and a guru in Vermont—but I had never heard of anything as patently psychotic as Royce's vision. Maybe Joe Magnus reappearing in his life while he was living so peacefully with Santane had cracked Royce's mind, or maybe all religious fanatics must break apart on their roads to Damascus.

15

Ruby leaned against the back wall of her cell, arms spread against the raw cinder blocks. Wet gaps showed on both of the short sleeves of her paper dress.

"Can I sit down?" Without waiting for an answer, I sat on the naked mattress on her cot. The cell was bare except for the video camera in one corner and a metal toilet with no seat.

"They were all right," she said sullenly. "They were sleeping when I left. I just did what I was told."

"Please don't start with lies, Ruby. Are they giving you medications to help you calm down?"

"They're even giving me shots, but nothing does any good. How could it?"

I tried to quiet myself inside. "Why don't you come over here and sit down by me?"

Her steps were awkward, perhaps from the drugs, but she sat beside me on the cot. "It's like confession," she said. "When you sit beside the priest, you don't have to look at him through the grate. Even if you try, he just keeps looking forward."

"Are you saying you want me to keep looking forward?"

"Yes, please."

We stared at the cinder block wall, this one painted ocher. The unpainted back wall annoyed me. "Have you become a Catholic, Ruby? That's what I heard from your mother."

"The church was where I met Mr. Dabley."

The story that emerged in this first conversation was nearly as bizarre as her earlier tales. Two months ago, she claimed, she had been walking to her car in a parking lot at a small Catholic church in Bocca, Arizona, when a man named Claude Dabley approached her. She had been going twice a week to the noon Mass before her accounting class. Lightman didn't know about the accounting class and thought she still worked at a grocery store in Bocca. She knew he would be furious about her going to Mass, but ever since she saw the sacramental snake during the winter festival, she wanted to learn more about the Christian God. Jesus was always unselfish and fair to everyone, except to the moneylenders, and the smells and rituals of the Catholic Church calmed her. *This is my body and my blood* was a sickening idea, but the gods and ceremonies of the Nogalus were much worse. During the winter festival, when a giant puppet snake thrust its head through the doorway of her mother-in-law's house, she was terrified. She knew the figure wasn't real, but she felt a deep panic about it that she still couldn't explain.

"When you went to confession, did you tell the priest your secrets?"

"They wouldn't be secrets if I told him."

"Did you tell him who your father was?"

"No, but I told him about the man who kidnapped me, the one who said he was the hand of God."

I couldn't help but turn my head and look at her. "You were kidnapped, Ruby?"

She began to tear the hemline of her paper dress into little squares. "When I was fifteen, I hitchhiked over to Berkeley, and this crazy old man locked me in his car. Santane thought I'd run away again, and by the time she got worried, it was too late. Besides, we weren't the kind of people who called the police. Jerry claimed he was the prophet Jeremiah. He lived in a trailer in the woods, and his teeth had turned black. His mouth was the worst part, but some nice people helped me get away."

I tried to absorb what she was saying and gauge if any of it was true. "So, when you got back home, did you tell your mother what had happened?"

She stacked the tiny squares of paper on her knees and balanced four of them before they collapsed back into her lap. "It didn't take Santane long to make me confess, because I was pregnant. The old man kept saying, 'I'm the hand of God, honey, I'm your bad luck.' But maybe he wasn't bad luck, because Lucia came. Jeremiah was a white man, but then Lucia turned dark and her hair frizzled all up." She turned her head away and began to chew on her sleeve again.

"Go back for a minute, Ruby. Tell me more about the man in the parking lot at the church. You said his name was Claude Dabley?"

"He was dressed in a suit and tie, and his teeth were white and straight, like those people in toothpaste commercials. He was really skinny, and his face was swept back almost like a blade. He's the one who told me Daddy is still alive."

She rose, crossed the tiny cell and spit a piece of paper into the metal toilet. A third of her sleeve had disappeared. The squares of her hemline had dropped onto the floor, and I resisted the urge to pick them up.

She stared up at the video camera in the corner, suddenly distraught. "Why can't you at least let me have something to write with? Why won't you give me a Bible? How can I hurt myself with a Bible?"

"Ruby, let me see what I can do about it. I'm sure they'll give you a Bible, but I doubt they'll give you anything sharp, like a writing instrument. Would you like for me to ask for a priest to come see you?"

She made a strange harsh sound like a cough and then sat back down, burying her face against her knees. I wasn't sure whether or not to touch her, so I just stared down at the patch of gray mattress ticking between our legs.

"Please don't let them send a priest." She made that guttural sound again. "I know my father is alive, because why would Mr. Dabley say that if it isn't true? He told me to get a post office box in Bocca and write the number in the dust on my car. 'Don't wash your car,' Mr. Dabley said. He told me Daddy would write me a letter. He said Daddy knew I had children and wanted to see all of us, but it would have to be carefully arranged."

"You thought Royce was writing to you? Is that the letter Santane told me about, the one that came to the post office box?"

"When the first letter came, I showed it to her, but she said it wasn't his handwriting and that somebody was trying to trick me. She kept saying I was in danger. I hadn't seen her that upset since I was little."

I tried to imagine what Santane would look like upset. "Can you please stop chewing your dress?" I patted the dry part of the sleeve next to me.

When she turned, her gaze was burning, and I stood straight up. "You're the first person I've thought might understand," she said.

16

The second time I visited Ruby, she again was leaning against the back wall of her cell, but this time she held a small black Bible pressed against to her chest. "I know the whole story," she said. "Daddy told me. Cain killed his brother Abel, and he was banished to the land of Nod, and Daddy killed Joe Magnus's father, so I would have to go to Nod too." She thumped the Bible against her chest twice.

"Ruby, help me comprehend this. You're saying Nod was a real place?"

"Daddy explained everything to me. What happened to Joe Magnus's father was an accident, but even with all the meditation and praying, God wouldn't forgive him."

"Do you remember when Joe Magnus came to the cabin in Mendocino?"

"No, but I remember his beard and weird face. He looked like a big monkey, but a really mean one. Even his arms hung funny. Daddy told me I should never talk to him alone."

She began thumping the Bible against her chest as if it were her heartbeat. "When I was born, Daddy tried to deliver me himself, but Santane's vagina tore, so he had to take her to a hospital."

"Can you please sit down?" I sat on the cot again and patted the space beside me. Again, there was no cover on the thin gray mattress. "I'm surprised my brother would tell you something like that when you were so young."

Ruby did not move away from the wall. "He was very proud of it. And I delivered Lucia by myself in a hotel room."

"How could you possibly manage that? Ruby, I want to believe you, but you just keep telling me so many different stories."

"They're all true." She sat awkwardly beside me on the cot again, and again it was as if we were traveling together on a train. Her voice dropped to a whisper. "After Mr. Magnus came to the house, he and Daddy went into the woods. Mr. Magnus had a rifle with him because he was a soldier, but Daddy was a Buddhist. They brought back dead squirrels, and Daddy skinned them in the yard."

"Ruby, please tell me the truth. Where did Lucia's African American blood come from? You're saying someone kidnapped you when you were fifteen who called himself the prophet Jeremiah and that he was a white man?"

"Well, he looked and acted white, but then Lucia turned that chocolate color, so everyone started saying she was black."

"What do you mean, he acted white?"

"You know, like you do. Like all white people do."

Ruby described how they traveled to Nod in Joe Magnus's truck and she had to sit between the men, but she leaned as close to Royce as she could. "Daddy and I played clouds. One person says what a cloud looks like, and the other person tries to guess. We stopped at McDonald's, and I got a Happy Meal. There were two other children at Nod. One was this black boy named Stretch, and one was a white boy who had something wrong with him. We were in a building like a warehouse, only it was supposed to be a church. A lot of people had crowded inside, and a man was preaching. He had big white eyebrows, and his hair stood straight up because he had been shocked by the Holy Spirit. His name was Billy Valentine. They sang 'Onward, Christian Soldiers,' and people started raising their hands in the air and making noises. The children had to go up front first. Daddy made me do it. Reverend Valentine put his hand on my head."

"Have you told Santane about this?"

"I didn't tell her because she hated Mr. Magnus so much. She and Daddy would argue about him in whispers. She didn't want him to do it."

"To take you to that camp?"

"Or to have Mr. Magnus in the house. Daddy promised he wouldn't let anything bad happen to me, but she stopped speaking to him anyway." She studied the Bible on her knees.

"I see they gave you a new dress. Or whatever it is."

"I have paper underpants too."

"You're not going to chew your way out again, are you?" When she didn't reply I said, "What is it you want to have happen now, Ruby? What can I do to help you? I've hired a good lawyer. I hope that's okay with you."

"I have everything I want. My children are in heaven, and they're wearing little gold halos."

"You think they're wearing little gold halos?"

"Did you ever hear the song 'Jesus Loves the Little Children'?" She began to sing, "Red and yellow, black and white, they are precious in his sight. Jesus loves the little children of the world . . . and all those children have halos . . ."

I cut her off. "Do you still want to see Royce?"

She sighed and her hands went slack. "I know he can't come here. And it wouldn't really matter now." She touched the black cover of the Bible, tracing the gold word *Holy*. "I did want to go to the funeral. Did you go?"

"The ceremony was private, and Lightman didn't allow me or your mother to attend." I did not volunteer that Lightman had refused to claim Lucia's body.

According to Ruby, it was Mr. Dabley who had come up with the plan. Nogalus don't like having their pictures taken, but Ruby had pictures made before they moved to the reservation. The only reason she agreed to move there was to get help with the children. With Lucia, she had managed pretty well by living with another single mother, but after River was born, she and Lightman decided to move to the reservation because he had been offered an apprenticeship with a prominent knife-maker and his mother could help with the children.

At first Ruby did not find living with her mother-in-law so awful, but she kept wanting them to get remarried in a Nogalu ceremony because she said marriage by a justice of the peace did not count. Ruby kept saying "No, no, not yet," and then, when she saw the giant snake at the winter ceremony, she knew she could never marry Lightman the Nogalu way. The Nogalu belief system frightened her too much. Once Lightman had disappeared for three days, and when he returned, the inside of his mouth was burned black. For a while he could drink only the liquids his mother gave him, and he became too thin.

Mr. Dabley had told her that Royce wasn't killed in the fire at Whidbey Island, but he had been burned badly there. His right hand was damaged, so someone else had to write letters for him—because Ruby had asked about the handwriting. Dably said they had taken Royce to Brazil, but part of one foot had to be amputated. They'd saved his other leg, but now he needed a wheelchair most of the time. Still, Mr. Dabley insisted that Royce looked just like he always had, except for getting older and for the burns on his hand and foot and one side of his face. Being in the chair was sapping his strength, and he wanted to see Ruby again and meet his grandchildren while he still could.

"We'll have to arrange two separate trips," Mr. Dabley said. "We'll take the children first."

"No," Ruby told him, "no, no, that doesn't make any sense, and how could you handle Lucia and River without me?" He claimed a wonderful woman named Mary would accompany him when they came to pick up River and Lucia, and Ruby would have to pretend they had been kidnapped. Then Mary would take the children to her father, and within a week they would be dropped off at a hospital in the northwest.

Ruby hadn't believed what Mr. Dabley said until he gave her the rattles. Royce still had his collection from the snakes he killed as a boy. There were four sets of rattles that she had played with as a child. When Mr. Dabley handed her the smallest and palest of the collection, she felt struck, dazed with hope, and then something else gushed up inside her.

"I could feel it coming up inside me like a fountain. I thought I was going to start screaming, so I drove away, and I sat for two hours in the parking lot of Dunkin' Donuts, holding on to the rattles."

"Ruby, you were planning to let them take your children without you?"

"No, of course not. I told him I would never agree to that, and he would have to kidnap all three of us. Because I needed to see my father. Maybe I wasn't white, but I was part white. I don't know how Lucia got that dark, but it wasn't her fault. And Daddy had already told me that Jews were going to lead the revolution, so maybe I could convince him Native Americans should be given special treatment too. They live on their own reservations and aren't any trouble to anybody. And Lucia could be an exception because I was an exception."

This rush of information confused me. How had Ruby known Royce's views about Jews and the white apocalypse? Had he instructed her like this when she was only six years old? According to Ed Blake, it was Royce's pro-Semitism that had caused a major schism in the radical right and had put him in danger from his former allies. "Can you tell me more about Lucia, Ruby?"

"Lucia didn't make the mistake, I did."

"Lucia was a mistake?"

"No, I don't know."

My anger was quick and harsh. "You think Lucia was a mistake because she was dark-skinned and had nappy hair?"

"Don't say that word! That's a mean thing to say! Lucia had beautiful hair!"

"The way 'gook' is a mean thing to say?"

Ruby made a choking sound. "I did the right thing!"

"The right thing was to put your children inside a refrigerator?"

"There was a plan. They didn't come!"

"You did it, Ruby? You really did?"

Her wailing was so loud that two male guards came jogging to her cell. Ruby had buried her face into the torn edges of her dress, and I wrapped my arm tight across her shoulders. "We're okay," I said. "She's okay."

"I've called medical," one guard said. "You'll have to leave now."

"But she's finally trying to tell me what happened."

"You have to leave immediately," he said again, so I did, and Ruby's wailing followed me down the hall.

17

The lawyer I hired was a lean, morose man with thick black hair. His name was Billy Brock, and he was well-known for death penalty cases, although the death penalty seemed unlikely in Ruby's situation. Brock immediately advised Ruby not to answer any questions from law enforcement, even if he was present, and he also told her she should stop her conversations with me, a suggestion we both rejected. Later Brock told me that he didn't know whether Ruby had killed her children and didn't need or want to know. And once Brock was hired, I became increasingly reluctant to confide in Ed Blake.

I kept trying to work out a time line. According to the FBI, my brother had died in the fire along with the leader of the Silent Brotherhood in 1984, and Royce's body had been identified via DNA in 1986. Then, in 1993, government forces had set fire to a compound in Waco, Texas, that housed a religious cult called the Branch Davidians. Seventy-six people had died in that conflagration, two dozen of them children. Then, on April 19, 1995, four years ago, on the second anniversary of the destruction at Waco, a right-wing terrorist named Timothy McVeigh set off a massive bomb that collapsed the federal building in Oklahoma City. McVeigh's bomb had killed 168 people, 19 of them children. When

McVeigh was arrested some ninety minutes later, he had pages of *The Turner Diaries* inside an envelope in his car. McVeigh was scheduled to be executed, and his request that his death be televised had been turned down.

If, as the FBI claimed, the white terrorist movement had been disabled in the 1980s, if most of the members had been jailed or were dead, and any remaining extremist elements such as a compound at Elohim City in eastern Oklahoma were thoroughly monitored or infiltrated, how could the construction and detonation of a six-thousand-pound bomb on a bright blue morning have slipped through the FBI and BATF nets? Timothy McVeigh continued to insist he was an independent foot soldier in the war against the corrupt American government, but I had always wondered if he was. The many missing elements concerning the Oklahoma City bombing troubled me, and now I had a new and awful thought: What if my brother had somehow been involved in Oklahoma City? And what about Joe Magnus, one of the few figures still classified as a fugitive?

My current AA sponsor, a nice Charleston woman who drove a silver Mercedes and had her hair done weekly, drilled me repeatedly that I was not responsible for the world's troubles. "You and I are just these eentsy-beentsy specks, Ellen," she said in her heavy accent. "We are these tiny grains of sand. Your only task is to stay sober no matter what, so you must learn to yield to things you can't control. That certainly includes your dead brother. Your brother's actions were not your fault." I believed her because I wanted to, and a surprising peace had come to me during the years I'd been sober. Nevertheless, Estelle once remarked that I was "about the angriest white woman I've ever met."

"What do you mean?" I had said. "Because I wear these safari shirts? Most of them are really fishing shirts. I just like all the pockets."

"Yes, but you get them all in khaki."

"That's not true. I have an orange one and a green one. I even have a white one."

Estelle could not stop laughing.

I did not call my sponsor before I went to New Mexico, and I did not call her now.

18

The morning Ruby finally confessed everything to me, I returned to my hotel room and ordered a pot of coffee and a chocolate milkshake from room service. I still couldn't absorb what she had said. My breathing was starting to go out of whack, and I was afraid I'd hyperventilate, a frightening experience that had occurred twice in my early sobriety, so I spent a few hours consuming caffeine and sugar in my hotel room and picturing the slow surf of the beach in South Carolina, fighting the urge to get on a plane and go home.

When I had calmed down enough, or thought I had, I drove back to Albuquerque because I had agreed to meet Santane and Ed Blake for a meal at Giang's restaurant, and I couldn't think clearly enough to figure out how to get out of it. In a daze, I found myself walking beside Santane in the dry afternoon heat toward her husband's restaurant. She wore jeans and a T-shirt that said GIANG'S PLACE. I had not imagined Santane dressed like this. I asked, "Have you ever read *The Turner Diaries?*"

She didn't reply or even glance my way. I wondered if Ruby had told her the truth now too.

"I've read it twice," I said, "and I think it's one of the scariest books ever written."

Santane still didn't look at me, and I had trouble keeping up with her gait. "Of course I've read *The Turner Diaries*," she finally said. "But it's no stupider than a lot of other things."

"The author was Royce's first mentor. And Pierce's other novel, *Hunter*, is a how-to manual for murdering interracial couples. Did you read that one?"

She stopped mid-stride and turned to face me. "Listen, Ellen, I cut hair. That's all. My husband is a chef."

When she resumed walking, I had to jog to keep up her. "And I write about redneck junk food and go to AA meetings, but what we're doing can't be enough. It just can't be."

She did not speak or even look at me.

"Is it racist to say you're inscrutable?"

She stopped walking and pointed across the street to a Chinese place with a taco stand beside it. "That's our restaurant." Instead of crossing, she sat down on a low brick wall, and her face again took on its carved quality. "After Ruby received the rattles, it was clear to us that she and the children were in grave danger. But I will admit that I was not prepared to lose them by Ruby's own hand."

"So she's told you too?"

"Yes, but I already knew without knowing. I understand that you aren't able to discern much about my personal responses, Ellen, but this situation is extraordinarily difficult for me."

I wanted to say something sympathetic, but all I managed was, "Do you have any more of Royce's papers?"

"He burned what he didn't take with him. He made a fire in the backyard."

"Who took care of Ruby the day he left and you got hurt?"

"I had a white friend who wasn't scared of Royce. She kept Ruby with her own children. I was only in the hospital overnight. The emergency room doctor was worried about my cheekbone, but an X-ray showed it wasn't fractured. He set my arm and gave me painkillers and sent me on my way. Royce must have come back to the house later that night and put the letter I gave you on his desk. The printed letter. Or maybe I just hadn't noticed it earlier. I stayed out of his office, mostly, and he usually kept it locked."

"Where was Ruby when he was beating you?"

"To be fair, Ellen, he only hit me once. Ruby was hiding inside the hall closet. After he left, I kept telling her it would be okay, but she had slipped into a stupor."

"And after you got out of the hospital, you went back to the house?"

"I had to get our clothes and some money I'd hidden. Also, a ring of my mother's. I insisted that Ruby come inside with me because I wanted her to see that I wasn't afraid, but the truth is, I was very afraid. I thought Royce might be in there with Joe Magnus and Magnus might try to kill us. Ruby wanted to keep one of Royce's undershirts, so I let her do that. We didn't stay inside the house more than ten minutes. My friend took us to a women's shelter in Boise."

She tried to smile but stopped herself. "Here is what he was shouting at Ruby through the closet door: 'You are the biggest mistake of my life!' He shouted it twice. I can still hear it in my mind, and I'm sure Ruby does too. Of course, I already knew that was what he believed because he had taken her to that unspeakable camp, and she had heard some of the hideous things Magnus would say about us. But when Royce shouted at her through the closet door, it was as if he had thrust a spike into her heart. She was never the same again. Then he jerked the closet door open and saw her cowering in the corner like a dog, and I think he couldn't stand the sight of it, so he turned and hit me with his fist. My arm broke when I fell. Then he was gone, and I never saw him again. So now you know all of it."

I glanced up and down the street, the anonymous cars, the anonymous pedestrians. The ordinariness seemed so strange. "And now you think we are going to be able to walk over there and eat a friendly meal at your husband's restaurant?"

"Exactly," she said. "That is exactly what I think."

19

Because Giang had been so sophisticated about American clichés, the Chinese-American decor of his restaurant disappointed me. A cloudy fish tank with slow-moving inhabitants hulked near the cashier's desk, and Ed Blake and Giang sat at a back table covered with a red-checked plastic tablecloth. Blake wore a black police uniform, which made him look less familiar and more like an ordinary cop. Giang still seemed small and nondescript, but at least he wasn't wearing a chef's hat. They were drinking bottled Asian beer. A partially finished plate of spring rolls lay on the table before them.

Both men stood up. I shook hands with Giang but avoided eye contact with Blake. "So, Giang, I had assumed your restaurant would look more original."

"If it works, don't fix it."

"And I see you're feeling quite official." I reached across the table to shake Blake's hand. My glance at his gray eyes revealed his deep concern.

"So, what is this amazing food you want to introduce me to?" I said to Giang.

"Would you like a drink first?"

"I don't suppose you have a chocolate milkshake?"

"How about a beer? Or a glass of wine? Also, we have a full bar."

"A regular Coke," I said. "Two of them, please."

As I sat down the first gasp escaped me, and I began to take long, slow breaths, trying to imagine the sound of the rolling surf at the Isle of Palms. If I have trouble handling myself in public situations, this often helps: I concentrate on recalling the sound of the ocean as it pulls back from the shore on my inhalation, and, as the waves flow over the beach, I exhale. I try to pause at the top of each breath.

Blake touched my arm. "Are you all right?"

I kept my gaze on my empty plate, and when I looked up at him I knew my eyes had gone wild. "My mother said that I have a tender heart but that I would get over it." I suppressed a gasp. "Maybe she was right, because I care more about my family than I care about strangers. I'm just trying to look out for my own, but I don't know who my own are."

After a silence, Giang said, "This was a cruel thing for your mother to say. And also it is untrue."

The gasping stopped, but I still breathed shallowly, almost panting. "I thought wars were about territory and natural resources."

"Wars," Giang said, "can also be about tribes and religion."

Santane touched my arm, and I felt a kindness that had been absent from all of our previous interactions. "It has taken me a long time to accept this, Ellen, but Royce believed that what he was doing was right. Ruby may believe it too."

"It's just so unthinkable. It's unbelievably horrific."

"And you have turned thoroughly against your brother and his beliefs, have you not? You made this choice long ago, and you have lived by it."

"Then why do I want to find him? What good will it do me or anyone else? Maybe I just want to kill him." The two Cokes arrived, and I drank one straight down. Then I stood up and knocked my chair over behind me. "I've got to get out of here. Raincheck, please. Raincheck."

"Sorry, fish," I said, hurrying through the tables past the aquarium and finding myself outside on the hot street. Ed Blake had managed to stay right behind me. "Go away, Blake."

"I've really got to talk to you, Ellen," he said. "Something important has happened."

"I don't care what it is right now. Go away."

"Please. I need to talk to you."

I turned around and looked up into his face. "Listen, goddamn it, I am a temperamental, high-strung alcoholic, and my fucking sobriety is hanging by a thread. Don't you hear me? If I tell you to back off now, you have to back off."

The 4:00 P.M. meeting was almost half over when I got there. I sat in a straight-back chair in the corner of the last row, trying to stop my eyes from leaking. If I hyperventilated, I knew I would end up passing out and being carried to an emergency room, and I hadn't been through that drill in a long time. *Think of the ocean, the waves, the blue-gray sand, breathe in, breathe out.* I leaned over, head in my hands, eyes squeezed shut.

As the meeting proceeded, two women moved to sit in the chairs alongside me. They did not try to intrude, but one of them tapped my shoulder and gave me a tissue. The other handed me an empty paper bag that smelled like tuna fish. I didn't need the paper bag, and by the end of the meeting my panic had run itself out.

Daylight was fading and the air cooling off as I drove back to Gallup. I tried to ground myself more by focusing on details of my mother's care, but when I pulled up in front of the El Rancho Hotel, Ed Blake's car, a genuine police car this time, stood out front. I pulled in behind him and walked to the passenger-side window, which was open. "What?" I said.

"Ellen, I know how upset you are, but I think you should see the cave where this all happened. This is the only chance I'm going to get to show it to you."

I stared into his bloodshot eyes. "You're dogging me like this because you want me to see inside the damn cave where she did it?"

Then it was as if we were talking without words.

I handed my key to the valet and climbed into his police car. A shotgun was attached to a large radio that protruded between us, emitting static. Metal grillwork separated the front and back seats. "Just like in a fucking movie."

As we pulled away he turned on the blinking lights and let the siren howl. "For your movie," he said. Once we were out of Gallup, he shut off the fireworks display and turned off the crackling radio.

"Listen, Ed," I said in the sudden quiet. "I might be breaking now. I've broken pretty badly in my life before, and it's crucial that I not do it again, because then I might drink, which is the same as suicide for me. I just want to go home. I want to go back to Charleston and take off my mother's crazy makeup and eat boiled peanuts and sit in the dark and talk to my friend Estelle. Don't you ever feel like that? That you've fucking had enough? Really enough? That you just want to go home?"

"I've been wondering what was holding you together."

"My best friend Estelle is black and I'm white, and we don't even talk about it."

"Maybe your relationship isn't about that."

"This is my brother's mess, not mine. I've got to go back to South Carolina and try to get my bearings. Try to forget Ruby for a while. Walk on the beach. Stuff like that."

"Will that work?"

"I don't know."

"Of course you can go back to Charleston, Ellen, but first I want you to see where the children's deaths occurred, if you think you can stand it. Also, I have something else to tell you."

Beyond the tunnel of blacktop lit by our headlights lay the red and green hills preceding El Morro State Monument, but those hills seemed like a dream now, something I had conjured, and only this tunnel through the darkness held true. When we finally pulled off the highway onto a dirt road, I said, "This is the other way in?"

"You know about the two roads?"

"Ruby's told me a few things."

The dirt track was narrow and pocked, difficult to navigate. Thick brush scratched along my window. The darkness was too close; the cruiser was not made for this terrain. Once we nearly got high-centered by ruts as we crawled forward into our puny lights. Where we stopped, there was barely room to turn the car around. Blake shut off the motor and handed me a big black flashlight.

"More bad movie?"

"Could that be your sense of humor trying to peek through?"

"Can you tell me the other news now? I'm assuming it's bad. I know you'd tell me immediately if they've found my brother."

He walked ahead without answering. By the time we got to what I assumed was the barn, he had pushed aside three boundaries of yellow police tape. We entered through an open side door. The ovals of light from our flashlights revealed a dirt floor scattered with wood chips and straw. Sitting in the middle was a rickety two-seat linoleum-topped table and two chairs, faded green and rusty. An electric lantern rested on the table.

Blake picked the lantern up and flicked the switch. The dim light accentuated the room's bleakness. A mound of filthy blankets lay bunched against one wall. "This doesn't look like a place where kids did eighties-type drugs," I said. "It looks more like a place for shooting dope. Where's the refrigerator? Aren't we messing up evidence? Aren't we doing something we shouldn't?"

"This isn't the right room." He shone his light toward the far right, where a bureau had been shoved aside to reveal a much smaller opening. "It's back in there."

We stooped to get inside. Blake's flashlight revealed a small propane generator, and he flicked it on, but the light was blinding, the rumble alarming. "Jesus, they're not patrolling this place?"

When he shut it off, the silence seemed worse. "That was a crazy thing to do."

The flash of propane illumination and our lantern revealed the refrigerator with its open door, the metal shelves leaning against a dirt wall. To the left, I glimpsed cots with blankets, and in the room's center another table, this one made of raw pine. Four wooden chairs surrounded it. Big containers of water had been stacked to my right, along with crates of canned food. Twenty-pound sacks of dried beans and corn and rice and another propane stove were stored in the corner, where there were two more large propane tanks. "There weren't any weapons in here? Is this just a safe house, or was it a bomb shelter?"

"It's a safe house. A bomb shelter would have to be concrete, fortified, and airtight. No weapons, but we think they were taken out the day before."

"Any chance we're going to be caught?"

"Not tonight."

"I'm not as spooked as I thought I would be. Or maybe I'm so spooked I can't even tell anymore. Why did you want me to see this, Blake? Those are the beds over there. Ruby claims she put the kids on the cots side by side, right in their car seats." I sat down at the table. "And she sat right here. She says she stayed here for maybe a half hour the first time, while the children were asleep from the Benadryl."

"She's told you what really happened, hasn't she," Blake said. "I thought so, and that's why you fell apart in the restaurant?"

"She's told me." I focused on the yellow gleam of the lantern. "She says that when no one showed up she lugged each of them back out separately, still in their car seats, one at a time, sticking them through that narrow entryway. She said it was harder getting them out than bringing them in."

Blake said nothing, sitting in the chair next to me, his hand resting near the lamp.

"Then she fastened the seats into the car and strapped each one back into the belts correctly. She had to take each sleeping child out of the seats in order to install them into the car because kid seats are tricky. Then for a while she sat in the driver's seat with the door open, thinking about what to do next."

The line between magic and horror had thinned, and the light from the lamp made Blake seem eerily handsome.

"After a while, she says, she started the car and drove back out to the highway. I can't even glimpse her state of mind. She believed that Royce was still alive and that he was reclaiming her, but whoever was supposed to meet her here did not come. She began to think that something had gone wrong or it had been a cruel joke. So she drove back toward the reservation, but a few miles down the road she turned around, and this time, when she came back, she went through the front entrance, not even bothering with the secret way."

"Thank you for trying to tell me," Blake said.

"First, she unstrapped both children from their car seats and carried them together, one in each arm, while they were still unconscious. She says they felt weightless. Did I say that the generator was running when she first got here? That the room was all lit up? And the fridge was cold inside. She got the lamp from the other room just like we did, and she turned off the generator so she could hear better. She was worried Lightman might get home from work early. He didn't get back until four thirty, but what if he returned sooner? And she had told his mother she was taking the children shopping for clothes, but they were already unconscious in the car because she had put the Benadryl in their milk at lunch. She wasn't sure how long it would last. Without the lamp, this room would have been pitch-dark, even in daytime. She laid the children on the cots, and she says she sat here for so long that she thought that Lightman must have gotten back home, so she went outside and was amazed to find it was still afternoon. Next, she came back in here and picked up River and sat with him in one of these chairs. She says he was warm but very limp, and she's not sure what happened next, but she does remember picking up Lucia and sitting awhile with her too. And she also remembers going out to the car and pulling those blank deposit slips from the checkbook they kept in the glove box and writing on the backs of two of them GOD LOVES THE CHILDREN OF NOD. Deposit slips, for God's sake. It was the only paper she could find."

I pointed at the wire refrigerator shelves leaning against the dirt wall. "She didn't mention taking the shelves out, but of course she had to do that. She put Lucia in the refrigerator first, in a sitting position, with her knees up, her head tilted forward, and she put River in facing her, with his knees tucked between hers. She angled their heads toward each other. She said they looked really beautiful, folded together like that. It was as if they were sleeping. Maybe you saw the little tableau for yourself, her crèche. Then she says she prayed on her knees in front of the refrigerator. That may be the worst part for me, her praying on her knees in front of the refrigerator. Then she shut the door and turned off the light, and, when she left this time, she pushed the bureau back into place to cover the entrance. Outside, she says she drove straight back to the reservation crying and shouting the Twenty-third Psalm."

At some point, I had begun pacing the dirt floor and had picked up one of the sacks of dried beans to carry in my arms. Blake didn't try to stop me.

"Then, when she got back to the house, she found Lightman's hammer in his tool box and two rolls of duct tape, and she hit herself in the head so hard she blacked out. When she came to, she managed to tape her legs together, then her wrists and forearms. I don't know how she did it, semiconscious and bleeding from a cracked skull, but I do believe her about this. And with her arms pulled tight that way, she still managed to wind a loop of tape tight around her neck. Then she went to sleep, or lost consciousness. Maybe I just can't stand to think she went to sleep."

I dumped the bag of dried beans at my feet. "I just hope they didn't wake up."

Our ride back to Gallup was mostly silent, except for this exchange: "I know I've put you in a tough position, Blake, but I don't care. Please don't tell anybody, if you can manage that. Can you just assume I've told you personally, off the record?"

"It doesn't matter. I've been suspended. I'm not sure what the hell is going on."

When the lights of Gallup became visible on the horizon, I said, "I hope your suspension was the news you wanted to tell me."

He didn't reply, so I assumed we'd had enough for one night. But when he pulled to the curb in front of my hotel, he climbed out of the car and, before I could escape, drew me into the shadows under the eaves, locking his arms around me.

"I can't tonight, Blake. Really."

He held me like this, rocking my rigid body. "Tell me when you think you can handle something else."

I pulled away and looked into his eyes, which were dull with pain and exhaustion.

"I don't know how to tell you this except directly," he said. "Apparently, BATF has been bugging my house ever since you arrived."

I pushed him back so hard he stumbled. I sat down on the cement curb and put my head between my knees but soon realized I wasn't that upset. Maybe I had nothing left to react with. Blake hadn't moved from where he stood, so I looked over my shoulder at him. "Well, I hope they're impressed."

He stooped down beside me, so we were face-to-face. "I am very sorry, Ellen, and embarrassed for us both. Even my friend at the FBI isn't taking my calls. That's why I wanted to get you out there tonight, while I still could manage it. And this is what I'd like to suggest. Either come stay with me now or, when you get inside, ask for another room. Do you have cash? In the morning, pack your bags and check out of both rooms. I'll pick you up at six. Unless you want me to stay here with you now?"

"No. Too weird."

He stood up slowly. "Tomorrow there's more I want to tell you, some personal things, before you go back to Charleston."

20

The groggy desk clerk seemed unsurprised that, no, I did not want a room change but, yes, I wanted to pay cash for a second room. He was a plump young man with a brown face round as a moon. "Whatever you say, ma'am." He tried to summon a smile as he gave me a small white envelope embossed with the El Rancho logo. "This message came for you tonight."

I turned away from him to read the note that Santane had written in a calm, lucid hand. She asked me to take charge of Lucia's body. She had intended to discuss this request with me after our meal, and she hoped I was feeling better now.

> I simply cannot bring myself to bury this child, Ellen. I hope you will understand. I only ask that you not cremate her. The paperwork has been prepared and is waiting at the coroner's office. Thank you for coming, and for trying to help Ruby.

Blake's advice about rooms turned out to be good, because I fell onto the bedspread in the Humphrey Bogart room and slept soundly. When I awoke just before dawn, I returned to the Ida Lupino to shower but kept flashing onto the slasher scene in *Psycho*, so I sang Elvis Presley's "Blue Moon" very loud.

It was barely light out when I walked down the large, curved staircase. Ed Blake sat in the lobby with his back to me. He wore civilian clothes, no gun or badge in sight. He was lost in thought and hadn't heard me approach, so I hit the starter button on the old player piano behind him, which began to belt out "She'll Be Comin' 'Round the Mountain." He stood up, visibly annoyed. "Turn that damn thing off."

I turned it off, and he breathed deep, shrugged his apology, and said he knew a kitchen on the road to El Morro National Monument where locals drifted in during the early morning for take-out egg-and-bacon sandwiches. We could get good coffee there. El Morro was where he wanted to take me. "Have you been out to the big mesa?"

I tried to cheer him up. "Well, sightseeing hasn't been on my priority list."

"It's an important place to me."

We took my rental car, and, surprising myself, I even let him drive. Except for stopping for carryout coffee and sandwiches, we stayed quiet and passed the entrance to the Catacombs without comment. I was too drained to think about anything other than the fact that New Mexico was not where I belonged. Once we got to El Morro National Monument, he unlocked the big metal gate with his own key, drove us through, and relocked it. "A friend loaned it to me. Not legally, of course."

We needed almost an hour to climb the steep, rocky path. Blake volunteered that most tourists didn't make it past the watering hole at the base of the mesa, a dark blue spring edged thickly with green reeds. The spring had been key to the survival of both the Natives and their invaders, so the trail was lined with Spanish inscriptions carved into the sandstone as well as Native pictographs.

There isn't much to say about the view from the top of El Morro in the early morning except that it's beautiful. Not South Carolina, but beautiful. On the high mesa lay a partially excavated settlement where, Blake said, some fifteen hundred Natives had lived between the thirteenth and fourteenth centuries. The exposed honeycomb of rooms unsettled me. "These people must have been really short."

"I never know whether you're joking or not, Ellen. Of course these people were smaller than we are. This was seven hundred years ago. Do you realize they had to carry all of their water and food up here? Depressions in the rocks served as cisterns, and on the plains down there they grew corn. Archaeologists think maybe a big drought caused them to abandon this place."

We sat down on a large flat rock where we could see, in the rising light, extinct volcanoes and smaller mesas lining the horizon above the rapidly heating desert. The sandwiches were cold, but we ate them anyway, nursing our lukewarm coffee. Blake had brought along a small pack, and he stuffed our food wrappers into an outside pocket.

When I still didn't speak, he said, "Some anthropologists think these people were an anomaly. Their pictographs aren't like the other Pueblo tribes. It's possible they were forebears of the Zunis, because the Zuni language is different from the other Pueblo tongues, and the Zuni physiognomy is unusual."

I said as gently as I could, "Are you going to keep playing tour guide, or are you going to tell me what it is you're trying to say?"

"We're never going to know what these people were like." His face was so sad and suddenly much older. "What I wanted to tell you, Ellen, is the real reason that I'm not a federal agent anymore. You remember I already knew about your brother?"

"Yes, and your friend at the FBI office in Gallup gave you a copy of Royce's file. Mine too, unfortunately."

"That's right, but I haven't told you that I was in BATF before I was in the FBI, and how it might relate to your brother and Joe Magnus."

I stood up, spilling my coffee. "Jesus Christ, Blake, you were involved with Royce's case before this thing with Ruby happened?"

"No, of course not." He stood up too, but he had the presence of mind to put his coffee cup down first. "I wasn't involved at all. But all of the federal agents, even rookies like me, were aware of the Silent Brotherhood and the other white terrorist organizations. What I wanted to tell you is that I got fired from BATF because I found out there was a right-wing element operating within it. A rogue element. Maybe something like that is still happening. My friend in the FBI wasn't certain why BATF bugged us, but it was you they were following, not me."

"You know all this for certain? In the sixties we were right about the feds?" I began to walk away from him, skirting the edges of the excavated ruins. The inhabitants couldn't have been more than five feet tall.

Blake moved behind me, carrying his daypack. "Listen, there really was a lot to fear about the civil rights movement and the antiwar movement. Even from women like you. That's why there was a file."

"Lesbian nation, right? Sex without men, so fucking threatening. Why don't I climb down into one of these rooms so you can see what a larger-than-life woman really looks like?"

"Please stop walking away from me, Ellen."

I liked him so much and wished I did not.

"In the government," he said when I turned to him, "there was genuine fear that a revolution could get triggered in this country."

I looked up into his face. This man was making me cry and Ruby had not. "They thought white boys with college degrees and megaphones could start a revolution?"

"The white students weren't the problem. It was CORE and the Black Panthers that put all that paranoia on the government's radar."

"Those uppity folks might rise up?"

"It's not as ridiculous as it sounds. Okay, maybe it is. I love your fury about stupidity. It's such a relief talking to you. More than a relief."

He had begun to shiver, and I was shivering too, although we weren't cold. "Listen," he said, "I was a young, patriotic man, and in Vietnam I thought we were trying to save the world for democracy. But when the FBI burst into Fred Hampton's house in Chicago and killed him in his bed, I had my first doubts."

"You were in the Vietnam War? Is that something else you've left out?"

"Yes, but I was in navy intelligence, and I didn't get any closer to Vietnam than California. That was when BATF recruited me. Among the younger agents there was a lot of discussion about Hampton's death. Most of us approved of the decision to take him out, but we had serious disagreements about how it was done. He was asleep in bed, and they shot his pregnant wife beside him."

"I can't believe I'm even talking to you. You thought it was all right to 'take out' a Black Panther leader? It's bad enough that I have to deal with Royce Burns as my brother."

"This all happened a long time ago, Ellen, and we're both different now. I'm just trying to tell you the truth. I was a rookie BATF agent in North Carolina when there was a shoot-out between an organization called the Communist Workers' Party and the Ku Klux Klan. My job was to assist the local police behind the scenes. You don't remember any of this? It was all over the news. Anyway, a bunch of cars pulled up in front of the place where the commies were gathering, and the Klan guys got out of their cars and shot right into the crowd. One guy stood there firing with a cigarette hanging from his lip. Five of the six CWP leaders were shot in the head or heart. The only black male wasn't hit, and he was arrested for inciting to riot. Then the Klansmen drove away."

"That's a tidy scenario."

"Yes, but two video cameras were still running, which turned it into a public fiasco."

"Okay, I remember now."

"Here was my problem. I recognized the sharpshooter. He had been my informant on a previous case. His red beard was new, but I knew who he was. So I realized that someone must have sent him into this situation to assassinate the CWP leadership. I couldn't have been the only field agent who figured this out, but I was the only one naive enough to write a report. I was twenty-seven years old, and I thought we were the good guys. The CWP were just a bunch of loony intellectuals working in factories, trying to organize the workers. But because of my letter a big stink developed in BATF. The Klansmen got caught and were acquitted, except for the man with the red beard. Him they didn't find, of course. Then I got my first bad job review and was informed I was being transferred to Quantico because the FBI would be a better fit for me. In other words, I was forced to make a lateral move or I was done as a federal agent. But about your brother or you, no, I knew nothing at all. Not until Ruby's children went missing."

"I'm still so rattled about that file on me."

"Ellen, you went into hiding with a bombing fugitive."

"Her boyfriend was the bomber. She was never dangerous. We were just white girls who thought we were revolutionaries because we stole food from grocery stores and spray-painted buses with feminist slogans."

"Don't sell yourselves short. It wasn't the women's movement that was threatening, it was the overall picture. If the FBI leaders thought Martin Luther King was dangerous, can't you imagine what they thought about radical lesbians?"

"You're saying 'they' now?"

"I've always been saying 'they,' damn it, and now I'm probably going to lose my job again."

We stumbled along the mesa, past the excavation, into the untouched parts of the ruins. He pulled a packet smaller than a book out of his bag. "You ever see one of these?" He began to unfold a large silver square that looked like a piece of tin foil. It crinkled and flashed.

"A giant condom?"

He laughed. "No, it's a space blanket. Developed for astronauts and now used by backpackers and emergency rescue crews."

"I've seen them, but I doubt they keep anyone warm."

He wrapped it around us like a silver cocoon. "It wasn't only BATF I quit, Ellen. After a while I resigned from the FBI too. Then I joined the police force in Bowling Green, Ohio, where I had been based. As you might imagine, I went up their ranks fast. Within that world, I was a big deal. But I lost my heart for it when my marriage fell apart. So I came out here to rebuild myself."

He unwrapped us, spread the space blanket on the ground in a sandy place sheltered by a ledge of sandstone, and sat down.

"It's not that cold up here," I said as I sat down beside him. He arranged his daypack like a pillow and wrapped us both in the silver blanket. We lay on our sides, faces close together, as if this had been our intention all along.

I put my hand on his penis, half-erect inside his pants, and he began to stroke my breast. "A revolution is a woman who doesn't wear a bra."

I pulled my shirt up but didn't take it off, and he touched the mild scars under my breasts. "Had them lifted. Face too. Just because I don't wear makeup doesn't mean I'm not vain." I pulled his head up and kissed him on the mouth. "You taste like bacon."

He unzipped his pants and pulled them partway down.

I began unbuttoning his shirt. "Why do you always smell like Old Spice?" I held his unshaven face. "Listen, if Royce Burns is my brother, what am I supposed to do about it?"

We sat up to unlace and remove our boots, and soon all of our clothes were off. "I like being naked outdoors," he said.

I lay back, and he slid one finger inside me, then two. I groaned against my will but still managed to say, "No microphones up here?" The ground hurt my back, but I wasn't cold because of the space blanket. "Aren't we going to get sunburned?"

"Are you really a lesbian? I just don't understand what that means."

"Thank God for astronauts."

I tried to turn him over without uncovering us from our silver cocoon. "Isn't it time your back hurt a little?"

"Nope."

He kept me pinned beneath him while I half struggled against him, and he began to thrust with a steadiness, an intentness, looking down at me. I had to turn my face away. "If somebody interrupts us, I'll have to kill them."

"There's nobody else up here. Nobody alive."

We fucked for what seemed like a long time. I wrapped my legs around him and held on to his back so tight my arms began to go numb. I didn't want to come this way, helpless and pinned and aching in a way I couldn't remember. Then it was long and slow and spinning, and when I felt him come inside me, I came too.

Afterward we were silent, breathing, on our backs together and looking up at the clean blue sky. I turned on my side and studied his tough, salt-streaked face. Blackheads on his temples, nose hairs not plucked. Probably never had been plucked. He hadn't shaved, so my cheeks were chafed and burning. "Listen, Blake, sex can bond inappropriate people."

He sat up and stared toward the extinct volcanoes lining the horizon. "It's not the sex that's bonding us, Ellen."

I sat up too, touching the white rim of skin at his hairline. "What's your theory?"

"It's because I see who you are," he said, still looking at the horizon. "And you see me. So I think it's the usual stuff."

"I can't handle a connection like this, Blake. Too many trips around the block." I stood up and began to sort out my clothes. His semen ran down my leg, and I wiped it off with my underwear. "Maybe we should bury these up here," I said. "Leave another ghost behind."

He was sitting, naked, hairy, vulnerable. "I know how strong you are," he said, squinting because the sun was behind me. "It's part of what I like."

I handed him his white briefs. Fruit of the Loom. "I don't think our emotions are reliable right now."

He stood and balanced on one foot to step into his shorts. "Good luck with getting past this," he said.

PART II

There is never only one, of anyone.

—Margaret Atwood, *Cat's Eye*

1

Lightman Redstone had buried his son, River, on the Nogalu reservation in a private ceremony, but afterward someone bootlegged to the newspapers a photograph revealing a small wooden coffin surrounded by figures dressed in fantastical regalia. This blurry image revealed what seemed to be the head of an enormous beaked bird, a large snake, and a foreground figure conjuring nothing either human or animal. The group stood before a raw crevice near the base of a rugged mesa much slighter than El Morro. The bird figure was carrying a cross, because maybe all gods are useful in the death of a child.

According to press reports, River's grave would remain unmarked.

On the flight back to Charleston, I studied the most commonly available pictures of the children, newspaper copies of the photos Ruby had done in a studio before they moved to the reservation. River's picture drew me in less, possibly because his remains were not down in the cargo hold, but Lucia's image held me fast. She had the careless beauty of most four-year-olds, the openness of gaze and uncomplicated joy that come from waking up in the world. I sniffed the photo, which smelled of ink, not flowers. Lucia's baby teeth, small and even, shone against her skin. Ruby had not retreated from the claim that Lucia's darkness was inexplicable, that she had been kidnapped by a white man who called himself Jeremiah and claimed he was the hand of God.

She was drowsy with medication when she finally began speaking to me with any tenderness about her children. It was the day before she told me what had really happened in the cave, and whatever drug they had given her rendered her dreamy and haunting. She sat beside me on the cot, then unexpectedly lay down sideways and rested her head in my lap. I touched her uncertainly. Her hair was coarse and thick and black, the shaved place above her forehead bristling with new growth. The stitches were gone, but their tracks remained, crisscrossed and red and healing. I counted sixteen.

Lucia, she murmured, Lucia was a wonderment. She loved River too, of course, but Lucia came from God. Lucia's eyes were blue at birth, her skin pale, and as she darkened, her brown eyes always looked amazed. Did I know that Lucia learned to crawl backward before she learned to crawl forward? And that as a baby she slept with three pacifiers, one in her mouth and one for each hand? But Lucia was a wiggler, not a snuggler; River was a snuggler, River was a melter, River could melt into her like a plant taking root.

I rested my hand on her hair intermittently, the weight of sorrow in my chest like a stone.

The plane was not crowded, so I had an aisle seat. By the window sat a black man reading a book. Black was the correct word, but he was light-skinned enough to have freckles. He wore a gray business suit, and on his wrist was an expensive-looking watch with lots of dials, possibly a diver's watch. I couldn't tell what he was reading because of the light from the window. I wondered if he noticed me, what he made of my fishing shirt, the trout bag, the cowboy boots and turquoise bracelets I bought just before leaving.

"This is a picture of my niece," I said, thrusting the photo toward him. "Her name was Lucia. I'm taking her home for burial. She's on the plane with us."

He looked at me, startled, and took the picture from my hand. "I'm sorry for your loss," he said.

"I'm a white person," I said. "Or pink. Whatever you might choose to call it."

He studied Lucia more closely and frowned. "Is this one of the children whose mother put them in a refrigerator? Her body is actually on the plane with us?" He pushed the photo back at me as if it might burn his fingers. "You're a relative of Ruby Redstone's?"

"I'm her aunt. Royce Burns, the intellectual terrorist, he was my little brother."

"I'm sorry for the children, but I have no sympathy for Ruby Redstone." He turned back to his newspaper. "But you look like her. I didn't notice the resemblance before."

I picked up my trout bag and made my way toward the back of the plane. Hardly anyone glanced up at me.

In the tiny bathroom vibrating from the plane's engines, there was nothing to look at but my aging face, the one that Ruby's echoed so eerily. Despite the face-lift ten years ago, my skin was lined and weathered. I hadn't worn makeup since the 1970s, but sometimes I still considered having eyeliner tattooed onto me. Bob Dylan wore eyeliner, so it seemed okay. Now my eyes were dry and red, either from pain or from the parched air of the plane.

"Maybe I really am part Cherokee," I said out loud. My father had once taken me to a Cherokee tourist shop in the mountains of North Carolina, where he grew up. I'd been about five years old, crying because the altitude hurt my ears. He bought me a souvenir tomahawk, an oval rock strapped with rawhide into the top of a split stick. The edge of the rock was painted red. I tried hitting my arm to see if it hurt, but the rock fell out of the stick.

If I was part Cherokee, then I was Native American, because the man sitting next to me was black even though he had freckles and gray eyes. And if I wasn't white, then Royce wasn't white either, which would be a great joke on him. And maybe Ruby wasn't lying about the man named Jeremiah, or maybe Lucia's blood had been in our own family, which would be the best joke yet. But my brother and I were white, I understood that in my bones, and sooner or later I would have to figure out how to shoulder the burden of him and of our great-grandfather, photographed so proudly in his Confederate uniform.

I did not go back to my seat but sat in the empty, stiff-backed row by the toilets. Given what had happened to Ruby and her children, there were only three options open to me: guilt, avoidance, or action.

When we were little, I suspect that I did not love my brother. Our parents had wanted a boy; maybe they had always wanted a boy. "He's all boy!" my mother once shouted, when Royce peed in her face while she was changing his diaper. And what could that remark possibly mean? I worried a great deal about this as a child. I had always been called a tomboy, so was I part boy? If so, which part?

My brother, my brother, my brother.

Once our mother left me alone with him while I was using a large pair of scissors. "Don't let Royce touch those scissors. They're sharp." I cut out my drawing of South Carolina for World Geography class, handed Royce the scissors, and left the room. He stabbed his leg twice, but he didn't need stitches. "He wanted the scissors," I said.

Once Marie put Royce on the floor of the shower and turned on the water, but his shrieks brought our mother. "I was trying to wash him," Marie said, and I added, "I was trying to help."

I would have to cope with my desire to see Lucia's body before the undertaker rearranged her. Jimmy Beecher had been my sister's undertaker, and he had done an amazing job with Marie, but he insisted I leave Royce's remains sealed. So maybe I should buy the same child-size coffin for Lucia, and they could be like twins. And maybe I wanted to see Lucia's body because sometimes it is better to let what is ghastly be ghastly.

I began to love my brother after he killed Skip Magnus. I had been living in a lesbian commune in Northern California when my mother sent me the newspaper coverage. Royce's disputed hair had been shorn, and the pain coiled in his eyes connected us. When he got engaged to his debutante a year later, I flew home. He and Avery and I lounged around together in the yacht club's pool. I liked Avery, who was tall and leggy and not a bimbo. "I know you hate coming down here," Royce said, "but will you please come to our wedding?"

"Can I wear a tux? Can I be an usher?"

"No to being an usher, but you can wear anything you want."

His face was full of brightness and vitality. I knew he believed this marriage would save him. His eyes were hazel like mine, but what connected us was something I couldn't name, more like a tide sucking around my ankles. "When I'm home I always feel like I'm standing in the edge of the ocean, but I know it's only the shallow end of the pool."

"Jeez," Royce said.

Avery had a tinkling laugh that I liked.

"I told you," he said.

"I'm the only normal one in this family," I said, which sent them deeper into laughter.

"You're right," Avery said, "she's funny. Royce told me you were funny."

"Yes, even when I'm not joking."

Royce's gaze seemed so open, but I wore dark glasses, even at night. "Hollywood," I would say if anyone asked me, or, "light sensitivity, from when I saw the eclipse."

Royce and Avery listened patiently while I explained that marriage was part of a corrupt, vicious, capitalist system that turned women into property. After their wedding, I got very drunk, and Royce slow-danced with me in the dress I consented to wear.

When he disappeared the first time, I grieved for my brother, and when I located him living peacefully in Mendocino with Santane and their baby, the intensity of my relief astonished me. And when *The Burning Chest* was published, I fell for my brother completely.

I fell for my brother completely.

The Burning Chest chronicles the story of a young man much like Royce, who inherits a plantation and brings his young bride home. On this land, he creates the aristocratic life he thinks his wife wants. He has the original house torn down and a mansion built with a wide veranda and tall white columns much like Tara's.

The black caretakers on this imagined plantation are named John and Ruby Tillman, the names of the real caretakers at Blacklock, and the protagonist's story parallels Royce's in many ways. Royce did not write much about snakes in *The Burning Chest*, but he did describe his collection of rattles. In the novel, John Tillman gets committed to the state mental hospital, Ruby refuses to eat or leave their shack, and the protagonist then moves Ruby into the main house, where he tries to nurse her back to health while his moral compass churns. He begins meditating

using a Zen guidebook, and the descriptions of these meditations inter-
cut with Ruby's anguished ravings in Gullah gave the novel a luminosity
that drew much admiration.

Now I was sitting in the back of an airplane flying to South Carolina
to bury my brother's black granddaughter beside the coffin that I had
begun to think of as the Tomb of the Unknown Racist, and Royce's real
daughter was in prison for murdering her real children, and Royce was
almost certainly still out there.

2

Estelle picked me up outside the baggage claim area in Momma's ancient Mercedes, which sported a faded sticker of a Confederate flag with the words HERITAGE, NOT HATE across the back bumper. Inside the airport, I had bought a baseball cap that said CHARLESTON: THE HOLY CITY and pulled it low over my eyes, hoping no one would recognize me. Charleston, despite its prominence for tourists, remained in many ways a small town. Lucia's body had been quietly picked up by Jimmy Beecher's funeral parlor. I didn't know if anyone from the press besides Claudia Friedman would know or care that I had left New Mexico and brought Lucia back to Charleston with me, but I had called Claudia from a phone booth in the airport.

"Does this mean that I should come to South Carolina?"

"Can you afford it?"

"No."

"I think you need to get here. Maybe I can't promise you an interview with Ruby, but you'll have a story. I'm going to bury Lucia's body beside my brother and try to turn it into a big deal."

"Why?"

"Why turn it into a big deal?

"No, why are you helping me?"

"People helped me too, Claudia."

"Yes, but I hardly know what I'm doing."

"I think you've got promise written all over you. I've been sober a long time, and I'm a pretty good judge about stuff like that. Do you have an editor at the *Times* you can trust? Tell him that you're going to have an exclusive, and they'll probably pay your way down here. Call me when you arrive. Let me give you my numbers."

"I don't know what to say."

"Well, there's no crying in journalism."

I climbed into the passenger seat beside Estelle. "I can't believe you're picking me up in Momma's car with this bumper sticker."

"Mine's in the shop, and I was afraid to take the cover off yours."

"This isn't just to amuse yourself?"

She glanced at me, but I couldn't read her gaze.

"What," I said.

Estelle had straightened her hair and dyed it a reddish brown. Usually she wore her white uniform and tags because of the respect that came with them, but today she had on a sleeveless top and baggy shorts that let her thighs spread out on the worn leather seat.

She snorted with laughter.

"That good, huh?"

"Yo' mamma done lose her teeth. I took her out onto the balcony for some fresh air, and she whipped them out of her mouth and threw them right over the railing. Eleven floors. They could have killed a tourist!"

Estelle pulled onto the edge of the road—luckily we weren't on the interstate yet—while we had a good one. Tears on the face, that kind of laughter.

"It's been hard," she finally managed to say. "Listen to this. A local reporter learned my identity and located my family on Johns Island. I have six aunts, and the one who helped lead the hospital workers' strike in the sixties was featured again in the Sunday paper."

"I hope you saved the clipping. Nobody has tried to corner you personally?"

"No, because when I went out with your mother, she was the story. And when I'm by myself, I just act ignorant. It's all died down for the moment, thank God."

"I think that's about to change."

Once we had passed through the industrial areas of North Charleston and entered the city itself, even the asphalt sliding beneath us felt more familiar, more intimate. I opened the window, letting in the hot, heavy air while I stared down at the pavement. Palmetto trees lining the narrow street seemed so close I wanted to reach out and touch them. Palmettos are squat versions of the palms ubiquitous in Florida. The first time I went to Florida—I was fourteen and had not yet been anywhere farther than North Carolina—I'd been shocked by the tall, spindly trees. How could anybody get the coconuts down from palms like that? Of course, I had never seen anyone remove a coconut from a palmetto either, so I began looking for coconuts on the palmettos as we passed.

"Hey," Estelle said. "Get over it. Roll up that window."

"Do you know if palmettos grow coconuts?"

"I never thought about it."

"Estelle, can we go get some green peanuts? I think a big bowl of boiled peanuts and a couple of Co-Colas will do a lot for my mental health. But I don't want to walk into the store."

"I'll go in for you. But listen, seriously, what are we going to do about your mother's teeth?"

"One thing at a time. Peanuts, then Momma, then the body in the trunk."

"There's no body in the trunk. Are you needing an AA meeting?"

"Indeed, I am. But I'll go tonight or in the morning. Do you think Jimmy Beecher will give me any trouble about burying a famously murdered black child in the family plot?"

"He has to legally, I think. I'll bet he was more than willing to bury your crazy brother out there."

"Yeah, but Royce was white, and anyway, now I'm wondering if that's really Royce."

Estelle rarely went to AA meetings anymore, a fact that worried me. I still went to three or four a week, although I rarely considered drinking. But meetings quieted me inside and provided a framework for calm self-examination. At first, I had assumed AA was a cult, but at that period of my life I was hallucinating from drugs and too paranoid to enter a treatment center, so I just crawled around my apartment eating chocolate and experiencing what is called "the gift of desperation," because no one joins Alcoholics Anonymous and changes her whole fucking life without experiencing a bottomless desperation. In my early sobriety, I was so frightened that I spent several nights on the bathroom floor crouched under a blanket on the bright tiles, door locked, butcher knife in my hand. At dawn, I'd call my sleeping sponsor, who would murmur, "Did you have a drink or take a drug?"

"No," I'd sob.

"And did you go to a meeting last night?"

"Yes."

"Then you are a winner." She kept saying that word to me: *winner, winner, winner.* My terrors and rages would pass, she said, or at least lessen considerably, but I would have to walk through them without the relief of alcohol or drugs. "Try praying."

"But I don't believe in God."

"Pray anyway, because your body and brain have been damaged. Do these three things: don't drink or take drugs no matter what, go to meetings, and pray whether you mean it or not."

"But how will I know I'm recovering?"

"You'll know."

The terrors took more than a year to dissipate, and the rage, well, my temper could still blindside me. My early AA prayers consisted mainly of things like *Goddamn it, if you're out there, help me.* If I could remember to say or even think that, I would start to feel better. *So, hey, God, listen, I'm sorry for this foxhole stuff, but please don't make me admit to anyone that I talk to you.* Prayer seemed like the ultimate humiliation, the pathetic endgame. Yet slowly I did begin to recover, although during the first year I didn't feel much like a winner. More like a C minus. Gradually, that notion passed too, and, yes, I became a winner, at least against alcohol and drugs, while stability filled in slowly, like ink on a map.

After I had learned the AA lingo, meetings felt less threatening. For a while I assumed that sooner or later I would find out who was really running this outfit and where all those crinkly dollar bills went.

We passed a basket and were supposed to throw in a dollar or two, if we were able. I soon realized that we were like functional commies, and our slogans were more effective than Chairman Mao's. Mao had said things like *Learn swimming through swimming*, which may be useful advice if you don't want to be a brain surgeon, but *Keep It Simple, Stupid*, can function in any situation.

Estelle and I sat with Momma at the old mahogany table and ate boiled peanuts off paper plates. We had sent the health aide home. Momma liked to pick out the long peanuts with four or five wet nuts crammed inside one shell, and Estelle and I forwarded those to her plate. She began to growl with pleasure. Once, though, she surprised me by saying, "Hello, Ellen. How nice to see you."

Her teeth appeared too large for her mouth but didn't seem to bother her. I had sorted through the cabinet under her bathroom sink, where a thirty-year history of Merle Norman cosmetics crouched waiting, before finding an old set of teeth tucked inside a brown paper bag. I soaked the teeth in gin before giving them to her, afraid they would make her mouth sore, but I didn't know what else to do. I tried calling her old dentist, but he was dead.

Later, after Momma fell asleep, propped up on pillows and snoring lightly—her snoring could sound like a tin gutter being torn off a house—Estelle and I settled into the matching rocker recliners in her bedroom. We turned the recliners toward the sliding glass doors and stared out at the lights of the Cooper River Bridge. After a while Estelle said, "Why do you think she invited me to sit at the table today?"

"I don't know. Maybe because you don't have on your uniform?"

"I didn't think any human beings got to eat at that table, white or not. I've never even known her to eat there."

My mother's mahogany table was a source of great pride, like the hand-carved walnut piano no one could touch, although it was so out of tune it didn't sound much like a piano anymore. "Maybe it was the boiled peanuts. She told me that when she was a kid, her people lived on a farm for a couple of years, and one of her best memories was about all the children digging up the peanut mounds and washing them and boiling them in a big vat of salted water. But who knows, Estelle, tomorrow she might start calling both of us ugly names."

"She's never done that to me."

"She's done it to me."

"What did she call you?"

"Oh, just lesbian, unnatural, queer, stuff like that. My favorite line was, 'How did a lady like me raise a daughter like you?'"

I felt Estelle's smiling in the dark. "One of the best things about being raised by all those church ladies was learning to fight back without seeming like I'm fighting back. To keep myself contained and pray for my enemies and all that. Just to keep going forward."

"You pray for Momma?"

"She's not my enemy, but yes, I do, and I pray for you too."

"Jeez, Estelle, you must have missed me."

I heard the rocker clicking as she stood up. "Are we just going to keep sitting here like this?"

"I pray for you too," I said as she eased herself into my lap. "Oh my God, you feel so good."

Estelle and I often ended up in bed together if we were alone at night. This was a casual, friendly arrangement. For me, sex with one person rarely seemed related to sex with another, and Estelle, who had initiated this connection when we were still in Cambridge, seemed to feel the same way. We knew our attitude was unpopular, especially among women, and had learned our discretion separately at considerable cost. Ed Blake, though, Ed Blake might turn out to be a problem. He had unsealed something in me that felt dangerous.

Afterward, Estelle said, "You're wide open."

"Don't ask."

"Thank God for grown-ups."

"Estelle, do you ever think maybe we're going to mess our friendship up if we keep doing like this? I mean, I do pay you to stay with my mother."

"That's got nothing to do with you and me. And it's your mother who pays me, not you. You're just the intermediary."

"I'm the intermediary. I like that."

She reached toward the floor beside the bed. "Where's my underwear?"

"What do you think I should do about the body?"

"Yours? Nothing, please."

"You know who I mean. Lucia's body." I hadn't wanted to say her name.

She rolled over and looked at me, her dark eyes askance. "I don't understand your question."

"Do you think I should just bury her?"

"What else would you do?"

Estelle's drug of choice had been painkillers. Being a nurse practitioner, she could write prescriptions to false names and fill them for herself. Eventually, she graduated to snorting them and then to snorting heroin because *I just wanted to see how it felt.*

How did it feel?

Be glad you stayed away from it.

"We'd best get out of this bed now," she said. "Your mother has been known to wander around at night, and she's not so addled that she wouldn't recognize what we're doing. And, by the way, after tonight, while you're back in Charleston, I'm going to stay out at my own place."

"But will you go with me to the funeral home tomorrow?"

"Absolutely not. I told you I'm avoiding this whole mess. And I think you would have been wise to stay out of it too."

Momma's snoring stopped, and we were immobile until her motor restarted.

Then, in a low voice, I said, "I didn't think I still had this much anger about my brother lodged inside me. I thought I'd accepted all that detachment stuff in AA."

"Maybe it's a lot easier to detach from the past than it is from the present, especially when it's right in your face. And you've got a little girl's body to deal with."

"Tomorrow," I said, "tomorrow I'm going to declare war on my brother."

3

R oyce's ex-wife had always refused to talk with reporters, but she consented now to talk to me. Avery had not moved out of Charleston's
orbit, and I had always, in my trips home, tried to avoid her. Maybe I
blamed her for hurting Royce, or maybe I didn't want to know more
about their marriage and its many disappointments.

Avery lived on a houseboat that she kept docked out on James Island.
She suggested we meet out there, but I knew a boat would feel claustrophobic, so I recommended Magnolia Cemetery, which might also feel
claustrophobic, but I did want to visit the old graveyard. I planned to
bury Lucia in North Charleston, in our family plot at Carolina Memorial
Gardens, a modern place that had opened in the 1950s just before our
father died. Carolina Gardens offered no headstones, only ground-level
plaques in a wide green lawn with small, skinny copper vases bolted to
them. Most of the vases remained empty or held a few plastic flowers,
which created a nightmarish, spindly crop.

Magnolia, on the other hand, was ridiculously romantic. Mossy oaks
and heavy-scented magnolias shaded the paths that curved among the
graves. Sometimes a breeze wafted in from the river. These were mostly
Confederate graves, interspersed with a few Yankees and other peculiar-

ities, like a pyramid engraved with Masonic symbols, and a man buried under his cannon. But, since Magnolia is on the National Register of Historic Places, no one gets interred in the old section anymore. Only the crew of the *Hunley* had been buried here recently. The *Hunley* was an experimental Confederate vessel and, supposedly, the first submarine ever to sink another ship. A few years ago, when the *Hunley* was discovered and raised from Charleston Harbor, the six bodies of the crew were so well preserved that they still sat at their stations. Their burial had involved a great deal of hoopla, with hundreds of Confederate reenactors attending in their finery. One of my cousins wore his general's uniform and rode on a gray gelding he had named Traveller, after Robert E. Lee's mount. The crew of the *Hunley* had to be buried in concrete to prevent souvenir seekers from disturbing their remains.

I'd parked my canvas-draped car, the one Estelle had balked at driving, in the open area of the Dockside lot since Momma was only allotted one indoor space. My car stayed covered because I didn't want the paint to fade, and also because each time I removed it, the old Cadillac still provided me with a frisson of delight. I'd named her Nadine, and she was a nineteen-foot-long 1970 Deville convertible. Originally an unimaginative blue, I'd had her repainted ruby red with metallic flecks, her bench seats redone in white leather. I thought Nadine was hot, but among aficionados of vintage Cadillacs, she was what is called a cut-and-paste job. Nadine was wrong on so many levels, from her switched-out 460-cubic-inch motor to her six-speaker sound system, but for me she was like a beautiful old hooker, rusty and worn up close, fine from a distance.

It was 9:45 and already too hot to have the top down, but I dropped it anyway. Then I put white stripes of zinc oxide on my nose and cheekbones like war paint, hooked my white Holy City cap down low over my dark glasses, and listened to the motor purr before hitting play for Tina Turner.

Avery had arrived at the cemetery before me. She sat in a Jeep parked in the shade under a live oak. When she climbed down, I was surprised at how emaciated she looked. There was an aging hippie quality to her I hadn't expected. She wore no makeup except heavy eyeliner, and she kept her graying hair in a single braid that reached almost to her waist.

A men's long-sleeved white shirt protected her arms, a straw hat her face. Her boat shoes were not sufficient to prevent the peeling sunburn on her knobby ankles. Instead of a belt, a white nylon rope held up her baggy khakis.

"I don't think I've seen you since the wedding," I said.

She hugged me with wiry, surprising strength. "It's so awful about those children," she murmured, "but I do like your car."

We began to walk along the path into the cemetery. "At least it's cooler under the trees."

"I'm glad there's a breeze today," she said. "But even on still days, it can seem like the ocean is breathing."

"Wow, I sometimes think the ocean is breathing too. Is that what your boat thing is about?"

"We should get drunk together," she said. "I bet we could really tie one on."

"I've retired from drinking, Avery. With full honors, of course."

"I heard that somewhere." She lit a cigarette. "Want one?"

"More than you know. Regrettably, I've quit that too."

"What's left?"

"A few unfortunate light habits. But that does smell very good."

"I got married twice more after Royce, you know, but now I just keep a nice young man on my boat. Your brother and I were trying to be people we weren't."

"Momma says youth is wasted on the young, and by the time you figure out what you're doing, it's just too fucking late."

She smiled, revealing capped teeth. "I forgot you were funny. Your mother said 'fucking'?"

"Okay, a small embellishment on my part. But why does it have to be so fucking beautiful here?"

"In the cemetery?"

"All of it. Charleston."

"Ah."

"Don't you ever want to get out?"

"I did get out. I went to Barnard for a year. But everybody in New York was so busy. They seemed frantic, and not a bit friendly. It made me nervous."

"I think now I should burst into song. You know, like, 'What's it all about, Alfie?'"

Suddenly, Avery boomed out, in tune: "What's it all about, Alllllllll-fieeeeeee?" She strung out the word *Alfie* so that it echoed across the water.

"You are so unexpected," I said.

A tourist couple wandering the path ahead of us had turned, startled. "We're living Charlestonians!" I called to them.

"Let's sit on a grave and talk," Avery said. "I'm not sure what you want from me."

"I don't think I can sit on a grave just yet." We sat on a stone bench under the stinking magnolias and stared at the shimmering river.

"For one thing, I want to learn more about Royce's relationship with Joe Magnus when they were still in high school. Do you do know anything about it?"

"Were you in Charleston during the hospital workers' strike?"

I shook my sweating head.

"I wasn't either, but Royce was a senior at Porter-Gaud. I'm a year older than him, so I was already at Barnard. They had stopped making the Porter-Gaud boys wear those military uniforms, but they still had to wear khaki slacks and navy blazers with red neckties and white shirts. Royce looked very handsome dressed like that. Royce was very handsome. And during his senior year he was a local star because of his golf game. But Joe Magnus went to Rivers High School in North Charleston, and that was where all the trouble started. Joe Magnus was so nasty. He was such a disturbing man. I couldn't understand how Royce could be friends with him."

I didn't want to defend Royce, but I said, "Try to imagine it, Avery. Try to imagine their situation."

"I know, but it was an accident," Avery said.

"Yes, an accident in which Royce killed Joe's father in front of him."

She lit another cigarette. "Don't say 'killed,' please. Say 'caused his death.'" Her voice was so hoarse that I wondered if she had begun to tear up behind her dark glasses. "This is something your brother told me once," she said. "He said that when the broom handle hit Skip Magnus's temple, it was like a shiver came up the wood. It wasn't a hard blow, everyone said it wasn't a hard blow, but this shiver came up his arm when Skip's temple gave like that. Royce said the broom handle felt stuck in his brain too, and he would never be able to escape it." She wept openly, wiping her nose on her sleeve. "He couldn't figure out how to live with it, Ellen. Skip loved Royce. Everybody loved Royce. He had this sweetness . . . I don't know." Her voice toughened. "The truth is, I didn't even meet Royce until after the accident. The world is full of horrors, everybody knows that, but it's different when it's your own horror."

"What's your opinion, Avery? That the world is just a big series of accidents?"

"Maybe," she said. "But then it gets all tangled together, like a bunch of knots. I didn't know anybody else thought about stuff like this."

"My guess is everybody thinks about stuff like this. Why are you living on a boat?"

"I wish I had children," she said. "What I mean is, I wish Royce and I had children. Then maybe everything wouldn't have gotten so messed up."

"Or maybe it would have gotten even more messed up. Listen, it's too hot to stay out here. Let's ride down to Oscar's and sit in the cool dark."

Oscar's, a small restaurant venerated by native Charlestonians, was located near the City Market. You rarely see tourists in Oscar's. The de-cor is dated to the thirties or forties, but not in a designer way. It's mildly creepy unless you've been going there all your life.

We rode in the Cadillac because I didn't want to leave my car in a de-serted place. I turned off Tina Turner and spoke loud so Avery could hear me with the top down. "After the accident, Skip Magnus bought Royce a go-cart and brought it out to the plantation on Christmas afternoon, but our mother told him to take it home and give it to his own son. There was a lot of guilt and craziness going around."

Oscar's was deserted at eleven o'clock in the morning. We sat in a booth near a small stained-glass window, which gave us just enough light to peer dimly at each other. I ordered two Cokes, and Avery ordered a pitcher of beer.

"Beer? Back when you and Royce were married, I heard you were a pill addict."

"Yes, Placidyls," she said. "My mother and I both took them."

"My family took Ambars," I said. "For dieting. So it was amphetamines for us, barbiturates for y'all?"

"Doctors really didn't know what they were doing. Lots of people got addicted."

"Somebody gave me a Placidyl once, and I ended up in a diner shouting about some movie star, with a fork jammed into my cheek."

"You get used to them, but they were very hard to kick. I had a convulsion once, trying to detox myself without medical help."

"Did you do LSD and all that stuff?"

"Only marijuana. But I heard you did all of it."

"Yes. My brain's not completely fried, but it's been, let us say, sautéed. Even now, if I'm too tired, I can look down at a rug and see it jump into 3-D. Or wood grain starts moving like it's alive. After I got sober, I had awful anxiety attacks. But it's hard to know what's inborn and what's from the drugs."

Up close, our eyes uncovered by dark glasses, I glimpsed something. "I'm sorry," I said.

"Sorry for what, Ellen? Don't apologize for your brother."

"Avery, are you an alcoholic?"

She finished the first glass of beer and poured another while I glugged down my Coke. "I'll bet you see an alcoholic under every rock."

"Maybe I just see that you're unhappy."

"But you are?"

"Not at the moment, but I've been reasonably happy as a sober person."

"Do you remember the hospital workers' strike in 1969?"

"I wasn't here, but I saw it on the national news." I wondered why she was suddenly asking about this. To draw her out further I said, "I'll never forget all those black women walking down King Street in their white nurses' uniforms with the National Guard tanks rolling along behind them."

"It was Joe Magnus," Avery said. "Joe Magnus got Royce to help him set off a bomb during the strike. At least that's what Royce told me. Joe had been arrested for assaulting someone at the hospital march, and he'd been suspended for carrying a knife to school. Royce thought what was happening to Joe was his fault, so Joe was able to talk Royce into helping him set off a pipe bomb right over there." She pointed toward the Custom House. "Right where the Market Street meets East Bay."

I turned my head and squinted, as if I could see through Oscar's dark walls to the end of the block. "They really set off a bomb down here?"

"Well, they tried to. It didn't even make the news, except locally. And no one could decide whether it was an action in support of the strike or opposed to it. Royce said the bomb had not been much stronger than those TNTs we used to get for fireworks. He said they made it out of twenty M-80s."

"The ones that would blow off your fingers if you made a mistake?"

Avery smiled, her lips thin and chapped. "Can you believe what they used to let us play with? Royce said you just had to be quick and throw them before they exploded."

"I was always afraid I'd freeze. I threw the cherry bombs, but the M-80s, I wouldn't even light them on the ground."

"You want to know what it's like to be an aristocrat in Charleston? You get taught that you matter just for breathing. You believe you matter because a couple of hundred years ago your great-grandfather did something, and your house is a few hundred years old. It's ridiculous. There's nothing old in this country except the Indians. Excuse me, the Native Americans. Want to hear a good one? Fourteen ninety-two is when the Americans discovered Europe."

"I heard that one," I said. "I think it was Buffy Sainte-Marie, the folk singer, on *The Dick Cavett Show*."

"My family's house has been turned into a museum, and so what? We never had money, just the house, which we lost because of taxes. My father was an insurance agent, but he'd come home for lunch every day and we'd sit at the mahogany table in the dining room and he'd ring this little crystal dinner bell and the maid would bring us tuna fish sandwiches cut into squares. We ate with the family silver. Royce and I got two crystal dinner bells for wedding presents. But when we moved out to Blacklock, I started to realize I didn't want any of it. I had the plantation and the star husband, and I didn't want any of it. I don't think Royce did either."

"Avery, I don't understand. Why do you still live in Charleston?"

She looked puzzled. "Why, Charleston is the most beautiful city in America. Charleston is paradise."

4

Claudia had taken the night-owl flight through Atlanta, and she sounded jumpy with exhaustion and adrenaline. "You were right that my editor went for it, so here I am. Although the famous Del Mead may be close behind."

"Welcome to the Holy City," I said. "Take the Mills House shuttle downtown. You'll like the Mills House, but don't let them put you on the fourth floor because a man jumped out of a window on that one a few months ago. Get a tourist map of downtown and walk to the Battery and look at the seawall and the harbor and cannons. That's where the first shots of the Civil War were fired. The aristocrats watched from their verandas like it was a big fireworks display. It's beautiful down there. Go do that journalistic legwork."

"Don't make fun of me, and don't start ordering me around."

"You're right, Claudia. One of my character defects is a tendency to jump out of the car and start directing traffic. Metaphorically speaking."

"You and your metaphors," she said. "I need coffee and breakfast. Any suggestions about that?"

"I like this new, testy Claudia. Can I just say 'eggs and cheese grits at the Mills House' without sounding too bossy?"

"That will pass muster."

"And where does the phrase 'pass muster' come from?"

"It's military. Am I going to be quizzed further?"

"I'll pick you up in front of the Mills House at eleven forty-five."

With Nadine's top raised she was noisy, but at least the air conditioner still worked. I pulled up in front of the Mills House, got out of the car, and stood staring at Claudia standing on the sidewalk while she tried to think of something clever to say about Nadine. "Okay, I forgive you," she finally said as she tried opening the passenger-side door. "The cheese grits are good. And I tried the country ham."

"You'll be drinking water all day from the salt." I walked around the car to help her get in. "These doors are heavy, and this one's a little bit bent at the hinges. You have to raise the whole door slightly with the handle before you can make the latch work. Also, never push down the electric locks or we'll be climbing in and out of the windows."

I shut the door for her, walked back around, and got in beside her on the white leather bench seat. I expected her to comment further on Nadine, but instead she said, "How's your mother?"

"I see you've been doing your homework."

"Is there really a grocery store down here called Piggly Wiggly?"

"Yes, it's a chain. I think they might be up North somewhere too."

She nodded, staring ahead as we pulled into the traffic on the narrow street. "I assume it's too hot to drop the top on this contraption?"

"We'll have to wait till evening. We'll ride out to Folly Beach and go to a meeting. Right now we have an appointment at the funeral home. There was a Piggly Wiggly up in Moncks Corner that my mom and I stopped at once. They had a funeral cake in the display case with a rhinestone-studded lavender telephone on it and the words *Jesus Called*. I wanted Momma to buy it for me, but she wouldn't."

"How old were you?"

"About ten."

"You want me to believe you were acting this way at the age of ten?"

"Nope, I'm just trying to tell you about the Piggly Wiggly and how much I wanted a rhinestone telephone. Look, I've made you laugh."

Beecher's Mortuary had been burying Charlestonians since the end of the Civil War. James Beecher Sr. buried my father, and Jimmy Beecher Jr. buried my sister and Royce. Jimmy was a year behind Royce at Porter-Gaud, and they'd played on the golf team together.

Jimmy tried to hide his surprise that a *New York Times* reporter was accompanying me. He was dressed as an undertaker: discreet dark suit, dark tie, white shirt, wingtip black shoes. Claudia wore a white sundress, which I thought made her look unserious, a fact I planned to inform her of later. I was wearing khaki shorts and an ARMY shirt with the sleeves cut off. My face was still warlike with white stripes of zinc oxide. I kept on my Holy City cap but took off the dark glasses. After amenities—no coffee or tea, but water, yes, thanks—I said, "I want to get a special coffin for Lucia. You should have been faxed all the necessary releases. Also, I want her plaque to say Lucia Burns Godchild.

He hesitated, opening a manila folder. "Well, her grandmother's surname was Dao, Ellen. That's the name on the papers we received."

"Royce made us that name. You're a powerful man, Jimmy, and you can make this happen. The paperwork releases the body to me. I know the name Godchild is not on any of it, but this was the name her mother Ruby gave to enroll her in the Head Start program in California: Lucia Burns Godchild. My lawyer said there shouldn't be a problem. For the obituary she's Lucia Burns Godchild, daughter of Ruby Burns Redstone, and granddaughter of Royce Burns. I want a new plaque for Royce too. It should say Tomb of the Unknown Racist. It turns out Royce may not be who's in that grave, but I can't do anything about it yet."

Claudia wrote furiously. Jimmy stayed silent.

"Is Lucia's body here in the building?" I said. "Is it downstairs?"

He nodded slightly. "Yes."

"Listen, Jimmy, don't let me see her body before you work on her, even if I change my mind and try to make you let me, okay?"

He glanced at Claudia for support, but she did not look up from her notebook. "All right," he said.

"Can we go look at some coffins now?"

"Tell me what you meant," he said. "Your remark about Royce's remains."

"How soon can you get the plaques made? Can you get them in, like, two days?"

Arranging the release of Lucia's body had turned out to be somewhat complicated, since she'd never had a birth certificate. Like Ruby during the years Santane was hiding her, Lucia existed outside of known contexts. However, Ruby's own birth had been recorded in California as the daughter of Santane Dao, because when Royce took her to a hospital to be sewn up, they were unmarried. After Ruby ran away, she'd used a fake ID to get a driver's license, sent a fax of it to the hospital in Mendocino, and received a copy of her birth certificate, which said her name was Ruby Dao. But by the time she married Lightman, she was calling herself Ruby Burns. When Lightman refused to adopt Lucia, Ruby told everyone her daughter's last name was Godchild.

The coffin room, like all public areas of Beecher's, smelled suspiciously clean. Some dozen coffins were on display, and we wandered among them. Jimmy said there were more in storage, and he could show me photographs. "We only have two children's sizes in here," he said. "But, of course, we do have others."

"Of course." On the edge of my vision Claudia was scribbling again. "But I want a full-size one for Lucia."

"If you prefer," Jimmy said.

"This is the one I was remembering." I stroked an oversize purple-pink metallic casket with a mother-of-pearl polyester interior.

"That's an extra-wide model, Ellen, designed to hold someone over three hundred and fifty pounds."

"Do you have a regular adult one like this?"

He looked toward Claudia again, but her head was down and she was writing.

"If you don't, Jimmy, I'm going to have to bury her in this one."

"I do have the adult size, Ellen," he said, "but I hope you realize that this is a casket. Caskets are rectangular. Coffins are tapered."

"What difference could that possibly make?"

"Well, you buried your brother in a child-size coffin." He gestured toward a polished mahogany one.

"I know you don't like this choice, Jimmy, but we didn't have much of Royce to bury, whether that was Royce or not. Also, he was my little brother, so it all kind of worked out in my head. But I think Lucia Burns Godchild is a very large figure."

"Ellen, are you sure this is how you want to proceed in this situation?" Jimmy's hands were clean, his nails and cuticles trimmed, his skin soft with lotions.

"I'm sure."

We retreated to his comfortable office, where we signed a lot of papers. Lucia's gaudy casket was expensive. "Okay, can I see Lucia's body now?"

He glanced at Claudia. "You asked me not to allow you to see her."

"I've changed my mind. It can't be that bad. There was no violence. She died of oxygen deprivation, didn't she?"

"But she's been autopsied, Ellen. We certainly don't recommend viewing at this point."

"Has she been embalmed?"

"Yes."

"What do they do with a person's blood after they're embalmed?"

"It is disposed of sanitarily and respectfully."

"But isn't blood an important part of a person's body, Jimmy? What do they do with it, flush it down a drain into the sewer system?"

He didn't reply but tried to look sympathetic.

I pushed the photo of Lucia across his desk. "Can you make her look like this? I'm not sure anybody will be viewing her, maybe not even me, but I'd like her to look like her authentic self as much as possible."

"Do you have garments for her?"

"Fuck." I suddenly feared I might cry, and he saw that in my eyes.

He said gently, "Why don't we clothe her in a simple white gown? Something nice, with a little lace. We can arrange that for you."

I hated the idea of crying in front of him. "Will she need shoes?"

"We'll arrange some small white slippers. Like ballet slippers."

Outside, in the blistering parking lot, I opened Claudia's door for her. I'd left the windows open to keep the car cooler. When I got into the driver's side, I started the motor and air conditioner and raised the electric windows. "Please don't say anything right now." I concentrated on the ocean, the in breath and out breath, and later we would listen to the real ocean.

We drove all the way to a car rental place on East Bay Street before Claudia spoke. "I assume that lawyer thing was a bluff?"

"Yes, of course, but I do have a lawyer. I want to tell you something important, Claudia, that might help you with your career. In my experience, authority belongs to whoever decides to seize it. So seize your authority. At first, I didn't think that dress you're wearing, that frocky thing, was such a good idea, but maybe you can get people to think you're harmless. I saw that happen with Jimmy. He wrote you off as a good girl. I play it different. That's why I have all this stuff on my face. That's what the men's shirts and trout bag are for. Other than that I like them."

"What exactly is a trout bag?"

"A tailored canvas bag with a rubber lining, in case I ever want to keep dead fish in it."

I saw the glint of a smile.

"So, listen, Girl Reporter, you need to rent a car now. You'll need a car anyway, and I want you to do something for me. Participatory journalism. I'd like for you to go to some stores and buy a couple of dozen toys that would be appropriate for a four-year-old kid. Stuffed animals, things like that. Will you do it? Do you have a credit card you can use? I'll pay you back, or we can go get some cash for you now."

"Do you care what stores I go into?"

"No. But it all has to fit into that awful purple-pink thing."

"What's up with that?"

"I want Lucia to be happy in paradise. I thought a colorful ride might make a little kid happy."

5

A round 4:30, I picked Claudia up again at the Mills House. Nadine's top was down now. It was still hot, but the sun no longer beat
straight onto us. Claudia had changed into shorts and sandals, and she
wore, over a silky black top, a lightweight khaki men's shirt, unbuttoned,
with the sleeves rolled up. She opened the car door like an expert.

"You got what I asked?"

"I did my best."

"I've called a press conference for tomorrow." We pulled into the
stream of traffic. "Only local TV and newspapers. And you, of course."

"And maybe Del Mead," she said, as we reached the road that runs
beside the harbor. "He's supposed to be arriving late tonight." When I
didn't comment, she said, "I like Charleston."

"Of course, because Charleston is paradise. Did you buy that shirt
today, or did you bring it with you?"

"None of your business." She had to shout when we crossed the old
Ashley River Bridge and the wind began to blow us clean.

I settled back into Nadine and let the velocity hold us. We crossed
the Wappoo Creek Bridge onto James Island. At a stoplight, Claudia
said, "Where are we going?"

"Out to Folly Beach. I want you to see Folly Beach."

"Everything is so flat here."

"That's because the ocean used to reach a hundred miles inland. At the Isle of Palms you can walk out into the water a hundred yards and still be only waist deep."

"What's so special about Folly?"

The light changed, and talking again became difficult. "Folly Beach is washing away. When the Army Corps of Engineers built the jetties to keep the harbor open, they caused the sand to build up on Sullivan's Island and the Isle of Palms. Those islands have all the sand that belongs on Folly. Then the hurricane of 1938 ripped off the entire front row, the really big beach houses."

As the sun fell, the damp air cooled and began to feel wonderful. We stopped first at a restaurant on the Folly River, which divides the island from the mainland. The Sea Shack was the kind of place that spread newspapers on our table and dumped out a bucket of boiled shrimp and a pan of roasted oysters. I showed Claudia how to use the oyster knife and glove to pry them open and throw the shells into the bucket beside us on the sawdust-covered floor. "I think Charlestonians roast the oysters so we can eat them faster. Opening them up while they're raw is too much work."

"This sure seems like beer food," Claudia said.

I had ordered a pitcher of Coca-Cola, and she asked for sweet tea.

"Wow," she said, popping a shrimp into her mouth.

"See? The small local shrimp are always sweeter. Now you know something new."

"What did you do while I went shopping?"

"I took my mother to a dentist so he could adjust her spare teeth and make a cast of them. Next time we'll know what to do in an emergency."

"What?"

"Yesterday my mother threw her teeth off the balcony, but nobody recognized us when we were out. Her old Mercedes with the Confederate bumper sticker is quite a disguise."

"Do you know that being here with you does not feel any weirder than every other day of my sobriety? Being sober, I feel as if I've woken up in another world."

"I know exactly what you mean. You'll begin to see how everything just gets weirder and weirder, because the truth is, reality is so genuinely bizarre. Also, it's chock-full of people even crazier than we are."

"Well, that's a cheerful view."

"I'll say this. I've never had a bored day sober. And I was bored a lot when I was using."

"I can't imagine what an amped-up version of you would be like."

"One of my old friends says I'm completely the same but completely different."

"What is this thing going on with you and Chief Blake?"

She saw me react. "Nothing. None of your beeswax."

"There are rumors. You must know that."

"I do know that."

"Aren't you a lesbian?"

"Listen to me, Claudia Friedman. I am not your journalistic subject. I am your source. No profiles of me—swear it on your, I don't know, swear it on your sobriety."

She stopped eating and emptied the rest of my pitcher of Coke into her own glass. "That's hard," she said, "because you're so quotable. But of course, yes, I'll do what you ask. I give you my word. And if I ask questions that are out of bounds, let me know the way you just did. I'm pretty curious, but I won't pry." She held up three fingers as if she were saying the Girl Scout Promise. "On my sobriety, which I hope is not fragile, and on my life, which I know is not fragile, or it would already be over."

I tried to gauge her truthfulness. "Okay," I said.

It was almost eight o'clock, and dusk had settled in. "I didn't plan this correctly, damn it. I wanted to ride you up and down the front beach road so you could see what I mean about Folly Beach washing away. After the 1938 hurricane tore up the coast, there was this interesting class effect. The houses left after the storm were more modest. And it's not a beach you can walk along anymore, because they've put all these breakwaters out there to try to stop the erosion. It's treacherous. There are riptides. Deep holes in the water you don't expect. So, if you're going to find a serial killer in Charleston, he's probably hiding at Folly Beach. Lots of drugs out here, and active alcoholics."

As if on cue, a tall man with a thick beard staggered toward the door.

At our table he paused, leaned too close to my face, and said, "I know who you are."

After he left, we sat still for several seconds. "So, Claudia, I'm thinking we'd best get ourselves away from this place."

Outside I held a small canister of pepper spray ready in my hand, but the man no longer seemed to be around, and Nadine appeared unharmed. I tried not to show how rattled I was.

The Tuesday night meeting on Folly Beach was chaired by a woman named Rose. The job of chairing any AA meeting generally rotates every couple of months among its members, but the meeting at Folly had been run by Rose for almost two years because nobody wanted her to step down. It was hard to identify what was so compelling about Rose. She was middle-aged, white, late forties or early fifties, hair dyed brown, gray roots showing. She wore makeup and dressed inexpensively, and she always wore straw pumps with little flowers on the tops. She painted her toenails red, but her fingernails she kept groomed and natural. When she called the meeting to order and read the Preamble, people listened as if they'd never heard it before.

There were only about twenty people in the room, all white, most of them beach derelicts. "Any newcomers?" No one raised a hand. "Anyone returning after further research?" Two hands went up, both belonging to women in such rough shape I couldn't guess their ages. "Welcome back. Are there any visitors?" Claudia raised her hand. "My name is Claudia, and I'm an alcoholic and drug addict visiting from New Mexico."

"Welcome," the group mumbled, more or less in unison.

Rose's topic this night was "The Gift of Sobriety." She talked about how difficult it had been to put a week together when she first came in, how many times she'd had to raise her hand to say she was returning. "I'd get two, three days. Once I got a whole month. But I just kept coming back. Then I don't know what happened. One day I stayed. It took me a long time to surrender." I knew she was indirectly addressing the women returning. "We all come in here thinking we're different. We think this program works for other people, but it won't work for us. Anyway, that's what I thought, that y'all are nice folks and all that, but this can't work for me, I'm too far gone. And, of course, I had my secrets. I'll tell you the rough ones in private sometime, if you think it might help you. But here are a couple: I was a prostitute for three years. I broke into a drugstore and stole drugs with my boyfriend, and I got sentenced to a treatment center instead of jail for testifying against him. But you know what happened as soon as I was released from treatment? I got drunk and jumped off the Cooper River Bridge. Broke both legs, but didn't die."

The thing I like best about Rose's story—jumping off the bridge comes in second—is when she talks about having the opportunity, before her mother died, to take her to Magnolia Gardens in her wheelchair, steering her through the paths of flowers. I disliked the swaths of garish azaleas that flushed the Charleston landscape every spring. Each property seemed to have azaleas, clashing pinks and yellows and reds and oranges, and I found them as alarming as giant white magnolia blossoms. But Rose spoke about taking her mother to the Gardens when it was in full bloom, and how lovely it was with all the brilliant colors. She called the colors brilliant, and spoke about what it meant to share something like this with her mother, who had suffered so much over Rose's debacles. Rose's eyes filled with tears when she talked about the gift of being allowed to do this simple thing for her mother.

Soon after I heard Rose tell this story, I took my mother to Magnolia Gardens, and she loved it. She said it was so much better than the time I dragged her through the Holocaust Museum in Washington, DC.

6

The next morning, I held my press conference at the foot of the City Market, in the same place where, according to Avery, Joe Magnus and Royce set off a bomb while they were still teenagers. When I was a child, locals always referred to this two-block open-air building running down the center of Market Street as the Old Slave Mart, but as Charleston was transformed from a lovely old city preserved like a jar of figs into a tourist attraction displaying the scalding virtues of preservation, the slave market, we were now assured, had really been the Old City Market, and the actual Slave Mart had been over on Chalmers Street. No human beings had ever been sold in this space, only blameless vegetables and fruits and quilts and jams and baskets made by pleasant old darkies wearing Aunt Jemima scarves. During the preservation movement, the first block of the City Market was rehabilitated into boutique shops, and the second block, the one Avery had pointed at, was stuffed now with vendors selling tourist wares. Silver sand dollars on little silver chains were favorites, as were the sweet grass baskets woven by "basket ladies," canny black women who had begun to understand the value of their craft, brought to this country, like Gullah, from West Africa. The baskets were expensive, and though the women still sat on corners weaving them, the older ones teaching the younger to make the intricate patterns, they no longer kowtowed, ingratiated themselves, or bargained. These baskets were what I usually gave Yankees for presents, and next time I went to New Mexico I intended to bring one to Ed Blake.

By 10:00 A.M., the corner of East Bay and Market Street became congested with reporters and cameras. The midmorning cars moved by slowly, their occupants straining to see what was happening. I borrowed a wooden crate from a vendor, an elderly black man with professionally friendly eyes, and stood atop it, passing out my flyers with these basic lines:

BLACK GRANDDAUGHTER OF FAMOUS WHITE RACIST TO BE BURIED BESIDE HIM

Lucia Burns Godchild, the four-year-old granddaughter of deceased white supremacist Royce Burns, will be buried beside him Wednesday at 1 P.M. at Carolina Memorial Gardens in North Charleston. Ruby Burns Redstone, mother of Lucia and daughter of Royce Burns, is being held without bond in Albuquerque, New Mexico, charged with the murders of her daughter and her son. River, aged two, was buried last week in a private ceremony on New Mexico's Nogalu Reservation.

Ruby Redstone's mother was a Vietnamese immigrant with whom Royce Burns cohabited but failed to marry before disowning her and their child several years before his death.

The identity of Lucia Burns Godchild's father remains unknown.

All who are concerned about the continuing presence of racism in our society are welcome to come honor the burial of this innocent child.

Calling hours will be at J. Henry Beecher's tomorrow, from 3–6.

I read the flyer loud, which quieted everyone. Then I spoke more informally. "You may wonder why this announcement is being made at this particular location. I learned recently that back in 1969, my brother Royce Burns and his friend Joe Magnus, a terrorist who remains uncaptured to this day, tried to set off a bomb on this very corner. They were protesting a strike by a group of black female hospital workers who wanted to unionize and win pay equal to the white workers. My brother and Joe Magnus's attempt to set off a bomb here was so incompetent and ineffective it didn't even make significant news."

I paused and Claudia Friedman shouted her planted question: "What happened to Joe Magnus?"

"You'll have to ask the Bureau of Alcohol, Tobacco and Firearms about that. He's probably working for them now."

"Is your brother really dead?"

"I doubt it."

In answering other questions, I pointed out that my brother and Magnus had tried to bomb this street corner many years before Royce wrote his novel *The Burning Chest*, and, yes, it was a book I once thought very highly of, and, yes, it did seem as if Royce Burns had been two separate people, not a schizophrenic but a good man who had an evil one waiting inside him.

My anger blindsided me, or else I wouldn't have said what I did next. Maybe it was the heat, maybe it was the image of Lucia's small body being professionally made up by an undertaker only a few miles away, this child who had learned to crawl backward before she learned to crawl forward and who had tried to protect herself by holding three pacifiers. Lucia was dead, and so was River, the snuggler who smelled like running water. Or maybe it was because Ruby was my niece and my doppelgänger and a damaged young woman and she had suffered horribly because of my brother and then had committed an unforgiveable act of her own. Or maybe I was still trying to come to grips with the fact that her children had been left to die inside a refrigerator.

The evening news and the paper the next morning reported some of what I had said: "I challenge the Ku Klux Klan, the Silent Brotherhood, the Aryan Army, the Posse Comitatus, the CSA, the Confederate sentimentalists, and any other of you racist cowards out there to try to stop me from burying Lucia Burns Godchild next to this man you revere, Royce Burns. Do you think I don't know that y'all visit my brother's grave like it is some sort of holy place? That you recite Confederate doggerel out there the same way you do at Magnolia Cemetery during your pompous, silly reenactments? I know about the midnight pilgrimages to my brother's grave where you hold hands and sing 'Dixie.' 'Heritage, Not Hate,' my ass. Royce Burns was a terrorist who believed that white people were the only human beings."

I went doggedly on, trying to explain the links between Royce and *The Turner Diaries* and Timothy McVeigh and the Oklahoma City bombing, until I saw, out of the corner of my eye, a short, boxy woman leaning over Nadine, who lay stretched out on Market Street with her top down. This woman was dressed as ambiguously as I was, but she looked tougher than I will ever manage, either because I don't have the right genes or didn't have the right childhood.

"Hey!" I jumped off my soapbox and pushed through the spectators, but the woman was gone by the time I reached my car. I thought she might be one of Joe Magnus's sisters. There had been two of them, but there was no way to recognize them except by family resemblance.

Nadine assured me she was fine.

It would be several weeks before I would find out that my brother had not been a committed member of the Silent Brotherhood and that it was his fury over their assassination of Alan Berg that led to his presence at the fire on Whidbey Island. When the members of the Silent Brotherhood retreated to their temporary safe house—as federal agents pursued them—they found my brother waiting to argue race theory with Robert Mathews. Royce was trapped in the shoot-out because he intended to make it clear to Mathews once and for all that the Jews were crucial to the survival of the white race. He thought Mathews, a Christian fundamentalist, might be persuaded by a new argument Royce had concocted: the Jews were the original tribe of Judah, and the Europeans were actually the lost tribes of Israel. Mathews, however, remained implacably convinced about the Zionist conspiracy described in the fraudulent *Protocols of the Elders of Zion*. He might well have agreed that it was crucial to argue about Jews while other members of the Brotherhood were slipping quietly into the woods to avoid a fight they knew they could not win. Whidbey Island was a large area, but choosing a safe house on an island that required a ferry ride and then paying for it with counterfeit money did not seem entirely smart in retrospect. I like to imagine that Mathews and Royce were still shouting at each other when flares lit the sky and the FBI loudspeakers demanded immediate surrender of all occupants.

Estelle called me during her lunch break, furious about my news conference. "You are using this child as a pawn, Ellen."

"Oh, my God, Estelle, you're mad at me for this? You can't be mad at me."

"You hold a press conference and challenge the Klan and the entire gallery of right-wing nuts out there, and now you think you're going to have public calling hours at Beecher's? What on earth has happened to you?"

"It's a bad idea?"

"It's a stupid, dangerous idea. It's a racist idea."

"Racist? You've got to be kidding me."

"Lucia wasn't a symbol, and you, of all people, must know that. She was just a little girl."

"But that's what I'm trying to do, make her real. I thought you would understand. I'm trying to do what Emmett Till's mother did by exposing her son's body to public scrutiny."

"Have you lost your mind? Emmett Till's mother was black and he was her son, and what she did was revolutionary. You are a white woman riding in on a white horse like you think you're some kind of hero. You didn't even know this child, Ellen. This is not about Lucia, this is about you and your brother. This is about your ego and his."

"Wow," I said, because I didn't know what else to say.

In her wordlessness, the sound of her exhalation, I heard her anger lessening.

"I sure hope you're not right, Estelle. Don't you think white people have to stand up and fight against this kind of racial hatred?"

"I don't know how to evaluate this particular situation, but I do know you're being reckless and sound paranoid. BATF? You're now making public accusations against BATF?"

"Don't you think Lucia has been a pawn ever since she was born?"

"That's your excuse? No, Ellen, she was a little girl, and what you have done has created a contaminated, dangerous mess."

"I thought burying her quietly would be contaminated."

In her long pause, I felt our uncertainty about each other growing.

"Estelle, disapproval from you feels just awful."

She still didn't answer.

"I hope we're going be okay with each other."

"So," she finally said, "did your little *Times* reporter get here?"

"Yes," I said, no longer holding my breath. "She and Momma sat through *Wheel of Fortune* together shouting answers at the television. Momma thinks Claudia is a relative. You'll like her. She's young, but she's one of us. She's only got about six months."

"Was that thing you said about people singing 'Dixie' at your brother's grave out there in the dark true?"

"I only know for certain that it was still happening a few years ago, mostly around the time they do that 'Confederate Ghost Walk.' You know about this? A bunch of sentimentalists in Confederate uniforms walking through Magnolia Cemetery at night? They sell tickets and do these little skits, trying to reimagine the Rebels buried there. Once they actually walked the crew of the *Hunley* through the gates of St. Peter. They made what they thought the pearly gates might look like and recited drivel. It's been infuriating me for years."

"You've got big trouble coming, girl, and I'm staying out of it. And you'd best stay out of bed with that reporter you're crushing on."

"Oh, please. I have a few boundaries left."

"Right. I know all about your boundaries."

"Nice bluff. You don't know shit about my boundaries."

"Ellen?"

"Okay, I won't, I promise."

7

Claudia and I had intended to go to the 7:30 A.M. meeting downtown, but in the morning we found Nadine ravaged. I never locked Nadine because her doors couldn't be unlocked without a call to AAA, but I did raise the top and cover her every night, and Dockside was surrounded by an eight-foot wall. Also, she was parked within sight of the guardhouse.

Her beige canvas cover lay on the ground and her white top and leather seats had been slashed. She smelled strongly of urine.

"It must have been a crowd," Claudia said, writing in her notebook. "How could they have gotten in here? The guard checked my pass when I came in."

"Good question. And how do we know it wasn't somebody who lives in the building? Some of those blue-haired United Daughters of the Confederacy?"

"Well, if it was those ladies, wouldn't they have brought their kitty litter along? Then they could have put cat shit in here too."

Over her shoulder I could see an elderly black guard meandering toward us. "Oh, oh, oh," he said, rubbing his smooth hands together. "How did this happen? Oh, my stars."

"This is my friend Claudia, Mr. Saunders. We seem to be having a little trouble, and I'm afraid we're going to have to involve the police. Could you please call them for me?"

"I come on duty at seven this morning, Miss Burns, and I don't see nothing amiss. Course I ain't done all my rounds yet. And I never study with them reporters, I just do like Miss Estelle say."

"Thank you, and I'm sorry to be making trouble for you."

"Somebody else make this trouble, Miss Burns."

It took over an hour for a young policeman to arrive, take a report, and photograph the car, so we missed the morning meeting. "I don't suppose you're going to dust it for fingerprints?"

"No, ma'am," he said. "We don't do that for vandalism, but you will need to contact your insurance company."

"Let's just take my car," Claudia said.

"No, we'd best take the one with the Confederate sticker on it."

My mother's vehicle remained undamaged inside the underground garage. Her HERITAGE, NOT HATE bumper sticker was proving to be a piece of luck. But the attack on Nadine meant that it was possible that even my mother's car wasn't a safe choice at the moment.

Claudia's white Ford sedan had Georgia plates, and I didn't think it could be connected to me yet. I got into the passenger seat, and we drove through the gate.

"Don't you have your own place out at the Isle of Palms?"

"How exactly would you know that?"

"The point is, if I can find that out, won't other people know it too? It's not like you've been living in secret in Charleston."

"Okay, we'd better ride out there. No. Let's go to Beecher's first. Jimmy's going to be so pissed off. No, let's go to the drive-through window at Hardee's and get some sausage biscuits."

We sat in the Hardee's parking lot drinking coffee while Claudia took her sandwich apart, inspecting it. "What is distinguished about this sandwich? A fried egg, American cheese, and a mysterious piece of flesh."

"The biscuit. This is part of your Southern education. You get real biscuits like these out West?"

"Yes, Ellen, we have real biscuits in New Mexico. Very good ones, in fact."

"Well, they don't have them up North. They don't even have Hardee's. I thought you'd be impressed."

"Listen," she said, "you're sounding pretty rattled. Not that I blame you." When I didn't reply, she took a bite of her sandwich. "Okay, this is gross."

"Saturated fat," I said. "Might even be lard. Biscuits don't taste this good unless they're made with lard."

"All of the Nogalu bread is made with lard. Did you see those big red clay ovens in a lot of the yards at the reservation? Loretta had one, but Ruby didn't."

Ruby and Lightman's mobile home had rested on cinderblocks, and its metal exterior was painted a reddish color to make it blend in with the red dirt and houses of the reservation. Some dwellings in the village were made of dark mud brick, but many were simply painted trailers. Nothing distinguished Ruby's dwelling, other than the crime scene tape.

The funeral parlor looked placid in the early morning heat. It had been built of red brick in the 1950s. Pious and smug. Morticians are required to be serene and sycophantic—an angry mortician is a contradiction—so maybe I did not seem aggrieved enough this morning. I had taken off my zinc oxide war paint and was wearing white jeans and a white shirt.

Jimmy said the plaques had been done overnight by special order and they would arrive in time for the burial tomorrow, but he was wringing his hands while he spoke. "I don't understand why you ordered a plaque that says Tomb of the Unknown Racist. Do you really think that might not be Royce's remains? I think that might have legal implications."

"It'll all be okay, Jimmy, I promise."

"No, it won't, Ellen. We had a bomb threat during the night, and the building had to be swept for explosives. My father built this building. We can't have this kind of thing happening here. Visiting hours will have to be canceled."

"Why wasn't I called about a bomb threat? Why wasn't it in the news this morning?"

"I think there's some kind of agreement about not inflaming the situation you're creating. It's not fair for you to use my father's funeral home to try to stir up racial trouble. Your niece isn't the only decedent at Beecher's."

"So, did you have to evacuate the corpses?"

He looked dismayed. "What an ugly question. No, it wasn't necessary. Could I please ask you to cancel the visiting hours?"

"Yes, of course. Certainly. We'll just have to cancel."

"Thank you."

"Is Lucia ready for viewing? I mean privately. Just by me. And Claudia here."

He led us down the hall to a closed double door and followed us in.

8

According to Ruby, Lucia's skin had begun to darken about three weeks after her birth. Ruby used lighteners to try to keep the baby white, but the creams irritated her daughter's tender skin, and when Ruby tried them on her own face, one cream itched and the other made her skin look milky and strange. Lucia's eye color altered more slowly, muddying over the course of two months from dark blue to slate to brown. Ruby studied this transformation while she nursed. Nursing hurt her at first, but after a while it felt good.

"I'm edible," Ruby would say to Santane, who was not amused. Santane was furious when Ruby came home pregnant, and she did not believe Ruby's story about being kidnapped.

"You are trash," Santane said, but Ruby knew she didn't mean it, because once Santane walked all night carrying her, and when they were staying in the shelter, Santane had held her close. It wasn't like being at Nod, when her father left her all alone that time and she had been scared in her heart. Maybe Santane did not touch her and cuddle her and praise her the way her father did, but Santane protected her. That proved something, didn't it?

Ruby knew from the first that Lucia's hair was never going to be black and strong and straight. Lucia would never stretch her hair back into a braid or a bun the way Ruby could. Lucia's hair hardly even grew at first, and for weeks she was nearly bald. When it did begin to come in, the filaments were sparse and fluffy and wrinkled.

Ruby didn't know what to do about this darkening child. For a while, she thought Lucia must be partly Jamaican. She'd known a beautiful Jamaican boy in San Francisco with lovely skin, a thin nose, and precise lips she wanted to kiss. He kept his hair in dreads. When Lucia's hair got long enough, Ruby hoped to form it into dreads, but soon Lucia's hair grew into a fuzzy halo, a tawny color, and Ruby loved it spread around her like that.

I learned most of these details many months later, from the nun named Sister Irene, who found out a great deal during what she called her "debriefings" with Ruby, after Ruby had been moved into the general population at the women's prison near Santa Fe. Nevertheless, staring down at Lucia's body in the shiny purple-pink coffin, I knew instantly that her hair was wrong.

Jimmy stood obsequiously behind Claudia and me. The photograph I'd given him yesterday had been black-and-white, but the image was clear about her fine wispy halo of hair. Yet in whatever basement room Lucia had been dressed in this white cotton gown, someone had presumed to cornrow her hair.

"I don't think Lucia's hair was like that," Claudia said, clutching in each hand shopping bags from Kmart and Toys "R" Us.

"What did you do?" I said, not yet turning around to look at Jimmy. Oiled lines of hair, some decorated with cowrie shells, radiated across Lucia's head like the marks around a melon.

"Braiding is a service we offer free to all African American women, men, and children," Jimmy said. "It is dignified and elegant and quite expensive." When I didn't answer, he said, "The child's hair was badly matted. This kind of braiding dates all the way to the sixteenth century. We have a brochure. I'll give it to you."

"I think maybe you just wanted to pee on a hydrant like a dog."

He drew himself up. His black suit, gray brows, balding head, and gray tie all rose. He was not a short man, but I was taller, even in my sandals. "That is an outrageous thing to say to me. Coarse and extremely offensive. Beecher's is not a racist organization. I am concerned about security here, and I will admit that I believe this casket is not appropriate for Lucia. I went to school with your brother, and our families go way back. I took care of your sister myself. I'm just trying to help you."

Claudia dropped the bags and began to write rapidly again.

I said, "Maybe it's too late to cancel the visiting hours."

His anger was obvious now. "I've already notified the police that the viewing has been canceled. The police will be here in case there's any trouble."

I managed to speak quietly. "So, could you just leave us alone with Lucia for a while?"

He left in a huff, and we were alone in the viewing room. It was large and carpeted and filled with about fifty folding chairs. Nicely padded ones. Discreet sofas and plush armchairs had been arranged around two walls. Near the entrance was a mahogany table with a lamp and a condolence book resting neatly atop a lace runner. Black pens that read BEECHER's in gold lettering lay beside it.

We dumped the toys onto the soundless beige carpet. "Good job with these."

"Most of the women who work in these stores have children of their own."

"Right, so they can decide whether to spend their minimum wage on childcare or figure out some other solution. Extended family, maybe. Neighbors. Older kids taking care of younger ones."

"You always sound so angry," Claudia said.

"Not angry, just clear. You bought a stamp-collecting book? Aren't some of these choices more appropriate for older kids?"

"Well, the ladies in the store got pretty excited. They knew about Lucia and River, and one of them told me quite seriously that although children are allowed to age in heaven, they have to max out about ten or eleven, before puberty makes them crazy."

"That's a good piece of news about heaven. Were the women who helped you black or white?"

"One of each, and they seemed like friends."

Claudia tucked a blond Caucasian angel about ten inches tall on the silky cream polyester beside Lucia's waxen face. "There weren't any dark angels," she said. "I got dark-skinned dolls, but I didn't get the Native American doll because of its headband and feather. Is putting the white angel by her head too weird?"

Only the top half of the casket was open, and we were quickly filling it. "I think we need to open this bottom half to get the rest of the toys in. Will you do that for me?"

She raised the lower half of the casket lid, and we both stared down. Lucia's feet were bare. They had painted her tiny toenails with clear gloss. I looked at her hands and realized they had glazed her fingernails too. Below her feet, the coffin was starkly empty, and the polyester fabric was stained and torn. I picked up one of the bags and dumped what was left of its contents into the open space.

"Do you think they glue their mouths shut when they prepare the bodies? I'm glad she has no shoes on. I don't know whether that's good taste on Jimmy's part or if he forgot what he said he'd do. I think the makeup is amazing. She doesn't even look like she's wearing makeup. She looks like she's sleeping. They've gotten a lot better at this since they buried my sister. My sister looked good, but she looked very dead."

"I don't think he was trying to hurt you with the hair."

"I know, and what I said was crummy."

Claudia put down the stuffed bear she was holding and dropped her notebook on the floor. She took both my forearms and tried to make me look at her, but I studied her hands instead. "Nice ring." A large deep green emerald had been sunk flush into a heavy gold setting.

"My mother's. Let's go to the noon meeting. You need an AA meeting." When I didn't answer, she said, "I need to go to one too."

I gazed into her face, which had a Semitic cast. But maybe that was because I knew she was Jewish. Claudia had brown eyes and curly dark brown hair, fuller lips than mine, dentist-whitened teeth. Maybe she looked Greek. If her name was Raptopoulos and I thought she looked Greek, would that be racist? "Claudia, do you think you look Jewish?"

She pulled me firmly away from the coffin. "Ellen, you don't even know that you're crying."

9

I don't remember much about the meeting, except that Claudia spoke. It was high noon at Old Central, a seedy clubhouse on a side street in the expensive part of downtown, and Claudia talked for several minutes. She told me later that, although I didn't acknowledge anyone, I showed no signs of hyperventilating and held very still, head bowed.

Old Central meetings are strictly formatted. Anyone who "shares" has to go to the podium in the front of the room and use a microphone. Old Central was where I first got sober, and for a while I assumed all AA meetings were similar to this one. When I began to attend meetings in New York and other cities, I thought their customs were peculiar, and, even after eighteen years of sobriety, I still harbored the secret notion that only Old Central meetings were held correctly. At Old Central you waited to be called upon; someone who raised a hand was signaling serious distress. The first time I went to a meeting in New York City, I'd been bewildered because dozens of hands shot into the air. All these emergencies, I'd thought, how will they get to everyone? In Los Angeles, I'd been amused to discover that some meetings required the use of a kitchen timer to keep participants from talking too long. Applause in these meetings was frequent and frenzied. Charleston, however, is known for its graciousness, and natives are so courteous they rarely even beep their horns in traffic. Claudia, not understanding the urgent meaning of such an action, raised her hand, was recognized, and had to walk to the podium.

"My name is Claudia, and I am an alcoholic and a drug addict." She sketched in her story: born in Albuquerque, heavy drug user in high school, got away with everything, went to college (didn't name Brown), failed out, got hospitalized. Meth was her drug of choice, though, of course, she had an alcohol problem too. In high school, she and her boyfriend built a small meth lab that blew up, but she wasn't there and didn't get blamed. At college, she snorted Ritalin because lots of kids had prescriptions. "I felt virtuous because I didn't do heroin." She only needed one twenty-eight-day stint at rehab before going back and finishing college, but that was five years ago, and now she only had six and a half months sober, because how could someone her age who made good grades in high school and college and even went to graduate school be in such trouble? But life had just seemed so much easier taking speed. On speed, she could drink more without getting sick or blacking out. But she finally hit bottom—she hoped to God she had hit her last bottom—when her mother committed suicide last year. "Something inside me changed. I still skidded around for a couple of months before I came back. But now I just do whatever the program suggests. If I want to take a drink or a drug, I pray to a higher power that sometimes I believe in or else I call another person in the program. And if I have to, I'll drive to an emergency room and say I'm suicidal, because that's exactly what it would mean."

After the meeting, we went by Dockside to check on my mother, who didn't seem to realize I had been gone, although she did tell Claudia how much she'd missed her. The sitter today was one I didn't care for, but Momma always enjoyed her because she made bologna sandwiches on white bread and served them with the crusts cut off, along with Pepsi in a glass bottle—Momma's favorite lunch. I kept the ingredients around so the two of them could eat together while they watched *The Young and the Restless*.

Next, I called the insurance company and arranged with the guardhouse for an adjuster to examine Nadine this afternoon, but I already knew a cut-and-paste Cadillac wasn't worth much.

In Claudia's car, on our way out to my beach house at the Isle of Palms, I said, "You want to tell me about your mother's suicide?"

Claudia drove with both hands on the steering wheel, her knuckles tight. "This is some bridge. No, thanks."

We were crossing the first span of the Silas Pearman, which ran parallel to the Grace. Each bridge had two separate cantilevered spans, anchored by a small island in the middle of the river. "When we go back, we'll have to travel on that other one over there."

The other bridge, the Grace, was very steep and so narrow that passing was difficult, even with its two narrow lanes now heading in the same direction. When I was a child, the Grace Bridge stood alone and bore two-way traffic. My mother, like many other people, had refused to drive across it. "Who cares about Mount Pleasant and all those other beaches out there? Folly's just fine." Folly was not fine. She had stepped in a hole there when she was a child and nearly drowned, and her father had been hit by a trolley when he went out to Folly to get oysters. He died soon afterward.

Because of being hit by the trolley?

No, back then people just died.

"Listen," I said. "I'm pissed at Jimmy and a lot of other people, but I do know he's doing his best. Neither of us knows how to handle this situation. I'll try to make amends to him later."

"Where's all this anger and grief coming from, Ellen? You didn't know Ruby, and before that you didn't know the children existed."

"There's something I've been meaning to say to you. You're starting to sound a lot like me. The bluntness, the irony. Maybe you're easily influenced."

"My mother hung herself in her garage. I was the one who found her. You're not a bad model."

"That's unspeakable, Claudia. I don't know how you stood it."

"It was very, very bad, but it did get me sober. The only people I meet who make any sense to me now are in AA. You've got a wild temper, and I don't envy you that."

My hexagonal beach cottage was raised on stilts, as are almost all beach houses on the Carolina coast. It was basically just a cabin with one small bedroom partitioned off, leaving a combined living area and kitchen. There was a green plastic carpet like the quack grass on a mini-golf course. The wood paneling inside and the balcony outside were what attracted me. Sooner or later I intended to remodel this place, maintaining the trashy beach feel, but the plastic rug was too much.

The woman I'd seen inspecting Nadine at the press conference was sitting on my wooden steps. She was wearing a white duster and dark glasses. Her car was parked in my spot. Claudia pulled up at the house next door. "What do we do?"

I decided the woman wasn't glaring and that only my nerves were making me think that, so I opened the car door. "Let's go meet her."

The woman pulled off her dark glasses and stood up as we approached. "I think my brother has come back," she said. "My brother, Joey." Her sweating skin was rough, her small eyes sweet.

"I saw you at the press conference," I said. "I thought you were one of my problems," I said.

"I'm so sorry. I shouldn't have told Joey about your car."

"Isn't he a fugitive?"

"He's still a fugitive or something like that, but they don't seem to bother him anymore. They might have to now, because of all this publicity. Messing with your car was kind of, well, you might say, off the reservation. But he probably didn't do it himself."

Claudia stifled her laugh.

"You call him Joey? I thought everyone called him Magnus," I said.

She said primly, "That is only his surname."

"You better come on in. It's way too hot out here."

I kept the air conditioning turned high because I didn't want to walk into a hot house, and the cost of electricity did not make my list of concerns. Claudia introduced herself to Joe Magnus's sister, who, it turned out, was named Lily. She said that her sister's name was Violet and that Violet lived in Minnesota. "She married a Yankee. Can you imagine living in a place like Minnesota?"

I opened the fridge for three cans of Coke and handed one to each of them.

"Jailhouse Rock" blared, and they both wheeled toward my phone, which featured a little statue of Elvis wiggling his hips and singing into a microphone. His tiny silver jacket had a tag explaining that the imperfections in the weave of raw silk were natural. His forelock fell across his forehead. The voice mail kicked on, and Joe Magnus's voice filled the silence. "Hey, asshole, tell my fucking sister to pick up the fucking phone. Lily, I know you fucking went out there."

I picked it up myself. "Hey, asshole, where's my fucking brother? Why aren't you in fucking jail? Dead would be even better."

"I didn't authorize trashing your car," he said. "I saw it once, though. Bet you thought it was fucking cool. Not so cool now, are you, bitch?"

"Listen, cuntsucker, you want to talk trash with me, we can do that. Are you coming to take a look at your boyfriend's little monkey this afternoon or are you too chickenshit to show up?"

"I'll be represented," he said.

"You'll be disappointed. Beecher's made me cancel the viewing because of your stupid bomb threat. I guess you've graduated from making bombs that don't work to throwing around threats."

Claudia and Lily had both moved around to stand where they were facing me. They were waving their arms, signaling no. Lily was saying, low-voiced, "Hang up, hang up," and Claudia was saying in a low voice, "Fuck, fuck."

"I don't make threats," he said, and hung up.

"What have you done?" Lily wailed while Claudia scribbled.

10

Lily Magnus Biggers was so undone by her brother's phone call that she sat down in my black leather barber's chair and babbled that she had never believed that "nigras" bore the mark of Cain or that the world was only six thousand years old. Her despair at speaking these heresies was visible. She said she loved Jesus and thought that intermarriage was wrong, but killing people had to be wrong too, and she'd seen the picture in the paper of that little girl, that sweetheart.

She said that when Joey got expelled from Rivers High, their mother sent Lily and Violet to a church academy. It had only two classrooms, one for grades seven through ten, the other for eleven and twelve, and the principal's office was in a trailer. But after he got involved with the pastor's niece, Lily and Violet had to be homeschooled. She thought Christian academies must be a lot better now because Violet was sending her kids to one, but she and Vi didn't know how to read or write very well, and she was sorry about that. "I can read ads in the newspapers, because they've got the pictures, and I can count money. I handle money fine. I was a cashier at Piggly Wiggly before I got married. I'd better leave now." She stood up.

I tried to imagine this woman, who looked butch to the bone, married to a man. "What's your husband like? What does he do for a living?"

She seemed confused. "He's a bus driver for Greyhound. It's a good job. With benefits. And he's a Christian."

"You have children?"

"We have a girl, Millie. She's ten. She's a sweetheart too."

When we left the cottage, I didn't bother to lock the door. One of the few things I could remember about my father was him saying that locks only keep honest people out. I wasn't supposed to drive Claudia's rental car, but I did it anyway.

"Cuntsucker?" Claudia said gingerly. I was trying not to drive too fast down the road that ran along the beach. The speed limit was twenty-five, and I was in enough trouble. "Is that term original with you?"

"I don't know, it just popped out of my mouth and I knew he would hate it. Where's your famous Del Mead?"

She giggled with a hint of what seemed like hysteria. "He's working by phone." She held up her mobile phone.

"And you're going to fill him in?"

"Not yet, but I have to start doing it tonight. He's in the air. I suppose you know how this kind of journalism works. I'll get credit for the research."

"You think I should have one of those phones?"

"How can you not already have one? And you need to get a security system for your house out here. Today. Get it right now."

"I don't want to be any more reachable than I am, and those phones give me the creeps. My brain has enough problems. Anyway, what is there to steal from my place? If they burn me down, I get to rebuild brand new."

"You want to lose your Elvis phone? The cool chair? That original photo of Marilyn Monroe? Yes, I recognized it—it's from her last shoot. Don't you think rebuilding would be a lot of trouble? Not to mention, what if you happen to be there when it burns?"

When I didn't answer, she called ADT herself—"They're the best"—and handed me the phone. I arranged an emergency installation for later that afternoon. The door, I explained, was unlocked, so maybe they could install some new locks too. I gave them Claudia's number as a contact.

On the way off the island and back into Charleston, I called Ed Blake at his house and left a message. "So, have you been officially fired yet? This is Claudia's fancy mobile phone. Use this number to call me back. Also, get a new one of these things. I'll have my own by tomorrow morning, but now I know I'm getting old. I remember party lines, where, like, eight families shared, and you could listen in on your neighbors. Your government pals listening to us were being retrograde."

After a silence, Claudia said, "You stake way too much on being tough and clever."

We were passing through the flat reaches of Mount Pleasant, and the bridges were now visible. "It's an act," I said.

"I don't think it's an act," Claudia said.

Part of what was nerve-racking about the Grace Bridge was the lack of leeway. Railings came right up to the lanes on both sides, creating a chute. It was impossible to walk on the bridge, and two cars could barely fit side by side. "Here's a quote for you when you get to do your big story, Claudia: 'Charleston is where the Ashley and Cooper Rivers meet to form the Atlantic Ocean.'"

"I get to do a big story?"

"If I can swing it and we can get Del Mead off your back. You do keep surprising me. I was an asshole at twenty-eight."

We were going steeply down into the turn where the two spans are anchored and the second span rises.

"You're still pretty much an asshole," she said.

I glanced at her profile. Nothing visually remarkable about this young woman. Short, probably ten pounds overweight. Face okay, not lovely. Hands stubby and nervous. "I know," I said. "I don't seem to be able to help it right now."

She did not look away from the bridge as we descended the first span, and I made the turn effortlessly. "Please keep looking ahead. Please," she said. "Okay, you're right. I can't believe this bridge. I was struck sane when I found my mother hanging in the garage. Some people go crazy from trauma, but I got struck sane. And I do intend to be a writer, assuming I can stay sober. Not like your brother. I want to write about real things."

"What did she look like?"

When I glanced at her, she was staring at me in a way I hope never to see on another person's face again.

We topped the second span. "Sorry. Really. The asshole thing."

"Her tongue protruded out of her mouth. Her face was dark red and blue. Shit had run down her legs."

"I'm so sorry, Claudia. I'm sorry for asking."

"My father is retired now. And I could have flown here without the *Times* helping me.'"

"You mean you come from money?"

"You make so many assumptions about people. Yes, I have a trust fund, enough to be a first-class drug addict, but not enough to buy beach property in Hawaii."

"You'd hate Hawaii."

"I did," she said.

"Claudia, I just don't understand. Why did Ruby do this? I can't grasp what she felt. I know she loved her children. Did she think they'd be resurrected?"

"Here's my theory," Claudia said, sounding relieved as we left the bridge. "And if I do get to write a real story, you'll see it there. I think sometimes events coalesce into a single moment, and in that particular moment a thing happens that only later seems inevitable. Ruby's children dropped out of the world like a hole had been torn in a piece of fabric. But it wasn't inevitable. If the people had been there to meet her like she expected, it wouldn't have happened. If she had told anyone else about it, it wouldn't have happened. Or even if the children had woken up, it might not have happened. Ruby made a choice, and then she covered the whole thing up by hitting herself in the head so hard she fractured her own skull."

"But given her history and my brother's, doesn't that seem like destiny? I hate that word, but I feel like we're all being moved around by forces we don't understand. My father believed that you're born with a number on your back and that is the day you'll die, and there's nothing you can do about it."

"Well, those are the two basic theories. Free will and predestination. Philosophy 101 at Brown."

"Children don't have free will, Claudia."

We were safely riding down Cannon Street. "That's because children aren't people yet," she said, "so they don't have agency."

"Let me think about that. You mean they don't have State Farm insurance?"

"That's what I mean," she said. "That kind of remark."

11

We barely had time to rearrange the toys. I didn't want to throw the white angel away because that might be bad luck, so I set it behind the trash can. Claudia took a lot of pictures, including one of the hidden angel. "A junk camera," she said. "I can't believe they didn't even send a photographer."

"Get a close-up of Lucia's face. Get a shot of those cornrows."

Jimmy came into the room, agitated. "There must be thirty people out there already. Two policemen are here. They keep telling them we're closed and that the viewing is canceled, but they're not leaving."

"Good. I'm glad."

"Can you please ask them to leave, Ellen?"

"Sorry, Jimmy. I hope you don't have any other viewings being disrupted by this."

"You might have thought of that first, but luckily, no, we do not."

"I'm sorry I was so nasty to you before. It was ugly. It was wrong."

He didn't reply but followed me down the discreet hallway. Our feet were soundless on the carpet. When we got to the big mahogany double doors, I said, "Jimmy, let them in. What harm can it do? There's no other viewing happening right now. The police will keep order."

His face quivered. "I will not have my father's business turned into a circus." Claudia took a photograph of us standing like that at the door. "Stop," he said, holding his hand in front of his face.

"People want to see her," I said. "They want to honor her. And you said there are only about thirty people."

"I've made commitments," he said, his voice rising. "We cannot do this. What about the bomb threat?"

"I don't believe the bomb threat," I said. "I think someone made that up. Who needed an excuse to cancel this? The police? The mayor's office? The chamber of commerce?"

"I am not a liar, Ellen."

"Jimmy, I don't think you're lying, but somebody else might be. Please let these folks in."

He stood there stubborn and red-faced while Claudia photographed us. I opened the door and stepped out.

There was no crowd outside in the hot air, just several groups of people, mostly African Americans hanging about in twos and threes. A policeman, also black, was talking with two women who had a young child with them. I saw a white reporter from the *Post* who'd had the sense to arrive early. Everyone seemed to turn to me with one face.

I spoke quietly, but they heard me. "Beecher's has decided to allow the viewing to begin now, even though it's thirty minutes before the official opening. I want to express my gratitude to James Beecher Jr. for his cooperation in this matter."

I turned and attempted to open the massive mahogany door, then mimicked surprise that it was locked.

"Please feel free to come forward and line up while I make the final arrangements with this nice policeman."

Everyone hesitated, looking from one to the other to decide what to do. Then the door opened, and Claudia stepped quickly outside. The door slammed shut behind her. "I hope you know what you're doing," she whispered. "Every employee of Beecher's has gathered. You've got a dozen white men in black suits standing right behind this door. Okay, one of them is black." There was a trace of amusement in her eyes.

"So listen," I whispered, "are you still running that fancy recording pen?"

She looked startled, then not. "Of course, but I wish the sound quality were better. How did you know it was a recorder?"

"So what do you take the notes for?"

We were hiss-whispering, which was hilarious in this context. "For settings. Expressions. Your Elvis phone. Lines that might not get caught."

The policeman, very dark and glistening, reached us. His uniform hung on him, and his eyes were so sad I wondered if he was sick. "I'm so sorry, Miss Burns. We can't allow anyone in. It's a direct order from the Public Safety's office."

I turned and knocked hard on the door. "Jimmy! We'd like to come in now!"

A photographer appeared by my side, his camera winking. A siren sounded, and police cars turned into each end of the street. While they cordoned off traffic, two TV cameramen suddenly appeared within ten feet of us.

A policeman drenched in sweat approached. He was young and white and angry. He said I would have to come with him now.

"You're arresting me for having a funeral? I'm not going anywhere unless you're going to arrest me. Why don't you arrest this *New York Times* reporter too?" I turned to one of the video cameras. "An outrageous thing is happening here. The police have arrived to prevent the viewing of the remains of Lucia Burns Godchild, granddaughter of the notorious white supremacist Royce Burns, my very own brother. I hope every sane Charlestonian who can hear me will come down here right now. Beecher's Funeral Parlor, on Rutledge Avenue."

I found out later that this invitation to the public was not sent out directly over the air, but local stations did interrupt their programming to say that a demonstration was forming in front of Beecher's Funeral Home concerning the viewing of Lucia Burns Godchild, and that police had been called to the scene.

Within minutes many young people, mostly white, began to glide in from side streets—dozens of them—and soon a real crowd grew as we watched. They were probably students from the College of Charleston and the Medical University, because many carried book bags. Scattered among them were men and women in white lab coats, nurses' uniforms, and green scrubs, as if they had walked straight out of their offices and laboratories at the medical university and hospitals nearby. Estelle was one of them.

She marched past everyone else, up the steps and under the awning. No one stopped her. Later she told me she just kept saying, "I'm her friend. Let me pass." Her eyes were puffy. "You damn fool," she said to me. "I'm here."

She turned and faced forward, and the three of us stood there side by side. "What now?" Claudia said, under her breath. She was holding her notebook in front of her, her pen poised but not moving.

"I have no idea," I said, trying to speak without moving my lips.

Someone called out, "Let us in!" Others took up the cry, and soon a chant of "Let us in, let us in" began.

Behind me the door opened, and Jimmy Beecher stepped out. "You are all welcome!" He opened both big doors and disappeared inside.

The employees in their black funeral suits had formed a loose line to the entrance to the viewing room. They held their hands folded in front of their bodies, as if they were praying through their navels.

Estelle took charge and began to wave folks forward. "Come right on in. There's no problem. We are so glad you're here. We are so glad you've come." She turned and whispered in my ear, "I'm going to wring your neck like a chicken's."

The young whites came forward first, either out of a sense of entitlement or because they had less to lose. I shook each person's hand and said, "Welcome, welcome, thank you for coming."

Black women began joining the line. Claudia greeted two women wearing Kmart name tags. "Take your name tags off," she whispered.

"I'm going inside to stand beside Lucia," I murmured to Estelle. "I hope you're going to manage to forgive me for all this."

Once inside the hallway I told one of the employees to find Jimmy Beecher and tell him to come greet the visitors standing beside me. "Tell him it will look better for him."

I stood by Lucia's pink-purple coffin, jumbled with toys, alongside Jimmy, who stayed for the first half hour, while several hundred Charlestonians took my hand and thanked me and also Jimmy, then moved silently past Lucia's body, some weeping, some murmuring about the toys and the coffin. The two men carrying video cameras put them down before they got into line. Three policemen did too. Not all of the white people were young; many were contemporaries of Royce's and of mine, or even older, and they all said, *Good, good for you, what a good thing to do, thank you so much for doing this.*

No press had remained outside, so only a single policeman saw what happened. An elderly black woman in an emerald silk dress ended up lying facedown on the sidewalk while two white men shouted at each other and a small group of black youths formed around them. When the sound of sirens echoed through the viewing room again, a few people went outside to see what was going on. Then we heard shouting, lots of shouting, and people poured out of the room. Claudia left too, of course, and even Estelle, and I was alone with my niece.

I touched Lucia Burns Godchild, my index finger held lightly on her forehead, which was cool and firm. Then I leaned over and kissed the place I had presumed to touch. "I'm sorry about your hair," I whispered. "I would not have let them do that without your permission, but it does look good. You're beautiful, honey." And I closed the coffin myself.

12

Within hours we learned that the woman in the emerald green dress had fainted from the heat. There had been no altercation, and Estelle had arranged for Lucia's remains to be transported to Bertie's Home for Funerals, located only a few blocks away, which she said had been burying black Charlestonians for over eighty years. Since the end of state-sanctioned segregation, Bertie's had also begun burying white people.

The original Bertie had been Estelle's great-great-aunt, and Bertie's Home for Funerals remained in the Manigault family. It was now run by Estelle's great-grandmother, a cane-thin, sharp-featured woman we all addressed as Miss Manigault, even Estelle, who bore no family resemblance to her.

"Why don't I know anything about this?" I asked Estelle.

"I told you about my great-aunt leading the hospital workers' strike in 1969, but I didn't know if you could get over all your racist assumptions at once."

It was almost dark. A message on Claudia's cell had confirmed that my new alarm system was successfully installed, and I could pick up keys tomorrow morning for the two new locks and instructions. All of my windows would now be monitored, there was a video camera in the big room, and the fire alarms, both interior and exterior, were wired directly to the Isle of Palms fire and police departments.

Ed Blake had called back on Claudia's cell without leaving a message, and Nadine still lay mauled in the Dockside parking lot, where I had tried to cover her up.

After we left Bertie's Home for Funerals, we went directly to my mother's place and ordered Chinese food. Momma greeted us indifferently, but when she realized that Claudia, Estelle, and I intended to sit at her mahogany table again, she made a grunting sound, which meant that she might be upset. I told her we had ordered General Tso's chicken and she could have all of it, and I'd gotten those boneless spareribs she liked too, so, for the second time, the prized table was liberated. My mother ate with her face too close to her plate, making snuffling noises.

"Sit up straight, Momma."

She sat back and looked at each of us. "Is it my deal?"

"What other racist assumptions do I make?" I said to Estelle.

Estelle turned to Claudia and said, in a Gullah-inflected accent, "Miss Ellen think we all be po' an' ignorant down here."

"That's what I think?"

"Of course that's what you think, Ellen. Not all of us go north to get educated the way you and I did. My schoolteacher aunts wouldn't like to hear that." She picked up a dumpling with her chopsticks, plopped it into her mouth, and said, "Also, you assume I haven't opened my clinic because I don't have enough money for it, but I have relatives who would back me if I made a direct case to them."

I tried to make a joke of it. "I'm overpaying you for no reason?"

"I promise that *your mother* is not overpaying me."

Claudia, unruffled by the earlier intensity and chaos, now seemed rattled too. "I've got to eat fast. I want to get back to the hotel. I've got to call my editor, but I do have a couple of questions."

"It's all in the brochure and the newspaper clippings that Miss Manigault gave you," Estelle said.

"I don't mean about Bertie's," Claudia said.

"You've been indispensable, Claudia," I said. "This wouldn't have happened the way it did if you hadn't been here."

"That's more what I mean," she said. "I suspect I've crossed over into what used to be called gonzo journalism. Do you really think this is finished?"

Before I could reply, my mother's face rearranged itself in subtle ways. She looked at me for a moment with recognition and grief. "Ellen Larraine, I saw you on the television. How could you say those awful things about your brother?"

Her old self disappeared before a reply was required, but this was the first time I'd seen genuine pain in my mother since her spaceship landed.

After Claudia left, Estelle helped Momma get ready for bed while I put away the leftovers and loaded the dishwasher. I felt odd. The floor seemed to be vibrating slightly, and twice I looked to my right, thinking a light flashed behind me. I needed to go to a meeting, but it was too late for that tonight. I would go in the morning.

Estelle took two packed suitcases with her. "I'm staying away from here for a while. Do you realize it's possible that I've put my own family at risk in this mess? And please do not go to bed with that child. I know your ways. She will not handle it well."

"I don't know if there will be any more trouble, and I sure hope your family isn't at risk now, Estelle. But I did what I did, and you did what you did, and I am more grateful than I can say. I promise that we'll put Lucia in the ground quietly tomorrow, with no public notice. Miss Manigault seemed to know exactly what she's doing."

At the front door Estelle hugged me, but I felt her distance through our breasts. "So," she said, still holding me, "what was the purple coffin for?"

I stiffened slightly. "Was that a racist thing to do?"

"Borderline, maybe. I don't know what white people should be doing."

"I wanted it to be pretty. And bold. I wanted it to be childlike."

"Here's what I do know," she said, pulling away from me. "I am going to drive your Momma to the burial tomorrow because I know she trusts me. After that, you are going to have to find someone else to manage your life for a while."

"Thank you from my heart, Estelle," I said, unsure whether I had permanently damaged our friendship, our relationship—whatever it was.

13

The trouble did not come with Lucia's burial, and it did not come with an attack on my house or car, and it did not come to Bertie's Home for Funerals or to Carolina Memorial Gardens. It came to my mother and Estelle.

Estelle was driving Momma back from the uneventful burial in the old Mercedes with the HERITAGE, NOT HATE bumper sticker on it, and Momma was happy because she had liked the graveyard with its neatly mown grass. Their car was three blocks away from Dockside when someone fired a small-caliber bullet at them. The back window on the driver's side shattered, and the bullet grazed my mother's forehead just above her left eye. The car's windshield began to crumble, and tiny fragments landed all over Estelle and Momma like diamonds. My mother was wounded slightly, but head wounds are bleeders and she fainted from fright. Estelle pulled the car to the curb. She was shaking visibly from adrenaline when Claudia and I got there. We'd only been a few blocks behind, and we reached them just after two police cars did. Maybe the shooter hadn't recognized Momma's car, or maybe he thought my mother would be easier to terrorize than me. In any case, I went berserk.

I stood on the street alternately screaming and swearing, then touching my mother's cheek and whispering. When she awoke and saw all the blood, she fainted again, and I began to howl, literally, which thrust Estelle and Claudia into a preternatural calm. When the ambulances arrived, Estelle told the paramedics that she was a nurse practitioner, she'd been the one driving and she was fine, but they should take me with them now and they would probably have to sedate me. At some point someone gave me a shot.

Once my mother's head had been cleansed of blood and a butterfly bandage had been laid across her shallow wound, she didn't seem to mind keeping on her bloody clothes. She was quite cheerful in the ER, but I was stoned, droopy, furious, and bewildered. "Have I lost my sobriety? Goddamn it, Estelle, did you make me lose my sobriety with that shot? Don't you dare write anything about this, Claudia. I was baying like a hound in the street, wasn't I?"

"This was a medical decision," Estelle said. "And, no, you have not lost your sobriety. You'll be fine once you sleep it off."

Estelle and Claudia took us both back to Dockside. Estelle cleaned Momma up with a soapy washcloth, then got her into her nightclothes and under the covers. I lay on top of the white bedspread in my boots and bloodied shirt, refusing to move, mumbling over and over, "What have I done?"

"Please," Estelle said, "for everyone's sake, just finally shut up."

During the night I awoke dazed, lying facedown on the carpet beside my mother's bed. Estelle had left the hall lights burning. My head felt stuffed and bursting. Watermelons burst when they are overripe. Something important had happened, and I didn't know what it was. A groove. Something is happening, but you don't know what it is. I'm not Mr. Jones, I'm Ellen Burns, and it's raining. I'm Rain Burns, but Rain was a fugitive and I'm not a fugitive. When my girlfriend shot herself, I gave her mouth-to-mouth resuscitation and tasted the blood.

I tipped to the right, stumbling around the apartment. Once I fell onto my butt. When I found my mother's bedroom again, I tried to come back to the correct decade. Momma had a groove on her forehead. My girlfriend's head was broken, and I touched the red jelly when she died.

"Wake up, Momma. Wake up. Wake up." Maybe I hadn't spoken, because she didn't stir. Once, in an AA meeting in California, I met a woman with a groove in the top of her head. She had tried to shoot herself, but the gun decided to point itself upward, so her skull was missing a piece, a channel that showed at the top of her forehead. Jordan had tried to fire into her temple, but the gun pointed itself farther back, so she blew off the base of her skull, where the fundamentals are.

The blood on my shirt was my mother's blood, not Jordan's, and someone had shot at my mother's car. Holy mother of God, someone had shot at my mother's car, and she was hurt and it was my fault. I had challenged the white supremacists, and my mother had been shot.

I lay back down on the carpet.

"Ellen?" my mother said, turning toward her side and gazing down at me. "What are you doing down there?"

"I can't sleep."

"My head hurts," she said, touching the butterfly bandages.

"Mine does too."

"Come back up here, honey. Take off that dirty shirt."

I didn't want to admit that I couldn't take off my shirt, but I did manage to crawl around the bed, up the side, and onto the white embossed spread.

"Get over here closer to me."

The expanse of her king-size bed looked too grand, but I got across it.

She didn't mention the shirt again.

Momma slept like a queen, raised on a wedge of pillows because of her acid reflux. I managed to get my head onto the pillows beside her. "I'm sorry, Momma," I whispered.

"Oh, I know that," she said.

14

Although Estelle had claimed to abandon us for the time being, she was worried enough about my condition to stop by the condo the next morning before she went to the hospital. "What happened," she said, watching me struggle down the hall.

"Nothing."

"Is there someone else here who can stay with your mother?"

"I don't think so. Why?"

"I'll call someone. You're going back to the ER. You're listing to the right."

All day I drowsed, listening to the noise of my breathing, watching my own blood get drawn, staring into the top of the rumbling MRI casket. When I woke up in a hospital bed, it was night, but I felt okay. I sat up warily and got out of bed. The overhead light made me squint. My reflection in the mirror revealed that I was standing up straight. I grimaced, and both sides of my face seemed the same too.

He was young, this neurologist, with dark brown eyes that seemed to have something veiled behind them. I was glad Estelle stayed beside me. Claudia had been called back to New York.

"So let me get this straight," I said. "You're telling me that part of my brain is now dead?"

"Well, Ms. Burns, you have had several events we call transient ischemic attacks, or TIAs. And yes, you have actual damage. These are not the kind of events that come from bleeding but from capillaries getting blocked, and as a result, an area of the brain doesn't get enough oxygen. So you have an infarct, which means you had a small stroke, and, yes, that technically means that a portion of your brain is, well, yes, that very small portion is now dead."

"Then why do I feel okay? Did I have some extra brain?"

I thought it would be hard to make a neurologist laugh, but I did.

"There are certain redundancies," he said.

I snorted while this sweet doctor's cheeks colored. "That's really it," I said. "When I was a kid my mother kept saying I was too smart for my own good."

"It's a result of evolution," he said, still enjoying himself. "The damage is in a deeply primitive area. Be glad it wasn't the part that speaks and reads. That one doesn't carry any spares."

"It's not a personality change," Estelle said. "She's been like this ever since I've known her."

The doctor wanted me to stay in the hospital for at least another night while they ran tests and observed me.

"Sorry, doc, but I've got too much going on. I'm Ruby Redstone's aunt, and I buried her daughter yesterday. Also, I've got to make arrangements for my mother. I tell you what, I'll quit eating red meat."

"I know who you are," he said.

"Wow, that makes me feel even better."

"I tried to come to the viewing," he said, "but the line was too long."

"You're from South Carolina?"

"Columbia." He grinned, and we said in unison, as if we had been rehearsing, "Sherman burned Columbia."

He looked both pleased and alarmed, like someone waiting to sing karaoke. "I think we've got a mutual admiration thing going."

"Hey," Estelle said. "What am I, the wallpaper over here?"

I did not know yet that they were lovers.

•

Dr. Daniel Peters and Estelle convinced me to remain in the hospital overnight and then to spend a week at my mother's condo recuperating while he ran more extensive tests. "You need to get grounded," Estelle said. "Before all of this happened, you were almost peaceful. Well, okay, not peaceful. Also, start eating something besides fast food."

So, for the next week, I made lunchtime bologna sandwiches with the crusts cut off for my mother and opted for healthier fare for myself. Momma and I watched *The Young and the Restless* every day, and I caught up on the story. "I remember when this soap first started," I said. "I was in high school, and we were living out at Blacklock. I loved the theme music, and because I was so restless I thought it was going to be about me."

She didn't answer, just watched her show.

"You won't remember this," I said, "but a few months after Daddy was killed, I was coming down the stairs and I heard the TV say that a nuclear attack had started and the bombing would start in fifteen minutes. I didn't know it was just a made-up show and not real news, so I tried to figure out how I could get all of us out of the house in fifteen minutes. At school, they had made us get under our desks, so I thought maybe we should get under the dining room table."

Momma kept her eyes fixed on the TV or her sandwich, biting it with her too-large teeth. "And once I was driving out to Edisto Island through one of those tunnels of oak trees and there was this gigantic lightning storm, and people were pulling off the road, but they all had out-of-state plates, so I thought they were Yankees who didn't know about lightning. Then lightning hit a tree right beside me, and it dropped across the road behind me. You can't imagine the noise of the lightning strike and the tree falling. It fell in slow motion. I saw it in the rearview mirror. I was crying hysterically, and I was afraid to stop and afraid to drive on, and my leg was jumping so bad I had to hold it down with one hand and drive with the other. Then after a while the storm turned to a drizzle and there were just these big fat drops, and it was like nothing had happened. But something had happened, I knew something had happened. I stopped at this little country store, one of those little stores out on the islands, and the lady inside said, 'Some storm! I hear a tree dropped right in the road.' I bought a Co-Cola and drove on out to the island where my friends were staying. I kept telling them that something important had happened and I'd almost gotten killed, and all they said was, 'Why, it hardly rained out here a bit.'"

She turned and smiled. A commercial break had started. "Dog whistles," she said.

"I know you understand me somewhere in there, Momma. What am I responsible for? What should I do about Royce if he's still alive?"

"They are loud, and people don't even know they're hearing them."

"I know you're in there, Momma. Are you telling me what to do?"

She blinked at me and smiled.

There was a patch of mayonnaise on her cheek, so I leaned over and wiped it with my napkin. "Don't you just hate it," I said, "that they've changed the theme music for *The Young and the Restless*? I have never felt the same way about this show."

At night, I cooked the foods she liked, meatloaf and pork chops and grilled cheese sandwiches. She hated fish, but sometimes I cooked salmon separately for myself. Most of our groceries were delivered by Harris Teeter, and I asked the sitters to pick up anything I forgot.

I helped Momma put on her makeup in the mornings and take it off at night, and I watched her brush the old teeth, and gradually these activities rubbed the edges off the frantic feeling that had been driving me since the night Ruby interrupted our viewing of *Wheel of Fortune*.

Estelle checked up on me by phone once a day. I did not leave the condo except for AA meetings, even when Carolina Memorial Gardens called to say the plaques on the graves had been installed. Royce's original nameplate could not be legally removed, they claimed, but they had mounted the TOMB OF THE UNKNOWN RACIST plaque right above it. Lucia Burns Godchild lay identified correctly beside him.

After making numerous phone calls, I managed to get Nadine towed away for repairs. Her seats and rugs would be replaced, and a new white canvas top had been ordered. The urine in the gas tank proved problematic, so the mechanic ended up replacing the tank, which he claimed was worn out anyway.

I felt sad about Nadine, not just because she'd been damaged, but because I realized I would get rid of her once she was repaired. But Nadine was a car, a notion, a goof, and anyway I'd always wanted a 1960 Cadillac in that nubbly pink color called Desert Sand, and maybe I could afford that now. Or maybe I wanted a 1960 Lincoln with those suicide doors that opened sideways.

Estelle said she would not return to taking care of my mother yet, but "Maybe I'll come back when you begin staying at the beach again," and she claimed to be going to AA meetings out on Johns Island. She said she hated how slow the people talked.

"Yeah, well, you don't talk so fast yourself. I'm the only Southerner who talks as fast as Yankees do. And people down here talk slow whether they're in meetings or not. Here's what I think is the real issue. Are they all white people?"

"Okay, they're not, so maybe I don't stand out as much as I was afraid I would, but I'll bet I could go home and do my laundry while they're reading 'How It Works.'"

Ed Blake and I called each other a couple of times, but it seemed we couldn't think of much to say. I didn't want him to know I'd had a small stroke, so we talked mostly about Lucia's burial, which had made the New Mexico papers and television news. "Was that your friend Estelle?" he asked. "And that was Claudia too. She's sure getting around."

Momma, alas, remained in her sweet oblivion.

I tried not to think about Ruby during the week I stayed home for tests, and I tried not to think about my brother. But the more I tried not to think about him, the angrier I got. Then I began to get angry with Ruby too. When I called Estelle to say I was thinking about returning to New Mexico, she said, "Ellen, your anger is going to kill you. Why do you think you had a stroke at fifty-four years old? You've got to let go of your brother and of Ruby too. It's basic AA, you know that."

I told her that a nun who worked at the prison, Sister Irene, had contacted me, and she thought it was important that I visit Ruby.

"That's an excuse," Estelle said. "You're not going back for Ruby. You're still looking for your brother."

15

Before I made a final decision about whether to return New Mexico, I wanted to speak again with Joe Magnus's sister, Lily Biggers. She was listed in the phone book out in Goose Creek, where the Biggers clan was based, but I asked her to meet me out at my beach cottage because I wanted to check on the house and test the new alarm system.

Again, she was sitting in my driveway when I got there. No raincoat this time, just ruthlessly feminine clothes, pink-flowered shorts and a pink tank top against which her large breasts strained. Girlish sandals and pink nail polish. "Thank you so much for coming," I said as we climbed the steps. The decals that read PROTECTED BY ADT had prevented more direct action, but a piece of white paper at the base of the door said NIGGER LOVER in large red letters.

Lily saw the paper before I could crumple it. "Sorry," she said. Cold air blasted us when I opened the door. Pulling directions out of my pocket, I hurried to shut off the new alarm.

"You really keep the air conditioning on like this all the time?"

"Yes, I feel obligated to do my part to destroy the ozone layer. Why are you apologizing for your brother?"

She looked confused as I pulled three Cokes (two for me) out of the refrigerator. "I don't know," she said. "Aren't you?"

"You think I'm apologizing too?"

"Yes."

"Maybe I am, but somebody has to try to confront these men."

"Why bother?" she said. "You won't be able to change anything."

"I'm not so sure, Lily. I keep thinking about the Oklahoma City bombing. Did you know that the guy who blew up that big building and killed all those people had pages of a novel called *The Turner Diaries* in his car? And Royce was some kind of protégé of the author before they had a big fallout over the Jews. Did you know there was a leg in the wreckage at Oklahoma City that they've never been able to identify? These white supremacists, Lily, they're our brothers. I don't mean just them. There are right-wing militias developing all over the country. And we both know it doesn't take many of these guys to make terrible things happen."

"Do you mind if I sit down?"

"Sorry. Take the big seat." I pointed to my art deco barber's chair, chrome and black leather, reclinable, spinnable, and raised on a short pedestal like a throne. But Lily chose to sit as far away from me as she could, leaning against the far end of my unremarkable sofa. I considered her decision and sat on the other end. "I'm still so freaked out about all of this, Lily. About what happened to Royce's daughter and her children. Because here I was believing Royce was dead, and then there's his daughter right on the TV, and I go out there to try to help her and it turns out she killed her own kids, and I have to bring one of them back to Charleston and bury her."

When she didn't say anything, I said, "So, what is it like for you having Joe Magnus as your brother?"

"I'm a girl, so I'm not very important to him. He still tries to protect me, though. Like when he called here." She seemed uneasy now, even alarmed.

"Lily, do you know where your brother is?"

She rose carefully and put her Coke on the end table. "I think maybe I ought to leave."

I stood up too, partly to block her way. "Listen, my mother has been shot, my car has been trashed, and I've had a goddamn stroke. Can't you give me a little leeway here?"

When she peered into my eyes, I realized she was wondering whether I was dangerous.

"You swear too much," she said. "You shouldn't do that."

"I'm sorry. I'm sorry I keep swearing. Really."

She made her assessment, stepped forward and put her arms around me. I began to cry mechanically, the way a baby can sound like a cat.

"You didn't cause it," Lily Biggers said, "and I didn't either. So how can we be responsible?"

"Excuse me. Excuse me, please."

I went into the bathroom, threw water on my face, blew my nose, and returned to the living room, where Lily had retreated to the safety of her corner of the sofa. I sat back down too, and we talked while I drank both Cokes.

"Joey has a bunch of fake IDs," she said, "but he usually stays away from Charleston."

"You're sure your brother was here?"

"Well, he said he was, but then I realized we had only talked on the phone. That's why I came to your press conference. Because I thought I might find him there."

"Lily, this is very important to me. Is my brother alive?"

"Well, I know there's bad blood between him and Joey. It's some kind of fight that's been going on all these years. I'm not sure what it's all about, but Joey hates him."

"Is it about our fathers?"

"I don't know."

"Have you seen my brother since he died?"

She looked uncertain, even frightened. "They got him to Brazil because of the burns, but I'm not supposed to know even that much."

I moved over to my barber's chair, tilted it back, and began to spin slowly. "Then he's alive, and I don't know what I'm responsible for."

16

I didn't want to be lying in Ed Blake's bed again, but that's where I was. We'd just had bad sex. He was on top, missionary position. He came, I didn't, and as soon as his dick shrank, I pulled it tight against my clitoris. "Hey, that doesn't feel good."

I rubbed his penis against me until I came too, sharp and hard. Afterward, I said, "See? We can always have sex that excludes each other. Then we won't get so tangled up."

I sat up on my knees and squinted down at him. He was a ridiculous man, with his stubbly face and bulging gut. I leaned over and slapped his face.

He hit me back pretty hard, and my cheek burned.

"I'll bet your government buddies have known all along where Joe Magnus is, haven't they?"

"I think I'm going to need a drink for this," he said.

"You'll need more than a drink." I tried to hit him again, but he grabbed my arm.

"I don't like this stuff," he said.

"You already knew my brother is alive, you fucking liar."

He turned me loose and raised up on his elbows. "Burns is alive? How do you know?"

"Joe Magnus's sister told me."

"How would she know?"

"I trusted you, Blake. How could you do this?"

"I haven't lied to you, Ellen. I did not know your brother was alive, and I'm not sure I believe it yet. Who is this woman you're talking about? What did she say? Nobody I'm in contact with at the FBI still has Royce Burns on their radar. They insist they killed him at Whidbey Island. I've told you the truth about that."

"Could the FBI's DNA evidence be wrong? Could they have faked it?"

"I don't know. I don't know what the hell has happened."

"And who is in his fucking grave?"

He clutched my arm so hard it started to go numb. "Places like BATF, probably the FBI too, I've told you, they have pockets inside them. Who's going to root them out? Some of those guys were contemporaries of Hoover, and he thought a race war was coming way back then."

I sat beside him and turned my back, clutching my knees as if we were in a soap opera.

"I'm getting a beer," he said. He pulled on his boxer shorts and left the room. "You want a Coke? You want a six-pack of Coke?"

When he returned to the bedroom, I was fully dressed. "I can't do this anymore, Blake. I'm sorry I let this happen again."

"You could have fooled me."

"It's not the sex."

"Then what is it?"

When I didn't answer, he put his beer on the end table by the bed and began to dress without looking at me.

"I wouldn't mind some coffee," I said.

For a while he disappeared to his kitchen, where he made quesadillas with beans and cheese and salsa and leftover chicken from a carcass in the refrigerator. We sat out on his porch to eat it. Even in the shade it was too hot, but I didn't want to go back inside his house. "You have a good view," I said, as if I'd never seen it before. I'd left Charleston at 5:30 A.M., and I was so exhausted that the wood grain on the floor started moving.

He said, "Can I ask you now about what Magnus's sister told you?"

"Not much more than I already said. She hasn't seen Royce herself, but the way her brother stays so furious, I know Royce can't be dead. Basically, she just confirmed what I already knew in my gut."

"But when he was declared dead, didn't Joe Magnus hear about that?"

"Lily said that Magnus—she calls him Joey—claims that was all bullshit the feds concocted to screw around with some men who belong to a local militia. They buried 'Royce,' and then the FBI or BATF or whoever it was gathered information just by paying attention to whatever idiots showed up at Royce's grave. I don't know if I told you this, but a few months after we buried whatever that was, people started coming to the grave and leaving miniature Confederate flags. Then a couple of Saturday nights about a dozen of them went out there to sing 'Dixie' and recite some doggerel poetry, and pray for the future of the white race."

"How do you know about this? Were they arrested?"

"No, but my cousin Logan told me about it. Logan's not a militia guy, he's just a Confederate reenactor. I mean, he's not out there in the woods training for combat, but he does own his own cannon. He's a furious sentimentalist about the Civil War. I don't know why he told me. I ran into him in a cafeteria. Maybe he was just trying to piss me off. I mean irritate me."

"Ellen, the militia thing is becoming an increasing problem. It's hard to know where the breakdown in Oklahoma was. There's a lot speculation that BATF could have prevented the bombing but somehow dropped the ball. In the eighties, all the terrorist organizations like the Silent Brotherhood and the Aryan Army and the Posse Comitatus supposedly got stopped, but now we're getting these vigilante terrorists like McVeigh. He probably wasn't operating alone. One of my more cynical friends thinks that the rise of the white militias is a response to what happened at Ruby Ridge and at Waco, because, in those cases, white people were the ones the government killed."

"Can you imagine if we had black or Hispanic militias? Black or brown people marching around in the woods training with machine guns?"

There was a silence.

"So," I finally said, "are you ever going to tell me what's really on your mind? What really brought you to Gallup, New Mexico?"

He reached over, took my hand, and rubbed the back of it. The sensation was not pleasant.

Everybody has a story, and Ed Blake was dragging his behind him too. Although he had described much of his professional history, he had said little about his marriage and daughters. I knew his time in New Mexico had been hastily constructed: the kit log house, the unimportant job, the solitude he'd chosen. "It's beautiful out here," he said. "Peaceful. I like the dry air."

He waited so long that I wondered if he would be able to tell me. Finally, I pulled my hand away because he was hurting me.

"Nothing as original as the Burns family. I lost my son to leukemia when he was in the eleventh grade. I didn't handle it well."

I couldn't think of anything to say. "What was his name?"

"His name was Edward, like mine."

"How long ago was this?"

"Four years."

"So, when you showed me pictures of your daughters in your living room, you chose not to show me pictures of your son?"

"I can't keep pictures of him where I would have to walk by them."

"Are you on decent terms with your wife about all this now? What about your daughters?"

"No, I lied about that too."

After he found out his son was terminally ill, Blake told me, he fell in love with, got obsessed with, a rookie on his own force. Her name was Olivia, and she was not much older than his daughters. What attracted him, he thought now, was that nothing bad had ever happened to her. She had always wanted to be a cop, got her degree in law enforcement and forensics, intended to work her way up, and could run a five-minute mile. Nothing bad had ever happened to her, and when he was with her he felt as if nothing bad had ever happened to him either. At the hospital, she'd been out of uniform in the lobby, on her way to visit a friend who'd just had her breasts enlarged, and within ten minutes there he was, the chief of police, staring down into a bowl of soup in the cafeteria while this young woman patted his arm as if he were an old man. "I was completely undone. I did every slimy thing you can imagine. Even the night of our son's funeral I spent with her."

"So you abandoned your daughters the way Royce did Ruby?"

"No, no, I didn't denounce them or tell them they were abominations or anything like that. But, yes, I abandoned my wife, who surely didn't deserve it. I left her in her own hell the night our son died. The girls had come home from college, so I told myself they would be more comfort for their mother, she was better off with them. I doubt that was true. And, of course, they needed me there for them. But I think I was only able to stand any of it because of Olivia. I ruined her career. A situation like that follows a woman much more than it follows a man."

"What happened to her?"

"She got married. She's still a cop, but she'll be writing tickets for the rest of her life."

"And you have a log cabin in the middle of nowhere."

"And an ex-wife who cleaned my clock financially. But I deserved that."

"What's the situation with your daughters?"

"They may have begun to forgive me, to some degree."

"So, Blake, I'm beginning to understand our connection better. My past is full of things I can't take back. When something's done, you can't undo it, even if you're sorry."

"Right. You can't unring a bell. So here we are."

"One of the AA promises is, 'We will not regret the past nor wish to shut the door on it.' Can you imagine thinking like that?"

"That's crap."

"It's not crap, but as long as we're telling each other our secrets, here's another piece of my mine. My brain doesn't work quite right. When I was about five years sober, I began to see imaginary kids following me around. Three or four of them at first. Then half a dozen. A lot of therapy later, I began to understand that pieces of my psyche had split off and were confronting me. I'm lucky I wasn't hospitalized, but it wasn't schizophrenia. It was just vivid and scary as hell."

He looked relieved that I had changed the subject instead of trying to find a way to offer him comfort. "What made it stop? Has it stopped?"

"The kids told me a bunch of stuff I didn't want to know, and then faded out. But every once in a while, one of them pops back up. What I mean is, my wiring's not right, and whatever was funky got exacerbated by all the drugs I took."

"Psychedelics?"

"I was a garbage head. If a drug or a drink would make you feel different, I wanted it. Except for heroin. Those scare-kids-straight movies in high school worked for me. But another thing that stays weird for me is metaphors. Metaphors become like real passageways in my head. I mean, metaphors can just be plain old metaphors, or they can make me feel as if I've stuck my arm in too deep and pulled out a living fish."

"Can you give me an example?"

"That is an example."

"Another example?"

"Okay, when I take off my mother's makeup at night, I use these little Q-tips to remove her eye shadow, but if I look too long at her eyelashes they can start looking like a burned forest, or they can turn green and become a sugarcane field. I can smell it, but I'm still sitting there taking off her eye shadow. Later, when I'm by myself, I can go back into the cane field because I like it there a lot."

"Is it always a cane field?"

"No, of course not, the cane field is an example. Cane fields aren't good places for walking."

"I guess I really don't understand."

To temper my snippy reaction, I said, "Be grateful about that. But I suspect that a lot of people's minds work like mine. They get it trained out of them or forced out of them, and then sometimes they go crazy. If I'm really tired, the physical world can turn translucent. A gauzy curtain I can see through. Am I scaring you yet?"

"Maybe. What do you see?"

"A reddish gold landscape. Sandstone. Big rectangular stones on the horizon. I don't know. Words that describe it slip around."

"It sounds a lot like New Mexico."

"I hope it's not New Mexico."

"Maybe I understand better now why you're so afraid of your brother."

"I may be eccentric, Blake, but I'm not morally deranged, and I manage to stay in the real world most of the time. I don't think Royce was ever in the real world again once those snakes crawled up his legs. Me, I only have to stay sober in AA and try to get regular sleep. As you can imagine, I saw a lot of doctors when the imaginary kids started showing up. The medical conclusion was that I have a sleep disorder. I think that's pretty funny too, because what the fuck is sleep? We spend a third of our lives doing something we can't even remember. The truth is, I wouldn't trade anything for the way my mind works. Royce's problems are very different. And, yes, I suppose my deepest fear is that I'm like him. What if one day diamond snakes start crawling up my legs?"

We were sitting in the near dark; it had been afternoon when we'd emerged. Only the frame of the porch was visible against the star-scattered horizon.

"You're not crazy, Ellen. You're just very intense."

"Yes, I've heard that before, but only as a criticism."

"I don't think I've ever felt as connected to anyone as I do to you."

I stood up, wanting to leave, but he did too and moved to stand very close to me. I could smell him and feel him, but I understood now that we were only looking for redemption, and my distance from him held steady.

17

Santane's face had aged, and her hands shook as she handed me another manila envelope. She had withheld these pages before, but she now thought that had been a mistake.

I sat in the same chair I had last time, and again she served me tea with a teabag. Dust lay like powder across every surface, and what looked like Japanese landscape prints hung haphazardly on the wall.

I described for her Lucia's burial and gave her several pictures Claudia had taken, including a close-up of Lucia's body in her coffin. Santane hardly glanced at the photos, and she seemed to know nothing about the controversy in Charleston. "I don't understand why you didn't give me all of Royce's papers before. Am I in for more surprises from these?"

"We had a plan," she said. "You should probably know that we had a plan. Ruby wanted to leave Lightman but she could not accomplish that easily and still take River with her, because River was a Nogalu, and he was being monitored so closely."

"You had your own plan to get Ruby free of her marriage? Please tell me why you have withheld these papers."

"Ruby remains a child in many ways. She's so . . ."

"I know. Something's off, and it's not just a matter of maturity."

"After a while, the Nogalu women lessened their surveillance. When River began to walk, Ruby came here twice with Lightman and the children. Lightman seemed satisfied and must have spoken to his mother, because after that Ruby could take the children off the reservation, although she had to let Lightman or his mother know whenever she did. We knew that if Ruby simply came to us with the children, Lightman would reclaim River instantly, whether legally or illegally. Our plan was to send them to San Francisco, where Giang and I have many friends. Over several months, Ruby brought to me the possessions she could not leave behind. Her father's undershirt. Some jewelry. A few clothes and toys."

She paused, but I knew not to speak. She now told me a story that was at least thirdhand, so I didn't know whether to believe it. She said that Lightman had stayed home from work one day and insisted on taking Ruby to the Catholic mission on the reservation. Maybe he had found out she'd been going to Mass or taking the accounting class. The mission was old and disintegrating. The steps were gone, and the door hung loose on its hinges. It was dark inside, but a cross still hung above the altar and the confession boxes were still there. Someone had painted enormous, brilliantly colored pictures of the Nogalu ceremonial costumes on the walls, including the gigantic snake that had frightened Ruby so badly. Lightman told her that when the men donned these costumes, they transformed into the actual figures. He said he was telling her something sacred, and that someday he would change like this before her eyes.

"Ruby believes in magic. Or in something like magic," Santane said. "You know what she's like, this Jeremiah thing. I have no idea what she was actually doing for the two years she says she was kidnapped. But she believed what Lightman told her, and she was afraid of what would happen to River as he grew up. What she says about Lightman's mouth being burned in some ceremony, maybe that isn't true either. But I do believe Lightman took her to the old mission to threaten her. He said that if she ever tried to leave him, she would die."

I could see dust in the air, fine dustlike motes of light. I put my cup on the table and moved my finger through the dust settling there, tracing a cross and a snake with my finger, not yet looking at her.

"Okay," she finally said. "I did not give you these papers before because I could not bear to read them. Whenever I tried, over the years, I could not. But now I have. At Nod, they were going to sterilize Ruby."

18

Jurisdiction over Ruby's crime had been ambiguous. El Morro National Monument was on federal land, but the pockets of private property inside were technically New Mexico and therefore existed in legal limbo. The FBI took this opportunity to bow out of Ruby's case with the understanding that her lawyer would negotiate a plea with the state for life imprisonment. This was what Ruby said she wanted. The process was ongoing, but the deal was basically done.

The state prison for women where Ruby was now incarcerated was surprisingly humane. It had air conditioning, for one thing, a privilege that had recently been taken away from the women's prison in South Carolina because, as their warden said, "It's not like these women are on vacation."

The New Mexico warden, Janine Pitts, turned out to be well-known in prison circles. Foreign visitors often toured her facility, trying to identify the elements that made it run so smoothly. Each day the warden walked through the prison, making herself visible and available. She had a broad, inquisitive face, a thick New York accent, gray hair that stood out in several directions, and a hitching gait. In our first conversation, she sized me up favorably and within a few minutes called Sister Irene into her office. Sister Irene wore the dowdy blue suit and white blouse that would later become so familiar to me.

Janine Pitts said they were considering moving Ruby Redstone into the general population, but there were two major concerns: first, would Ruby be safe from the other inmates, and second, would she be safe from herself? Maybe I could help them with the second question. The prison psychiatrist had said yes, Ruby was ready, but Janine Pitts wanted my personal opinion. She said that all that seemed to agitate Ruby now were Sister Irene's attempts to talk to her.

I found Sister Irene's gaze unnerving myself, and I had begun dreading seeing Ruby again. My anger and judgment had stiffened. I wanted to leave Ruby behind now. Her grief had been real enough, but stubborn dishonesties and fantasies remained in what she had chosen to tell me. I believed that Claude Dabley was a real person because he had given her the rattles (now in my possession), and the rattles had convinced her that Royce was alive, but how had her lies about the kidnappers originated? The fake kidnapping plan seemed too stupid for someone as elegantly minded as my brother. Yet Ruby's story remained as vivid as watching a film, and the duct tape bindings and fractured skull she claimed to have accomplished by herself remained troubling.

Janine Pitts said that Ruby's treatment now involved a number of medications, and they had found a cocktail that seemed to calm her without knocking her out. Ruby had begun confiding in one of the guards, and she was speaking fairly often to an inmate near her in suicide watch. They were hoping she would soon begin to "debrief" with Sister Irene. Since the solitary confinement of suicide watch could make anyone psychotic, integration into the population was always the goal.

According to Janine (she asked me to call her Janine), the prison systems were now dealing with an increasing number of mentally ill inmates. "Guards don't carry guns in here. Many people don't realize that. A lot of what makes a prison work is cooperation," and the presence of so many schizophrenics and manic-depressives was straining the system severely. "Here's something most people don't know. State prisons can swap inmates like baseball cards. Holly Bright, that school teacher in Alabama who convinced her student to murder her husband, was in prison down there, but their exercise yard was too close to the highway, so somebody took a shot at her. I traded two schizophrenics for Holly Bright, but another mentally ill inmate here beat her up. Holly's jaw was wired shut for almost a month, but mostly she was afraid I'd send her back to Alabama."

Sister Irene said, "They can earn their GEDs here. We have college courses and a nursery. What's hardest for all the mothers are holidays, because they can't be with their children. But we do have a taping program. They make audio tapes for their kids, and on Christmas Eve, a group of local volunteers hand-deliver them all over New Mexico."

"So you have a nursery?"

"Yes, and women who arrive pregnant can keep their children with them until the age of eighteen months. Work in the nursery is considered a great privilege. Inmates prize working in the nursery."

"This doesn't sound much like prison," I said. "Or maybe I've just spent too much time in South Carolina."

Sister Irene laughed, a low barking sound, and I examined her more closely. Her light blue eyes were unsettling, but there was something engaging in her toothy smile. "It's prison, all right," she said. "They're locked up, locked down, they can't leave. You wouldn't like it, I wouldn't like it, and they don't like it either. They hate it. But for some of them, prison is the first place they've ever felt safe."

"That's a terrible thought."

"It's the truth."

When I knew Sister Irene better, when I began to stay sometimes in the apartment above her garage, she told me a long story about an inmate who had become her good friend. "Lila Ames came up to New York from Georgia in 1931. She was nineteen years old. Her parents were sharecroppers, and her grandfather had been a slave. She'd saved up a little money and come to New York on the train. She lived at a rooming house up in Harlem, got a job, made a few friends, bought herself a sky-blue dress. You should have heard how she would say the words *sky blue*. Soon she had a boyfriend who took her to nightclubs and she bought other dresses, but the blue one stayed her favorite. It had rhinestones that looked like little diamonds. So one night they were out in his car. He had a car, which she thought was wonderful. A light yellow convertible. She should have known that he was big trouble, but she was nineteen years old from Georgia and living her dream in New York City. So one night her boyfriend goes into a small grocery and Lila stays outside in the passenger seat with the top down, and he kills the owner. She hears shots, realizes what happened, and jumps out of the car running. They both got caught, both got the death penalty. The boyfriend was executed, but Lila's sentence was reduced to life. Back then you couldn't sentence someone to life without the possibility of parole, so after twenty years of pristine behavior she became eligible, applied, and got released. But soon she realized that she had no people up here or anyone back in Georgia who could help her. She didn't know why the cars looked so different or how anything worked. The subways. The stores. Imagine. Somehow, she got herself settled back in Harlem but couldn't handle it. She wanted to go back to prison. So she goes down to the local police station and asks them to send her back, but they tell her they can't because she's on parole. She goes outside, gets a rock, and throws it through the station window. She gets arrested, her parole is revoked, and then she's back here, where she feels safe. I met her many years after all that happened. The parole system is based on the idea that prisoners will always apply for it, because who wouldn't want to be paroled? But Lila just refuses to apply, and they have to keep her here. Janine thinks the situation is amusing. If she's had a drink or two—Janine can really drink—she thinks the situation is a hilarious joke on the system. We both like this inmate very much, and every other Friday I bring her a crab cake sandwich because she said that going crabbing was all she missed about Georgia. We have lunch together in the common room or in the chapel. I used to take her for rides through the countryside, because everyone knew she was no risk of escape, and Janine got it arranged."

"What was her name again?"

"Lila. Lila Ames. She's almost ninety years old now. She can hardly walk, and she's nearly blind. It's just too hard to get her into the car anymore."

19

Ruby sat quietly on her cot, a Bible open on her lap. Her uniform now was made of blue cloth, probably polyester, and no video cameras peered down at her. A cotton sheet covered the thin mattress. She had a pillow and a blanket, arranged neatly. I stared at her through the bars, and at first she did not even look up. "Hello, Ruby."

Her eyes studied me quietly. The guard standing beside me grunted and unlocked her cage.

Before I even stepped in, I said, "I buried your daughter."

Her eyes did not change. "Thank you."

The guard locked the door behind me, and I was trapped with her. There was no chair, nowhere to sit except the toilet or the bed, and I did not wish to sit beside her again. "I put Lucia in the ground next to your father."

She stayed still. "That's not my father. Can you be hanged in New Mexico?"

"No, Ruby, you cannot be hanged in New Mexico. They prefer killing people with drugs."

"I was just wondering."

"You're not going to be executed. I hate it now, the fact that we look alike. That we're in the same family."

Her eyes smiled faintly. "I understand."

"Ruby, please help me comprehend it. How could you do that to any child, much less your own?"

"I don't remember some of it," she said, "and what I remember seems like it happened to someone else. I think I did it because I love them. Lucia and River are safe with God."

"You think Lucia and River are up in the sky now wearing their halos?" I thrust the picture of Lucia lying in her coffin in front of Ruby's face. "I thought you might want this."

She took the picture, laid it against the open Bible, and gazed at her daughter's image, framed by the text of Corinthians. "Her hair looks nice that way. Was that your idea?"

"Do you understand yet what you did?"

She said simply, "Yes, I put my children inside a refrigerator where they smothered, and I am responsible for their deaths."

I sat down beside her and held my hands over my face. "But why, Ruby? Help me understand."

"I never knew I had an aunt. I thought it would keep them perfect."

"That's why? To keep them perfect?"

"I would have done anything for Lucia and River, but I couldn't handle it any more. Lightman. His mother. Santane. The rattles."

"Then why not take your own life? Why take theirs instead?"

"Suicide is a sin, Aunt Ellen. And I couldn't leave River with the Nogalus. Who wanted Lucia besides me?"

"Your mother would have taken Lucia. She would have taken them both. Please don't call me Aunt Ellen."

"But she wouldn't have wanted them. She might have started to love them, but I couldn't take that chance. Lightman wanted River, and I couldn't let that happen. No one wanted Lucia except God and me. Now they're safe in a way we can't even imagine."

"They're not safe, Ruby. They're dead."

She laid the photograph gently on my knee. "Thank you for bringing this, but please take it with you. I want to remember my daughter with her lovely eyes open."

"I know that you've lied to me. You've lied about a bunch of things. Royce would never have concocted a plan like that kidnapping. And why put the notes about Nod inside their shirts?"

"I have not lied to you, Aunt Ellen. There may be things I haven't told you. I did not tell you that I drove out to the camp the day before it happened, that I went by myself to make sure that I knew the route. I knew that the kidnapping plan was weird, but Mr. Dabley had the rattles. When I got out there, two men I'd never seen were carrying out guns and boxes. They were hateful men. One of them snarled at me, and the other one said my father was going to get what was coming to him."

"And after that you still gave the children the Benadryl and took them out there the next day?"

"Those men were moving out, so I thought it was part of the plan. And I needed to see Daddy. I needed to talk to him."

"You still believe it was Royce who wrote you those letters?"

"Could you bring me the rattles? And his shirt?"

"Ruby, you were right. Royce is alive, but no one can find him."

She stared down at her lap. "Did you know 'Jesus wept' is the shortest verse in the Bible?"

"Yes, I know that."

"I understand now why Jesus cried."

"Ruby, do you remember Nod? Do you remember the camp?"

She studied her lap, as if the answer lay in Corinthians. "Daddy thought I didn't, but I did. There was this man, he was so skinny he looked sick. He had a voice sort of like music, and he gave me something to drink. I got so sleepy my eyes closed, but I could still hear them talking and moving around. I had on my baptism gown, and my hair was wet. I remember my hair being wet, but my dress wasn't, so maybe that's not a correct memory."

"Are you making this up for me right now?"

"I never told Santane. They took off my underpants. I was lying on the altar. There was a bright light, but Daddy came and stopped it."

"Do you know what they wanted to do?"

"Daddy was yelling at them. He had a snake around his arm. 'She's my daughter! She's my daughter!' I'll never forget it. I was only six. I think I was six. We were still living in secret places, and we had to pretend Daddy was someone else. That was when I found the pictures and he made Rommel get down in the hole. But after he left, I could always remember him shouting, 'She's my daughter!' and then I could go to sleep."

"They were planning to sterilize you."

"Yes, I realized that much later. But Daddy wouldn't let them. Then, after Lucia was born, when she got so dark-skinned, I knew I'd ruined any chance of ever belonging to Daddy again. River would belong to Lightman no matter what, but Lucia only belonged to me and to God. The duct tape was in the trunk with Lightman's toolbox. It felt like somebody else was hitting me in the head and tying me up."

"But why try to hide what you had done?"

"So he would come."

"You still thought Royce would come?"

"He said he loved me more than anything."

"He didn't, Ruby, he didn't love you more than anything. He's alive, and he didn't come, and he won't come, and he doesn't love you more than anything."

"I know he loved Santane, and I'm not nearly as yellow as she is. I could have had my eyes fixed."

"Let me get this straight. You thought that if the children were gone, then maybe Royce would claim you? Ruby, don't you understand that during all those other years, he could have contacted you and didn't?"

"Yes, but he sent Mr. Dabley and the rattles, so he must have changed his mind."

My gorge rose, and I feared that I would throw up. "You thought you would get rid of the kids and get your eyes fixed, and then he'd come?"

"Please get his undershirt and bring the rattles to me," she said, staring down at the Bible. "I need them."

"She killed them because they weren't white," I said to Blake. "Whatever crazy plan went on and whether my brother was involved or not, she killed the children in an attempt to please him. I don't know how to stand it. Maybe it's taken me all this time to face it clearly. Estelle has probably guessed it all along. Ruby put her children in that refrigerator because she thought that was what Royce would want her to do, and then maybe she could get him back. She looks like me, and he's my brother and we're white, Blake, white people like you and me. I drove my brother to school. I defended him against our stepfather. He was a wonderful kid. I always say I hated him, but I was just jealous. He got more privileges because he was male, but so what? Then he wrote that wonderful novel. Maybe I could detach better if he weren't my brother. If I believed in Satan, I'd think Satan had grabbed him with those snakes. I just want white terrorists to be somebody else's problem. Let me watch the news and go *tsk tsk tsk*. Let me change the fucking channel!"

"Ellen, you are not personally responsible for racism in America."

"He sent Ruby those rattles. Who knows what he and his people are capable of? I keep thinking that my brother and his followers are somehow tied to Timothy McVeigh. Is there any way you can find out who is really buried in my brother's grave?"

"Maybe no one. I think it's true they found your brother's DNA at Whidbey Island. I've checked several sources. But apparently all they found were fragments. So, who knows what they sent to you to bury? It's possible your brother escaped when the house caught fire and Mathews chose to stay. In any case, their followers think they're both heroes. Look at McVeigh and the people like him. If your brother got burned and managed to live through it, he might be very important to these people. He might be viewed as a martyr who can still lead."

20

The new batch of Royce's papers was fragmented and semicoherent. There were drafts, illegible hand notations, soliloquies of rage and self-pity, and rapturous encounters with his destiny. There were also a few facts.

Royce's research traced the origin of the Silent Brotherhood to the Christian Identity movement, which had been rooted in the nineteenth-century British Israelist movement. The British Israelists had been pro-Semites who believed that the Northern Europeans were the lost tribes of Israel and that the Jews were the original tribe of Judah; therefore, the Jews were white and could not be the enemy. But, in the 1920s, the Israelists had evolved into the Christian Identitists, who, caught in a global tide of anti-Semitism, began to declare that Anglo-Saxons were the chosen people, and they devised elaborate theories to account for the existence of the Jews. One biblical hypothesis involved an ongoing fight between the archangel Michael and the fallen angels; a more evolutionary theory postulated that white people emerged from *Homo sapiens*, but Jews and the dark races emerged from lesser lines of humanoids.

Royce, studying this material, arrived at his peculiar conclusion: the mistake about Jews was the vital flaw in the white supremacist analysis, and anti-Semitism was a disastrous path. Like his mentor, Royce subscribed to the notion that evolution would transform men into gods if the white race could purify itself, but his views about Jews thrust him into open conflict with both Pierce and Mathews.

Each of these three men believed he held the crowbar that would move the rock of history, but Joe Magnus was infuriated that Royce had stepped so rapidly into a leadership position. The most coherent and talented piece in Royce's papers was his novelistic attempt to imagine his old friend's point of view:

FOR JOEY

This was how it had always been, Royce in front of him, and Royce knew shit about coons, never sat next to them in school, never faced gooks, never learned that killing could be joyous. He'd only killed Joe's father.

Joey had despised his father, good riddance, but he hadn't understood that he would lose his chance to join the Marines and get stuck taking care of his mother and sisters. But then his draft notice came, so he got out of that mess. He loved basic training, loved that it was so hard, and when he felt the thudding of his heart before he slept at night, he felt happy.

Vietnam was stinking and hot and strange, and he learned not to trust anyone. He'd only been in country four months, cited for bravery, made his first kill, when the lieutenant he trusted got wounded. The new lieutenant was a half-breed from West Point, and Joe made one little joke about fragging him and a dishonorable discharge followed. Now he couldn't ever live in Charleston, but fuck them all, he'd go out West and find the righteous men he'd heard about.

He was a good soldier in the Brotherhood too, until Mathews made him kill a white man. Lonnie mouthed off in a bar about one of the bank robberies, probably so drunk he didn't even know he was talking. But a few nights later, Joe and another man had to walk Lonnie out into the woods to dig up a cache of arms, but instead they hit him with their shovels and buried him. Not a good feeling.

Then Royce became a star, writing those stupid articles. How could Royce be a leader if he had a gook kid? Something had to be done about Royce's kid, so Joe started saying that half-breeds needed to be fixed. Not killed, just fixed,

so they wouldn't be able to make more garbage. They clipped the black kid,
the one named Stretch, who wasn't really Jonesie's, just someone he'd picked
up as a pet, and they were going to do Royce's girl next, but then Royce came
in with that fucking snake, and that little doc—he was a veterinarian but
righteous—got more scared by the snake than he would have been by a gun.
So Royce got to take his kid away.

   Mathews decides we have to be separated, so it's me he sends to Elohim
City to meet this Strassmeir guy who knows how to make bombs, and he tells
Royce to study poisons and learn to make something called ricin.

Killing Lonnie sounded too detailed to be made up, so I assumed it
was an event Royce had actually learned about. His need to understand
Magnus was touching but nauseating too, because he could do it with
such empathy. I glimpsed once again how difficult it had been for Royce
to grapple with his humanity, and to try to extinguish his capacity for
personal love.

But this was the most disturbing fragment I found in his papers:

Of course we must breed eugenically. Mixing races dumbs us down and will
lead to genetic chaos. How can it be in society's best interest to make room for
the impaired? And the dark races are impaired by definition. Sentimentality
is always weakness, Ellen . . .

Had my brother really written my name in these pages Santane gave
to me? Had he addressed me this way, directly? Was it possible that,
during all these lost years, my brother and I had remained lodged in each
other's brains like splinters?

PART III

We have met the enemy . . .

—WALT KELLY, *Pogo*

1

At first I couldn't find him.

It seemed easiest to base my search in New Mexico, since Sister Irene wanted me to keep seeing Ruby, and whatever had happened between Ed Blake and me still felt ragged, unfinished. Ruby's prison was located near Santa Fe, several hours from both Albuquerque and Gallup, so I alternated between staying at the El Rancho Hotel, which had begun to feel like an old friend, and sleeping at Sister Irene's house, at first on her living room sofa.

Assuming I was still being monitored, I changed my room regularly at the El Rancho, which might have been silly but did let me sleep with a lot of stars. I tried the Kirk Douglas room, then the John Wayne, the Katharine Hepburn, the Rita Hayworth, and even the Ronald Reagan, before settling into Troy Donahue. I searched every room meticulously, yet found only a dead spider under Errol Flynn's carpet. Ed Blake had suggested, somewhat uncomfortably, that I might stay at his house when I was in Gallup, but I declined. The rooms at the El Rancho didn't have refrigerators, so I bought a mini-fridge to stash my Cokes and ice cream. The manager let me store my belongings in Troy Donahue whenever I was away.

At Sister Irene's, whom I'd begun to think of as The Friendly Nun, the sofa was soft and lumpy, and the third time I arrived, she had arranged for someone to "refocus" her meditation and prayer space above the detached garage. Off the large single room were a toilet and shower, so she'd added a bed, a small refrigerator, a toaster oven, and a microwave.

"You're moving me in?" I said, not quite sure how to accept such largesse.

"Well, it's not like there are any motels near the prison," she said. "And you won't be here that often. I might find a guest space useful. In any case, I can still pray here most of the time." She pointed at what might be described as an altar. It was a worn art deco vanity from which the round mirror had been removed, and on the wall behind the remaining circle of wood hung a large extraordinary bas-relief cross holding an unfinished Jesus whose tilted head, outstretched arms, and nailed feet were barely discernible, emerging from a polished piece of maple. Jesus's crown of thorns extruded nubs of lightness, as did his nose, brows, knees, and right hand. The dark sheen of the rest of his form surrounded these smaller elements. The chair that had originally belonged with the amber wood vanity had been pulled back, and a padded kneeling bench was placed on the floor before it. Several rosaries hung from the drawer knobs.

"I hope he's not planning to spook me."

Her smile looked like laughter. "It's just a piece of wood."

"Right, and I'm just a pile of protoplasm."

Sister Irene's eyes continued to bother me. They seemed too clear, the whites too clean, the blue irises too deep, but I decided her disconcerting gaze was an accident of birth. Later that night, as she heated frozen fried chicken dinners for us and socked down several beers while I drank my Cokes, she seemed to be floating around her kitchen in a bright, billowing muumuu. Her short hair was gelled straight up. "You know this one?"

She sang:

Oh, dear, what can the matter be,
Seven old ladies were locked in a lavatory,
They were there from Monday to Saturday,
And nobody knew they were there . . .

"I'm not much of a singer." I sat at her breakfast nook, holding very still.

"I'll bet you know this one." She flounced through the door into the living room. I followed her and sat on the sofa I'd used on my last visit. Joni Mitchell's album *Blue* began to play on an old-fashioned turntable.

"Sister Irene," I said, "are you trying to tell me you're gay?"

"I am, indeed." She sat down across from me on the ottoman of an armchair, and I shrank back like Lily Biggers had on my sofa.

"I'm queer as I can be," she said, "and proudly so. But I'm celibate, so don't be nervous."

"I'm not nervous."

She laughed. "Ellen, I don't have that many people I can be my real self with, even for a few minutes, but you're obviously such an old outlaw, I knew I'd enjoy having you around."

I said, as if I were holding out a crucifix against a vampire, "I'm a sober alcoholic. And I'm not much of an outlaw anymore. Well, mostly not."

"Of course I do have to remain closeted at the prison, though I'm sure some of the inmates suspect. Or maybe they just sense how deeply I love women."

"Does Janine Pitts know?"

"Janine will have to tell you her own story, or not. We're good friends, although I'd never heard of her until she became warden here. She's been warden for ten years, and I had already been here twelve when she arrived. Her presence has been a gift for me, and also for the prison, but I think she needs to retire. She developed a bleeding ulcer a few years ago, and with the stress of a job like hers . . ."

"Sister Irene, can I tell you that my life keeps getting stranger, even by my own standards?"

"Well, for some of us the world may seem more inexplicable than it does for others, but my guess is that it's all ordinary."

"That sounds like something I'd say, but you're a gay nun in a flowered gown who works in a prison, so of course you'd think it's all ordinary. Ha, I've made you laugh."

"I've been laughing ever since I saw you carrying that trout bag."

"You knew what it was?"

"Every year I go trout fishing in Montana for a week with two other nuns. They both have trout bags like that one. I prefer a creel."

"I'm not speechless," I said.

We drank three cups of instant coffee while I briefed her on the history of the Burns and Magnus and Tillman families. I didn't say much about Ed Blake except that he had helped me and that I trusted him, off and on. I skipped over our sexual connection and our suspicions about rogue governmental complicities, but I described what it had been like when he took me into the cave, and I gave her a brief version of Ruby's account of what happened.

"It's basically what she's told me," Sister Irene said. "Maybe a few differences."

"What kind of differences?" When she didn't answer, I said, "How can you be a nun? How can you even be a Catholic?"

"I love God and trust him."

"Him?"

She shrugged. "Have it your way."

"What about the Catholic doctrines on women? And the politics? You and I are evil in the eyes of your Church. We're abominations, and that's the word Ruby claimed those lunatics were using about her children. Aren't people like us supposed to be God's mistakes?"

"So you believe God makes mistakes?"

"Well, let me think. What about Hiroshima? Or the Holocaust? Or Rwanda? Oklahoma City, all those children in the day care center? I keep waiting for God's explanation on that one."

"I don't think like that," she said gently.

"I forgot the slave trade. I'll even bet you still take Communion and go to confession. Do you confess your sexuality?"

"Of course, when it's relevant, but I have been choosing celibacy for a long time now."

"Because you're an abomination?"

"You are such an angry person, Ellen. You're the one who keeps using that word. The answer is no. Though I admit I'm glad I don't have to confess to sexual activity, only to impure thoughts."

I didn't want to hear any more, in case she was rethinking her decision. "I'm glad Ruby's begun talking to you."

"She's such a dear," Sister Irene said.

"It's hard for me to see her that way anymore."

Later that night, when Sister Irene walked me out to the garage apartment, we discovered that some of her feral cats had punched out the screen of the window above the stairs. She opened the door and flicked on the light, and a snarling, furious cat raced straight past her, hurtling toward me. I turned like a matador, it missed me, and I slammed the door behind it. That left one other animal: a vicious, stunted gray mess with a single eye. "Relax," Sister Irene said, stepping between us. "She's just scared. Listen, Sweetie," she said to the cat, "it's all right. But you will have to leave. I'm sorry, but you really do have to go now." She backed Sweetie slowly toward the door, leaned across to open it, and the cat skulked out, glaring at me over her shoulder with her single eye.

"And you think she's the one who's scared of me?"

Sister Irene shut the window with the broken screen, crossed the room, and switched on a standing fan. "The other windows should air the room out sufficiently."

"Have the cats done that before?"

"I always forget how they smell. Don't worry, they can't come through the second-floor windows. They're not that crazy. Or that talented."

The feral cats hanging around the prison were supposedly managed by the guards—meaning that, unofficially, they were supposed to shoot them instead of nurture them—but the cats came anyway, drawn by the odors from the garbage pickup area. Then a couple of guards would start to feed one or another, and they would have to call Sister Irene. Someone had taken a shine to the little gray one with the single eye. They had named her Sweetie.

I was still rattled. "Let me get this straight. Somebody liked that little monster and named her Sweetie?"

"It's because I feed her. I'm her lifeline now, and she doesn't want any competition from you. Don't take it personally. They fight against each other too."

"Do I dare ask how many there are?"

"I'm not sure. Four or five at the moment. After a while they run away again because they like the woods better, and sometimes the coyotes get them. I don't think they'll bother you anymore. They usually avoid visitors, and they've never shown any interest in this space before."

"Maybe I messed with them in a previous life."

"No," she said, as if this were an entirely reasonable suggestion. "They're just scared of you. All violence comes from fear."

"Right, those earthquakes are terrified, just like those volcanoes and tidal waves."

"You've got a quick mouth," she said, sounding annoyed for the first time, which pleased me.

"I've heard that before."

She opened the door and looked out. "See? They're gone. What I mean, Ellen, is that intentional violence always has its roots in fear."

"My brother and the men in the Silent Brotherhood, the KKK, the Aryan Army, the white militias, you think they're just scared? What was Hitler scared of?"

"I'm not an intellectual," she said wearily, as if my argument was not even worth addressing, "and I'm going to bed." But when she left, she winked at me.

The Friendly Nun had winked at me, and the cats weren't finished.

For several hours, they flung themselves against the door, beating their displeasure like a drum. I'd never been attacked by cats before, but these were kitties gone wild, puddy tats who'd tasted savagery and embraced it. If their hostility was fear-based, it had transformed into something incomprehensible.

Jesus and I stared at each other, or I stared at him since he didn't seem to have eyes, until I lapsed into a restless sleep.

2

When I stayed at the El Rancho, I sometimes still had sex with Blake, but we were awkward with each other now, and these encounters usually felt sad. His job suspension had been lifted and there had been no further trouble about his employment, but whether or not the Gallup higher-ups knew he had been monitored by a federal agency wasn't clear.

The deaths of Ruby's children began to seem unreal, so twice I drove out to El Morro only to discover that both entrances to the Catacombs had been closed off with padlocked metal fences. The second time I parked half a mile away and hiked in, and there it was, a peaceful shabby farmhouse, quiet in its abandonment. Even the yellow crime tape was gone. When I got to the entrance to the hidden area, I discovered that it had been thoroughly boarded up. Heavy fencing had been sunk into a poured concrete base. There wasn't even a police notice.

I avoided Claudia less than Blake. Her long piece "The Tomb of the Unknown Racist" had been published under her own byline in the Sunday *Times Magazine*, where it garnered serious attention, and she was now a "special correspondent," a label she tried to wear lightly. We met several times for lunch. She favored Earl's, the local comfort-food joint, but I preferred the buffet at the casino. Mostly we talked about the quality of our sobriety. I could admit to Claudia how empty I felt off and on and how hopeless my attempts to find my brother seemed, while she struggled with what is called in AA staying "right-size"—that is, not letting her ego get in the way of her values, which for Claudia translated into something like "truth, justice, and the American way."

"You make me think of the way a blade of grass can crack a sidewalk," I said.

"Well, you did hit the sidewalk with a sledgehammer."

"I suppose I did. Why haven't you been twisting my arm to see Ruby?"

"Of course, I'd like to see Ruby, and I'm sure you'll arrange that if you think it's a good idea. But Ruby's not really the story anymore, is she? If I do get to talk to her, that would be terrific, but what I'm hoping is you'll take me with you on one of your find-your-brother junkets."

We were having lunch in the casino because I needed to be in an environment without windows and clocks. "Sometimes you make me wish I'd gone to Brown. At Duke, I didn't learn much about clarity. Of course, I did fail out."

"Your clarity is part of what I admire about you," she said. "You always stay certain that remaining sober comes first, but you've got a lot of courage. Look at what you made happen in South Carolina."

"That was rashness, not courage. I think Estelle was right about it. All I got was my mother wounded."

"It doesn't sound like your mother understood what happened."

"I, unfortunately, do."

"I'm still trying to figure out why you've so obsessed with finding your brother. What is it you think you can do about him?"

"I'm not sure. Hold him accountable? Make him stop?"

"Why you?"

"He's my brother."

"And how exactly will you change your brother? You think you have such great persuasive powers? Doesn't AA assert that 'Anger is the dubious luxury of normal people?'"

When I didn't answer, she said, "Ellen, are we going to have an affair?"

"Jesus Christ, no. Where did that come from?" I put my elbows on the table and held my head in my hands, staring down at my chicken cutlet. "Great. Now I can't be comfortable around you either."

"I'm sorry. I just needed to clear the air. I'm not trying to write about you, and I'm not trying to get involved with you that way. I'm really not."

I was still looking down at my plate, at this cutlet that used to be inside a real chicken going *cluck cluck cluck*, that lived inside a chicken prison where the birds couldn't move and had to eat hormones to make their boobs bigger. "Eating meat is so disgusting," I said, staring at the striations of exposed breast. "Meat of the bird, meat of the human, meat of the pig. Do you know we used to barbecue whole pigs in the yard when I was a teenager? John Tillman's son shot one of our cows as a protest. Meat of the children, blood going down a drain. They bleed animals after they're slaughtered, just like they do with people to embalm them."

When I raised my head, she looked alarmed. "Good. Be scared of me, Claudia Friedman. No, I'm not going to go to bed with you. I'm old enough to be your mother."

This remark hurt her, but she found it easier to be insulted than hurt. "Is it because I'm not pretty enough?"

"Don't be ridiculous. Wasn't publishing in the *Times* with less than a year of sobriety hard enough? Now you're trying to find a higher cliff?"

"I just asked a question. You don't have to act this way about it."

"Yes, I do, damn it." I stood up. "Listen, I like you, and I think you're smart, and I'm just trying to help you. Pay the bill. You can afford it."

When I saw her later that day at the 5:30 AA meeting, she mouthed the word *sorry*. Afterward, she approached me tentatively. "It's okay," I said. "Not a big deal." But it was a big deal.

I used to joke that if women could marry, I'd have had six or seven wives, I'd have been the Norman Mailer of lesbians, but that wasn't true. I'd married a man when I was eighteen and left him when I was twenty-five, and of all the women I've been with since then, there was only one I would have married. I don't mean Jordan, the fugitive, or Marina, the professor, or Heidi, the bondage dish, or Alexandra, the other bondage dish, or even Artemis, the artist I thought I would never get over but did. I would have married Meg, the social worker. Soon after I met Meg, I called my mother, still a reasoning being at the time, and told her I'd met someone new. Meg wasn't like anyone else I'd known. Meg was so quiet

I kept falling asleep around her. We'd be sitting somewhere, even in a restaurant, and I'd get so drowsy we'd have to leave.

"Is she white?" my mother asked. "Does she own her own house? Is she a stripper?"

"She's Jewish," I said. "She owns her house. She's a psychiatric social worker. She works with schizophrenics in long-term treatment."

"Well, that explains it. She thinks you're normal."

"I am normal, Momma. I'm a normal neurotic lesbian feminist."

"God help us," she said.

My voice rose an octave. "Meg was the first woman deep-sea diver in the navy, Momma. She was the kind of diver where you wear a full suit and a helmet and go deep and stay connected to the surface by a breathing tube. Like those little bubbling figures they put in aquariums, except the water's dark down there . . . She was the first woman ever to pass that training. Their equipment was made for men, and her boots weighed seventeen pounds each."

When she didn't reply, I said, "The navy was going to feature her on billboards before they found out she was gay. But they did let her stay in the navy."

"Well, that's a blessing," Momma said, proving that irony was not my exclusive province.

Estelle, it seemed, had cautiously begun to forgive me. She moved some of her things back into Momma's condo and took over supervising the caregivers again, so I didn't have to worry about going home for the moment, but we still remained distant with each other on the phone. Neither of us seemed to want to thrash through what had happened with Lucia's funeral.

If Blake began to seem mildly disgusting, Ruby did too. I had lost, with Ruby, not compassion but something deeper. She had begun to talk of killing herself, and when she did so, it was with the same eeriness she'd exhibited when I brought her the picture of Lucia. Ruby's conundrum—*conundrum* was the word she used—continued to be her belief that suicide was a sin, so the sinner would already be dead and couldn't ask for absolution. She believed Jesus had washed her clean about the children, but suicide might mean she could not enter heaven. "I just want to be with my children again, but I don't know how."

"Why do you believe these ideas about suicide, Ruby?"

"Jeremiah taught me, when I became a Christian."

"The man who kidnapped you? He helped you become a Christian?"

"Well, I do understand now that Jeremiah did not want to be who he was, and I didn't really escape from him, but I wish he hadn't lied about being white. And I wish he had been a cleaner person. The smell of his breath was awful."

Sister Irene continued to urge my visits with Ruby "to improve her spiritual condition." So, out of respect for The Friendly Nun, I showed up at the prison every week. At night, I barricaded myself away from the cats and studied the maple Jesus that Ruby believed had absolved her. Despite the odor of the cats, which I could still detect faintly, the room also smelled remarkably pure, almost like incense, which Sister Irene assured me she had never burned. "What is it then? The wood paneling? The oil on Jesus?" I finally concluded that Shakti, the life energy that some mystics believe can be accessed by prayer and meditation, had permeated the room. Its source did not seem to be the crucifixion but the bench in front of the bureau. The presence of Shakti was familiar to me from the ashram I'd visited when I went to see the guru Rama. I had been trying to learn to pray because my sponsor kept saying I didn't know how and the Boston *Phoenix* agreed to send me to interview him, because at that point Rama was still foolish enough to talk to press. I planned to write something funny and please my sponsor at the same time, but whatever happened at the ashram was too much like Royce's vision, and I had never told anyone about it except my editor on the phone, who had yelled, "Get out of there! You're drugged!"

When I first arrived in the ashram's parking lot, their "press representative" met me. From the farthest structure, I could hear chanting that was so compelling that this woman had to chase me across the parking lot. The sound suddenly stopped. "It's okay," she said, out of breath. "We chant all the time."

"But will it be the same? Will it be like that?"

The next morning, in the sanctuary, the chanting of Rama's mantra transported me again, and I began to see a lovely blue light whenever my eyes were closed. The sound vibrated inside my chest and spine and in the air surrounding me, and when we broke for lunch, I stumbled around, my face bathed with joy, saying to anyone who would listen, "Everything is perfect just the way it is!" This was embarrassing enough in retrospect, but this altered state lasted for two whole days, and by the end of the second day I could see the blue light at will with my eyes open. It was when I shared the perfection of the world with my editor that she shouted I'd been drugged. But I knew I hadn't been drugged. This state can have many names, among them grace, transcendence, enlightenment, and insanity.

During my private interview with Rama the last morning, I forgot my clever questions and dropped to my knees, mumbling, "What about nuclear bombs?" I keep a tape recording of that interview to review whenever I need a dose of embarrassment and humility. Rama said simply that if God wanted the bombs to go off, they would, and I did not have to worry about it. "Your thinking is not holding the sky up. What is breathing through you when you are asleep holds the world up. It has breathed you into this world, and some day it will breathe you out." When Rama left the room, he suddenly turned and hit my forehead with the heel of his hand. I could feel this light blow for months, and, if I lay on my back and turned my neck a certain way, I could sometimes again feel fragments of Rama's bliss.

Remembering this experience but unable to retrieve any part of it, I turned my head every which way, pondering Sister Irene's partial Jesus, waiting for a sign. Royce's vision had led him to evil, and mine had led me to AA and to a search for my personal goodness. If Ruby was my doppelgänger, Royce was my negative shape.

3

The first place I searched for Royce was Montana. Santane had given me directions to the cabin where they'd once lived, and also to another location in Idaho. I even drove to Whidbey Island to see where he was supposed to have died. The house that had replaced the one destroyed was unremarkable, its troubling history elided.

In each location, I visited libraries and read newspaper archives, called anyone I thought might know anything, and checked in with local police, and in all cases the answers amounted to the same reply: Royce Burns was dead. "That might be so," I said, "but please put the word out that his sister is looking for him."

These trips to the Northwest seemed like genuflections, mere methods of avoidance, because I knew in my gut that any threads leading to my brother's whereabouts were going to be found in Oklahoma. Although Timothy McVeigh had been sentenced to death for the Oklahoma City bombing, his accomplice, Terry Nichols, received life imprisonment, and a less complicit man, Michael Fortier, was given a lenient term of twelve years. His wife was rewarded with immunity for turning state's evidence. My several letters to McVeigh, Nichols, and Fortier went unanswered. I tried to locate Fortier's wife but could not. The Justice Department had insisted from the start that these four people were the only conspirators, because, according to Blake, reassuring the public had been their paramount concern. The authorities didn't want civilians panicked by the thought that other bombers might still be around. Nevertheless, agents from the FBI and BATF had continued to search extensively for John Doe #2, the man reported to have been with McVeigh when he rented the Ryder truck. The sketches of John Doe #2 did not resemble Terry Nichols or Michael Fortier at all.

McVeigh's bomb in the heartland of America had accomplished what William Luther Pierce promised in *The Turner Diaries*: "But the real value of all our attacks today lies in the psychological impact, not in the immediate casualties . . . That is a lesson they will not forget." Pierce might be a doddering old fool now, but because he had always presented himself as an author and a white organizer and the founder of the Cosmotheist Community Church, he had never done anything that would lead to his imprisonment. He still ran what remained of the National Alliance as a church in Hillsboro, West Virginia, but its members were primarily members of his family. Pierce declined to meet with me too.

Royce had been drawn to William Luther Pierce because he was the most educated and clear-minded of the white separatists. Pierce was not, however, the preacher who had induced Royce's ecstatic state. That was a man called Billy Valentine. Mathews had summoned Valentine and Pierce to the compound to meet each other and see if an alliance among them might be possible. Pierce had been looking for a charlatan evangelist, but Valentine, unfortunately, actually believed what he preached. Royce, who in his vision had demonstrated great power, was unencumbered by Christian beliefs, so Royce was the man Pierce chose to ally with. In any case, within a few months, Valentine began channeling a coming nuclear attack by aliens that he called "War of the Giants," so he split off his followers, who, over the course of two years, constructed an enormous underground bomb shelter in Montana. Seven hundred men, women, and children trundled inside on the predicted date, but nothing happened, and within a year Valentine had died of heart failure. The shelter, though it still existed, had since been abandoned.

Public records revealed that Timothy McVeigh had telephoned the Christian Identity compound called Elohim City in the Ozark Mountains of eastern Oklahoma a few weeks before the bombing. He had asked to speak to a man named Andy Strassmeir, a German national purported to have explosives training, and according to the last of Royce's papers, Strassmeir was the man Mathews had sent Joe Magnus to work with. The person who answered McVeigh's phone call had claimed that Strassmeir was not there, but perhaps the call had been some kind of signal. What is certain is that Strassmeir and Timothy McVeigh met at least once before. Strassmeir looked a lot like the sketch of John Doe #2.

"Here's part of what makes it stink so much," Ed Blake said. "Neither the FBI nor BATF interviewed Strassmeir. It's just an incomprehensible omission. They should have been all over him. Instead, they let him slip out of the country through Canada."

Blake had driven out to the casino to find me because I'd started avoiding him. Although I was losing steadily at twenty-five-dollar black-jack, I pocketed my remaining chips and followed him into the bar. We sat at a small table, and a waitress brought him two beers and me a Coke.

"So are you too now thinking that Joe Magnus and/or my brother might have had something to do with the Oklahoma City bombing?"

"I don't know about that," Blake said. "At this point Magnus is probably an informant for one of the agencies, and he certainly does not have a reputation for brains or discipline. And Strassmeir might have been an informant as well. Maybe different people were running different agendas. Maybe the left hand didn't know what the right hand was doing."

"But even if Strassmeir was acquainted with both Joe Magnus and McVeigh, what would be their connection to my brother?" I gestured toward his two beers, one draft, one bottled. "You're picking up extremism, Blake. Ever hear the expression 'one beer at a time'?"

"Ellen, sooner or later, you're going to have to deal with me. With the fact of me."

"You're a fact, all right."

"To answer your question, I doubt Strassmeir had anything directly to do with your brother, but since Strassmeir was not interviewed, an order must have come directly from above. So, here's the real question: If there was a government informant who knew how to make bombs and he was directly involved with Timothy McVeigh, does that mean McVeigh might have been stopped? I think only BATF has cowboys who are stupid enough to have bungled this. Or maybe I'm just learning to be as suspicious as you are. But there's no plausible explanation for not having interviewed Strassmeir." He picked up the draft beer but didn't drink it.

"Did you know all this before? I told you Oklahoma City was somehow connected."

"Well, I've done some poking around, and I do still have a few sources. I'm sure there are many fine agents in BATF, but something is really wrong about all of this." His head tilted forward, and he kept peering into my eyes, as if he were trying to understand something.

"I can't let you in anymore, Ed Blake. I don't know why." I studied him, this man who was kind and smart and trying so hard.

"I'd give up if I could."

"So, yes, okay, yes," I finally said. "What you see in me is pain. Before I met you, I had detached from a lot of painful events in my past, but that detachment was dependent on keeping a certain distance. You don't know this about me, and why should you, but it's not about sex. It's the language of sex that matters, and you and I speak something that might make me lose my bearings. The deepest anyone ever got inside me was a woman, and you remind me too much of her. She derailed me. I was sober by then, and she still derailed me. I didn't drink or use, but I spent nearly a year unable to function."

He smiled, still trying to make me connect with him from someplace other than the surface of my gaze. "Was she a cop?"

"No, she was a shrink."

I wanted to tell him about Meg but couldn't.

When Meg left me, I claimed I didn't know why, but I did. Meg's heart had enveloped me, or, in lesbian parlance, bottomed me. Also, she was witty and smart and accomplished, but I don't know if I would have cared so much about those qualities, given how she made me feel. "Feeling safe is so unfamiliar."

But after a while my restlessness returned, and several years later, when we were living in Vermont, Meg said she had concluded that my hypervigilance was hardwired. "Your intensity, the force of your personality, is not, as I had hoped, the result of the sexual abuse by your uncle, or the death of your father, or the fact that you cracked your skull when you were five." No, she said, my wildness was innate, and I had simply worn her out. Meg said I was like a tuning fork. Meg claimed she never knew whether I was going to take off for Iceland on some whim (it wasn't a whim, I just wanted to see a place where the crust of the earth was very thin) or end up with a shaman in Peru for two weeks. It wasn't good enough for me to go to Delos, the island off Mykonos that is now a museum and where only archaeologists can stay overnight. No, Ellen, the great Ellen, had to convince them to let her sleep out there. Meg said I lacked a healthy sense of limitation. She said I was exhausting. She said she'd been cheating on me.

"But you love me," I said. "I know you do."

"Well, I something you," she said. "You're a powerful person. But, Ellen, I think if I had loved you more, I could have handled you better. I'm very sorry. Maybe it's true I didn't love you enough."

She had loved me enough, I knew that, but while I was in Peru a friend of ours commiserated her right into bed. "I hope you're having stupid sex," I said. "I hope it's boring vanilla sex. I hope you have to watch porn to get off."

"I can't continue living with someone who thinks she has a license to do anything that comes into her head," Meg said. "I loved it at first, you know I did, but then you started treating me like I was home base, like I was some kind of holy object you would show up for and say a few worshipful things to, then take off again. You treated me like I was not a real person, Ellen. Not an actual living person."

"That's a lie, Meg."

"Feelings can't be lies. I'm telling you how I felt."

We sold the house in Vermont. I kicked out the tenant in my Cambridge apartment, buried myself deeper in AA, and within a couple of years developed a stalker who was following me everywhere. At first I thought she was harmless, just some Beacon Hill matron who imagined I'd be flattered. I had started going to meetings that were mostly African American and Hispanic (that's how I happened to meet Estelle), thinking that this strange white woman wouldn't follow me there, but she did. Her name was Diane, and she wasn't even an alcoholic. She just sat in meetings glowing at me. Sometimes, walking down a street, I could spot her behind me, followed by her small, bald husband trying to keep her in sight. Then, when Diane rented the apartment on the floor above me,

I realized I might have a serious problem. She began leaving presents in front of my door. I didn't open them, but once when I was carrying a package the size of a shoebox to the trash, I thought about a bomb. Maybe one day I'd open my door and she'd be standing there glowing and holding a hatchet. So, after Estelle moved back to the Low Country, I wasn't far behind.

Now I was entangled with a man. God's sense of humor was getting tiresome.

So, I invited Ed Blake to come with me to Oklahoma.

4

We started at the maw of what had been the Murrah Federal Building, though there was little to see now, other than bombed-out rubble and ongoing construction of what would later become the Oklahoma City National Memorial and Museum. These cranes and craters and trucks and beelike workmen could tell us nothing. The original explosion had sliced off the six-floor facade of the Murrah Building, exposing the interior in layers, and a month later experts imploded what was left of the structure with more explosives. The three bodies that had been missing were recovered. So was an unidentified left leg.

The leg found in the rubble of the Murrah Building was first described in a statement by the medical examiner's office as belonging to a light-skinned male less than thirty years of age. "This leg was clothed in a black military-type boot, two socks, and an olive drab blousing strap." A few months later, the chief medical examiner insisted to reporters that "DNA analysis by the FBI has shown conclusively that the leg is not male but female." And six months after that, experts began to claim that the leg had belonged to a previously identified female victim they had accidentally buried with the wrong leg.

"Who knows what to make of any of it?" Blake said. "What they're saying now may be absolutely true. I still think it's hard to falsify DNA analysis, although it sure would explain a lot about your brother."

There were other factors we speculated about on the three-hour drive east toward Elohim City. The significance of the date of the bombing, April 19, on the two-year anniversary of the governmental destruction of the religious compound at Waco, was already known, since Timothy McVeigh had proclaimed it himself. And the execution of Richard Snell on the same day as the bombing could have been a coincidence. But Snell had connections to Elohim City and to other white supremacists, and he sneered at the warden that "something big" was going to happen that day. If that report was true, then foreknowledge of the bombing must have extended beyond McVeigh and Nichols and into at least some of the terrorist web.

There had also been the complicated business about a man named Kenneth Trentadue, who supposedly hanged himself in his cell a few months after the bombing. Kenneth Trentadue's brother Jesse, who was a lawyer, had not believed the verdict of suicide, and he had insisted on the release of Kenneth's body, which, it turned out, exhibited multiple lacerations and bruises. Kenneth Trentadue had received three severe blows to his head, and his throat had been cut; the government's medical personnel continued to argue that these injuries were self-inflicted, but Jesse Trentadue believed that, in the course of a brutal interrogation, his brother had been murdered. But why? Because his brother looked so much like the sketches of John Doe #2? An inmate named Alden Gillis Baker, reported to have been Trentadue's cellmate at one time, claimed he actually saw the agents beating Trentadue and now feared for his own life. Later, Baker also reportedly hanged himself.

Except for these troubling conversations, the drive was long and boring, so Blake and I punctuated it with stops at casinos, where I could indulge what began to look like a gambling habit, and I told him more about my life than I should have. He sat beside me at the blackjack table playing absentmindedly with one-dollar chips while I described the night Jordan shot herself and mumbled about Meg leaving me for someone who wasn't even good-looking. I did turn the stalker episode into an amusing tale, but I couldn't think of anything funny about Jordan or Meg. I chatted up my visits to Iceland and the Peruvian shaman. I talked too fucking much.

Before we reached the police station in Stillwell, a small town on the edge of the Oklahoma Ozarks, Blake said, "Can I ask you something without making you angry?"

"I hope so."

"I don't understand what you mean about being a lesbian. When we were on the mesa at El Morro, I thought . . ."

"Yes, it was great." I was glad to be driving so I wouldn't have to look at him. "And, yes, it did mean something."

"It was great and it meant something, but . . ."

Two rabbits hopped alongside the road, but mentioning them would be avoidance. "All I can tell you is that the first time I fell in love with a woman, it was like I had stepped through a mirror into a different reality. In college, there was this woman I wanted to be with so much that my throat ached whenever I saw her. I assumed I was happily married, but I followed this woman around all the time, just so I could look at her. At the time I didn't understand that this was a sexual attraction because the only feeling I'd ever had that was anything like it was in art history class, when I first saw pictures of all those Greek statues. Maybe it has something to do with art, I don't know, but a shrink once said to me, 'You can't imagine what you've never imagined.' And I had never imagined being able to feel like that."

Blake didn't speak again until we were off the highway pulling through deserted country roads. "So you're saying I'll never be someone who can make your throat hurt?"

"I suppose it's as simple as that. I'm so sorry, Blake."

In the police station, we behaved with flawless professionalism. Blake showed his credentials, and a reluctant young officer phoned the only number he had for the Elohim City compound. When he got finally someone on that phone, he explained that he was bringing out some folks who wanted to speak to a resident, any resident. No, of course no one had to talk to these visitors, but he was going to drive them up to the gate. Yes, of course they were unarmed. One of them was a law officer from New Mexico, but the other was a woman.

We rode silently with this vacant young man through many miles of winding, paved roads, tucked deep into the heavily eroded crevasses of the Ozarks. Then we bumped down six miles of gravel road posted every fifty feet against trespassers. Eventually, we arrived at a red metal gate secured with heavy black chains, where two men holding shotguns stood waiting.

The deputy got out of the car and motioned us to follow.

These men were bearded and rough, but they were not unfriendly. "We just don't want any trouble," the large one said in a deep, booming voice. "We want to be alone with the Lord."

"We don't want to come through the gate," I said quietly, "though I'd love to see where you live. I heard you even have geodesic domes for houses, like hippies did in the sixties. Is that true?'

There was no answer, so I said, "I brought a letter for Joe Magnus."

"There's nobody here by that name."

I extended the sealed white envelope through the slats of the gate, but neither man reached to take it. "I don't think he's here now," I said, dropping it onto the gravel. "But he was here years ago. Could you spread the word around, please? Say that Royce Burns's sister is looking for him, and also for Joe Magnus. Let Magnus know that I'm staying at the Colcord Hotel in Oklahoma City. Tell him I have a cell phone, and the number is in the letter."

The next day, after more failed sex and silent poker, Blake said he believed Magnus wasn't going to show up, and there was business he needed to tend to in Gallup. He said he had come to the reluctant conclusion that I was paranoid about my brother and that Royce was probably dead.

"I'm paranoid? You're just realizing that now?"

"Ellen, listen, if there were some kind of conspiracy about the leg they found in the Murrah Building, don't you realize that they wouldn't put out three different stories, they'd simply cover it up? That we'd hear nothing?"

"But the rattles prove Royce is still alive."

"Even if your brother is alive, you're on the wrong track in Oklahoma."

"Then why did you come here?"

He didn't answer.

"You go on back," I said. "Magnus probably wants to find me alone. I'll just try to lose more money."

"You're sure you don't want to return to Gallup with me?"

"I'm sure."

During my stay at the Colcord, I went to AA meetings twice daily at the Kelly Club, founded in 1947 and visited once by Bill Wilson himself. No one at the Kelly Club had ever heard of my brother or of Ruby, which was a relief. And hardly anyone at the club was white, which was also a relief.

I contacted a reporter from the local paper, and the Oklahoma *Independent* ran an interview in which I explained that I was looking for Joe Magnus, who had been a friend of my brother's. And, yes, Joe Magnus was a federal fugitive but "just a minor one," I said, hoping to bait him.

The casino I liked best was called FireLake, and it was thirty miles east of Oklahoma City in Shawnee. I figured that if Magnus was going to show up, he'd do so at the casino. Instead, the third night after Blake left, Joe Magnus ran me off the road at two o'clock in the morning. I remained calm because adrenaline sometimes makes me calm, and enough adrenaline sometimes makes me beatific. I got out of my car smiling loopily. "Hi, Joe, I was hoping you'd come find me. Just don't hurt me, okay?"

"Cuntsucker? Really?"

"I'm sorry, but I really was very angry at that particular moment. I am genuinely sorry I said something like that to you, Joe. I'm trying to find a way to stop swearing because your sister told me to."

"What the fuck do you want with me, Ellen?"

"I'm trying to find my brother."

"He's dead."

"Like you are?"

"Nobody's claims I'm dead," Joe snarled, "but if you find your fucking brother, you tell him I'm going to kill him. And you stay away from my sister. You know I'll come after you if I have to."

He stood by his truck as if he were leaving, but then he changed his mind, left his door open, and walked straight toward me. He was a big man with a bullet-shaped head, his body outlined against his headlights, and there was nowhere to run, so I stepped toward him, not away. He halted about two feet from me, where I could see his dim face. I wanted to say something but couldn't. I was shaking so hard that I knew he could see it.

He took a rapid step forward and stiff-armed me in the chest, knocking me down, and then threw his full weight on top of me. I struggled for a few seconds and went passive. He was stronger than me; I was pinned. Up close he smelled like tobacco and acrid sweat. "I always thought you were pretty hot," he said. "You're as crazy as your brother, but you aren't so rotten." He stuck his rough tongue in my mouth, wiggling it deep, but then abruptly sat back up. "Royce's sister. I couldn't fuck you with somebody else's dick."

He rose to his feet, turning his back to me unsteadily. "Go on home, Ellen. You're messing with stuff you don't understand."

I sat up and shouted at his retreating form, "Were you involved with the Oklahoma City bombing? Whose leg was it they found?"

He acted as if he hadn't heard me.

"Whose leg was it?" I shouted.

When he got to his truck, he stood on the running board and said in a voice that carried across the distance, "You're crazy, and your brother is a fucking fool, but you keep this up, you just might get yourself killed."

He was driving a big truck, so getting out of the pocked field was a lot easier for him. My rental car had a crinkled fender and a punctured muffler, and it was dawn before I managed to return—very loudly—to the Colcord Hotel.

5

A day later I had calmed down, straightened out the mess created by damaging the car, let Blake know a mild version of my encounter with Magnus without pointing out that I was not entirely paranoid, and won $2,300 after someone taught me how to play craps. In Oklahoma, craps tables are as silly as their version of roulette. State law forbids the use of dice or balls in Oklahoma gaming (despite the fact that these casinos are on sovereign Native land), so, for the roulette facsimile, a dealer must spin a wheel with playing cards clicking around it like the ones kids used to fasten to bicycle wheels with clothespins. Craps, amazingly, is played without dice. At the craps table, a large fuzzy imitation die had numbered cards stuck to its sides.

I went shopping with the extra cash. Oklahoma City turned out to be an excellent source for cut-and-paste classics, and I spent several hours deciding between a 1960 white Lincoln with suicide doors and a 1966 Ford Fairlane. Both were convertibles with reasonably intact tops. The Ford was a slick two-tone green, but Jack Kennedy had been assassinated sitting in the open backseat of a Lincoln with suicide doors, and Jackie Kennedy had crawled across the trunk in her pink suit, trying either to get help or to escape danger, depending on how you read the footage. I bought the Lincoln. The doors fit tight, the top worked fine, and I didn't care that the bloodred seats were shredded with age. My cash sufficed for a down payment, more money was wired from Charleston, and I drove the car right off the lot.

Ed Blake had notified the FBI in Oklahoma City about my alleged run-in with Magnus, so that evening a nice young agent came out to the casino to interview me while I was playing roulette. I had abandoned the Colcord and was staying now at the casino's hotel so I wouldn't have to drive after dark. This agent was clean-cut, polite, wearing a cheap suit, and treated me as if I were elderly. I continued to play while we talked. Roulette is a slow game, and with bicycle cards on the wheel, it's tedious. After the formalities—"I'm Special Agent Mintern with the Federal Bureau of Investigation"—he actually said this, as if he were a character on *The X-Files*, I put twenty dollars on number thirteen.

"Miss Burns, can I ask why you are certain it was Joe Magnus who ran your car off the road?"

"The same way I know my own name."

"You recognized him, yet you hadn't seen him in many years? Did he identify himself?"

"Okay, so I couldn't have run into Joe Magnus—or, speaking precisely, he couldn't have run into me—since Joe Magnus is a federal fugitive. Yes, of course I recognized him, and anyway, who else would run me off the road claiming to be Joe Magnus? You think maybe it was Andy Strassmeir?"

His round cheeks and whiteness made me think of Ping-Pong balls, and his puzzlement revealed that he had never heard Strassmeir's name. That was what I had wanted to know. He said, "Would you be willing to come down to our office so I could record an interview in better circumstances?"

"I don't think so, son. I get very quiet in my head when I'm playing roulette. The canned music is obnoxious, and gambling is really about losing. Gambling is about trying to outrun statistical probabilities. It won't be any different for me, yet I still want to play. What do you think that means?" The wheel was going *click click click* while the music blared over the ringing and dinging of the slot machines.

At first, he didn't reply. Then he said, "Noncooperation may be unwise, Miss Burns. Joe Magnus remains dangerous, as you have learned, and we are trying to ascertain whether your brother could still be alive, just as you are."

"Noncooperation, yes, I suppose that's what it is. Okay, I'm not going to talk to you unless this wheel hits thirteen." The wheel turned interminably and finally stopped on five, black. "Oops, not thirteen, sorry. How old are you?"

"Thirty-four," he said.

"You look younger. I get it that you don't understand what's going on in this mess, and, if it's any help, I don't understand yet either."

He maintained his respect-the-elders demeanor. "I'm simply here to ask you to accompany me into town, Miss Burns. The possible reemergence of Joseph Magnus is a significant development."

"One more try at thirteen," I said. "We'll add twenty-two, the day of the month my sister died. What's your birthday?"

He said reluctantly, because he was probably breaking some rule, "The twelfth of October."

"Okay, forty dollars on twelve."

The wheel kept spinning. "Listen, kiddo," I said, "someone in BATF or some other agency has known where Joe Magnus is all along, and there might be agents higher on your own food chain who know too. And, nope, I'm not going anywhere to meet with you or anyone else from the FBI. You guys kept a fucking file on me." The card where the wheel stopped read twelve. "We just won something like fourteen hundred dollars. I didn't realize you'd be so lucky. Can I give you part of these winnings?"

"I'll have someone else get in touch with you, Miss Burns. As long as you understand now that you may be in danger."

"Do I seem like someone who would have the sense to quit?"

It wasn't Joe Magnus who showed up at the casino later that night; it was Claudia Friedman. I turned my head at the blackjack table, and there she was, standing right beside my chair. "Jesus, Claudia, what are you doing here?"

She was distraught. "I need to talk to you."

"What happened? Did you drink?"

"No. Can we talk?"

The dealer, Darletta, showed a six, and I had a seven and a three. I doubled down and got a jack, which gave me twenty, but she hit twenty-one. "Sorry," she said, confiscating my fifty bucks. I liked Darletta. "Born and raised in Shawnee, full-blooded Potawatomi, and I'm a betting woman. There's not much to do in Oklahoma besides sports and gambling."

I picked up my chips and tossed two to her. "How long are you on for tonight?"

"I'm off in a half hour. Back tomorrow at noon." The look she gave me made me wonder if she was hitting on me.

"See you then," I said, and headed for the all-night canteen.

Claudia said, "Please, can we just go to your room?"

I stopped and studied her. She was wild-eyed, desperate, and her urgency was repellent.

My small suite on the fifth floor had a seating area and a separate bedroom. I scraped up the clothes that littered the sofa and threw them onto the floor, grabbed the phone for room service, and then realized it was closed. "Want a Coke? I've got some in the fridge." I pulled open the small refrigerator, trying to decide what to do. "I'm not going to bed with you, Claudia," I said, without even looking at her. "First, I don't want to, and second, I promised Estelle that I wouldn't."

She sat on the sofa, and I handed her a Coke. "What? You promised Estelle? What has Estelle got to do with this?"

I didn't sit down, but I met her gaze.

She lowered her head and stared at the carpet. "I think I'm falling apart."

The chair needed excavating too, so I pushed the pile of newspapers and magazines onto the floor and sat down, keeping the coffee table between us. "Claudia," I said as gently as I could, "have you ever even been to bed with a woman?"

Her expression went through several painful and bewildered changes. "No, just a little fooling around in college. But I know this is right. It has to be." She turned weepy. "I couldn't feel this way if it wasn't right."

"Yes, you could feel this way, and you'll understand that better when you're older. The truth is, it's not right between us." I wondered where this kindly person had been hiding inside me. "Claudia, some things can feel very right and still be wrong. I think maybe your capacity for this kind of desire got triggered because I helped you in a big way for no reason that you can figure out. Then you had an enormous professional win, and that combination has knocked you over."

"I feel as if you've taken some power over me."

"I haven't." I handed her the box of tissues from the bedside table, and she took it without looking up. "But listen, if we were to get sexually involved, I might actually take power over you. I've been on both sides of that. I promise you that staying out of bed with me is the easier, softer way."

She glanced up because I was referencing a well-known passage in the AA Big Book: "We thought we could find an easier, softer way. But we could not."

"Why don't you tell me about your interviews with Ruby?"

She took a long wet breath. "Let me just say one more thing. Then we can talk about Ruby. I didn't know about feeling like this."

"I get that. I understand that."

She looked up and held my gaze. "We're really not? You're sure?"

"We're not. I'm sure."

"Because you don't want to?"

It seemed wisest to lie. Having someone weep with desire for me had opened the eye of lust inside me, and it was a gelid, amoral eye. I hoped she couldn't see me vibrating. "I don't want to."

Claudia managed to shift her gears impressively, and the face I knew better reappeared. "What Ruby has told me so far is basically what she told you. I think the 'Jeremiah, I'm the hand of God, I'm your bad luck' tale would be pretty hard to make up, but then again so was the kidnapping story. I'm starting to buy the assertion that Lucia looked white when she was born. Do you have any thoughts on that?"

I tried to appear relaxed. "You know you're going to have a book out of this, if you want."

"It turns out that children with mixed blood sometimes really are born looking white before they darken. And lots of babies have their eye color change. So her account is somewhat plausible."

I stood up slowly, looking down at her dark head. "I don't know if what's true matters much anymore, Claudia. But here's something I do know: we need to go downstairs and get ourselves a great big bag of tortilla chips and start playing slot machines. Do you like to play slots?"

She hesitated as if she wanted to say more. "I do feel better."

When we were on the elevator, I suggested that she check in to the hotel, but it turned out she already had. She had been at the casino for several hours and had been watching me while I talked with the FBI agent. "Don't do creepy stuff like that, Claudia. I mean it. I need to be able to trust you."

We ate two bags of tortilla chips and played penny slot machines until my fingers ached so much from punching the buttons that I had to keep switching hands. It takes great stubbornness to lose four hundred dollars on a penny slot. When it was late enough to be getting light outside, I said, "I'm going to bed."

"You go up first," she said without looking at me. "I'll come up separately."

"Okay, but Claudia, I'm speaking as your serious friend. There's only one thing that matters. Neither of us is going to take a drink or a drug, no matter what happens."

"Right," she said, pulling the arm of the slot. "I'm not supposed to drink, even if my ass falls off."

"Yes, and everything else is gravy."

She still didn't look at me, but I thought I'd worn her out. "Some gravy," she finally said.

6

In the morning, Claudia went missing. Her cell phone clicked straight to voice mail, and the clerk at the desk said she checked out early. I had a bad feeling. It was after eleven o'clock, so I drove the Lincoln back into Oklahoma City to catch the noon meeting. I left the top up so that I could call Ed Blake on the way. "Claudia turned up here at the casino yesterday, but I can't find her this morning. Something's off. I feel it."

Blake's silence meant he was digesting this turn of events. Then he said, "She's been interviewing Ruby. Is it possible she found out something we don't know?"

"I don't see how. She would have told me."

"She's a very clever young woman."

"That she is." Then I described for him the young agent the FBI had sent to interview me.

"I'd laugh if I thought that was funny. But Claudia saw you talking to him, so let me call over there and see if she's turned up."

The phone rang just as I rolled into the parking lot at the Kelly Club. Blake said, "She was there when the office opened at seven thirty this morning, but now she's gone again. They don't know where she was headed."

"What did she want from them?"

"She claimed she just wanted to see inside an FBI office for her research, and she wanted to introduce herself to Special Agent Mintern. He wouldn't let her come past the second entrance, but they did exchange cards."

"I've lost my sense of humor, Blake. I wish I knew what she's up to. Let's hope it's something harmless, like research in the library."

The AA meeting grounded me a bit, gave me a quiet hour to trust again whatever Rama said is holding the sky up while I'm sleeping. But something significant was going to happen, and I could feel it in my spine. *Thy will be done*, I kept telling myself. *Thy will be done.*

When I got back out to the parking lot, a man I'd never seen before was standing beside my big white car. He was tall and thin and wore a powder-blue suit and string tie. "You're Claude Dabley, aren't you?"

"You do look a lot like Ruby." He had a thin, gravelly voice, as if he'd had throat surgery. "Miss Burns, I must request that you come with me."

"Where are we going?"

"You're trying to find your brother, are you not?"

My heart was slapping hard against my ribs. "My brother is in Oklahoma?"

"You're going to have to trust me."

I looked behind me to see if anyone else was in the parking lot. A skinny old man named Tyrell, who had twenty-four years of sobriety, stood beside his rusty van watching us. He'd spoken in the meeting about this van, which now had 265,000 miles on it. He hadn't wanted to buy it but did so to please his wife. She died soon afterward, and he'd kept the van ever since. Now he thought it was going to outlast them both.

"You're kidding about trusting you, right? You left Ruby sitting in that cave and her kids are dead."

"Mistakes were made," he said. "We understand that. But he wants to see you. He wants you to understand better what happened, and he has a proposal for you."

"He's somehow going to make it all better?"

"He knows how angry you are with him." Dabley's green eyes were pale and watery. He did not look like a powerful man or even a smart one.

"Tell me about the mistakes right now," I said, "because I'm not going anywhere with you."

Tyrell took several steps toward us. "Hello. Are you a friend of Bill's?" This was a coded question about AA membership. What Tyrell had really asked was, *Ellen, are you okay?*

"I don't know anybody named Bill," Dabley said. "I'm a friend of Ellen's family. I was asked to meet her here."

Tyrell looked at me, his eyebrows raised.

"Can you stick around for a few minutes? But let me talk to this man privately."

Tyrell nodded. "Nice ride. Suicide doors, right?"

After Tyrell was out of earshot but still watching us, I said, "Listen, no more of this cloak-and-dagger bullshit. Just tell me how to find my fucking brother. Tell him I promise not to betray him. He knows my word is good. That's the best deal he's going to get out of me, and I intend to find him whether he cooperates or not."

Dabley didn't reply.

"I'm going back to Gallup now," I said. "I'll be staying at the El Rancho Hotel, which is a very cool place. When they were shooting those early western movies, the stars all stayed there."

Finally, Dabley said in his gravelly voice, "I'll give him your message."

"And listen, somebody make a better plan this time. Do a decent job on it. And the trust will have to flow in this direction."

As he drove away, terror seized me for the first time. Claudia was missing, and I was going to find my brother. I had been right; he really was alive. I crossed the parking lot and held on to Tyrell as if he were a life buoy. He seemed surprised but put his arms around me. "It'll be okay. Whatever it is."

I raced back to Shawnee, threw my belongings together as fast as I could, and headed toward Albuquerque, calling Estelle on the way just so I could hear her voice. I didn't explain anything but asked her to put Momma on the phone. My mother jabbered in my ear, "The yellow dog. I once had a dog that ate peanuts."

I started to sob, and Estelle took the phone back. "Ellen, what is going on? You sound awful."

"Nothing. I'm just homesick. Really, really homesick." I hung up before she could question me. Next, I called Sister Irene and left the message that I was on my way back to New Mexico. I was going to stay in Gallup tonight, but I needed to see Ruby in the morning.

The Oklahoma Visitors' Center seemed like a safe enough place to stop, so I went inside, said hello to a nice lady, and hid in a bathroom stall, where I composed my first text message on a cell phone. I hated the tiny buttons. In AA I had learned that, if I write an important letter, I should wait a day to send it, so I promised myself I would not send this message yet. *Blake, I am so grateful for your being in my life. I need to tell you that I do seem to be in love with you, or whatever it is. A real connection. I'm not sure I can say this any other way, but okay, I give up, I yield.* Since I had finally grasped the fact that I might die in this situation, I added, *I've had a wonderful life.*

7

The speed limit was seventy, the Lincoln rode rough but steady, and the retrofitted FM radio worked reasonably well. I passed the rest of the drive back to New Mexico listening to country music and fundamentalist Christian stations.

Rock of ages, cleft for me,
Let me hide myself in thee.

Jesus seemed like a pretty good idea at the moment. But the hours of driving exhausted my fear, and on the outskirts of Gallup I came to my senses and erased the text to Blake on my phone, replacing it with *I'll be in Gallup in twenty minutes.* He immediately replied: *Meet me at Earl's.*

Earl's Restaurant was about a mile down the strip. Blake stood on the curb, his hands thrust into the pockets of his windbreaker, his face lined with anxiety. "Where did you get this?" he said absently, patting the fender of the Lincoln after I pulled to the curb. Then he wrapped his arms hard around me. "Stay calm," he said, "but Claudia's been hurt. Her father left for Oklahoma on a chartered plane a few hours ago. I waited to tell you."

He released me and held on to both my hands. We stared into each other's eyes like a pair of scared teenagers.

"Ellen, the FBI is now insisting that you work directly with them. They'll protect you. You were right that your brother is alive."

"I've had a long drive to think about all of this, Blake. I did get very scared, but I don't believe I'm on anybody's list as dangerous. Tell me what happened to Claudia."

Claudia had been found lying beside her rental car on a dirt road in the Ozarks, forty miles north of Elohim City. Her jaw was broken, and she was unconscious. As beatings go, it had not been dreadful. She had not been raped, but someone had used a small blade to write *JEW* onto her forehead and carve *ZOG* into her arm.

"This is my fault," I said, beginning to hyperventilate.

He still held on to my hands. "Ellen, look at me."

Gasping, I looked into his face.

"Keep looking at me."

I held on to his ordinary face and began to quiet down.

"You need to hear me right now. None of this is your fault. These are very bad people we're dealing with."

My breathing slowed to the panting stage. "She's going to be okay?"

"That's not clear yet. The main problem was the force of the blow to her face. Somebody hit her hard enough to break the bone. She'll be in intensive care until she's conscious and they're sure they have any consequences under control. She does have quite a concussion, that's for sure."

A fresh wave of panic broke over me, but I controlled my breathing. "It's my fault."

"No, Ellen, this was about her. Their fury was about the piece she wrote in the *New York Times*. They left a note in her car about Jews and ZOG media, and they even mentioned the name of her article, 'The Tomb of the Unknown Racist.' But they spelled it *T-O-M-E*."

"Really? These are people who read the Sunday *Times Magazine*?"

"They're not all idiots, and they do have communications networks."

I let go of his hands and turned toward the restaurant. "Let's get off the damn street. I'm not sure what to do next. Maybe that's why Dabley showed up after the AA meeting. Maybe they were planning to teach both Claudia and me some manners."

"What are you talking about?"

He followed me in, and we settled into a booth with vinyl seats as shredded as the leather in my new ride. "I didn't want to tell you this until I got here. Claude Dabley, the man who set Ruby up with the cave disaster, showed up after my noon AA meeting in Oklahoma City today. I told you, somebody has been watching me all along. Dabley wanted me to come with him. He claimed that Royce wants to see me, and he tried to convince me to get into his car."

"Do you think it's possible Royce is in Oklahoma?"

"I don't see how. I think it must be true that he's got physical mobility problems, and Oklahoma would be too close to Magnus. Having Claude Dabley show up scared the hell out of me. For all I know, his connection is with Magnus or with Elohim City, and this Royce-wants-to-meet-his-grandchildren scenario wasn't even connected directly to my brother. Maybe it was all a setup. Maybe it was a way to try to draw Royce out of hiding. Or maybe you were right, and Royce is dead. I don't know how to figure anything out. I did realize I might be in big trouble now. Claudia was missing, and Dabley was standing by my car."

"Ellen, you'll have to let the FBI protect you until this situation is under control. They're going to let my friend be your point person. He's the one who works in the office here. His name is Wally Furman. I trust him."

"I'm surprised Claudia drove straight to the Ozarks. Even I wouldn't do that alone. She's got more courage than sense."

"Well, you seem to be her role model."

"Here's what I'm willing to do, Blake. It's what I told Dabley. I'll check into the El Rancho and wait. I don't care how your friend Wally decides to handle it. He can keep my room bugged and my car under surveillance, he can tie a fucking ribbon to my arm, but I'm staying at the El Rancho, and tomorrow morning I'm going to the prison to see Ruby. I'll stay with Saint Irene tomorrow night because I need to talk to her. I'll be back at the El Rancho first thing the next morning. And after that, whenever I leave the hotel, it will only be to go to AA or to Earl's Restaurant or to the casino."

"Can't you skip this trip to the prison? Why is it necessary? Can't you just stay here for the time being?"

"I need to talk to Sister Irene. I'm not sure why. And I want to talk to Ruby again."

Wally, it turned out, sat nearby, watching us. Blake signaled him to come over. "Blake, you hold hands with girls in front of your friends?"

"Please drop the macho act," Blake said. "I get so tired of it sometimes."

Wally Furman was about our age, mid or late fifties, but he was taller, tanner, fitter, and his hair was silver. "You look like a movie star," I said, shaking his hand. "Do you put something on your hair?"

He ignored my question and said he had just gotten word that Claudia was conscious. She hadn't recognized the man and woman who attacked her, but she was certain that the perpetrator hadn't been Joe Magnus. They had been a young couple, early twenties, maybe even late teens.

Wally left to make his arrangements at the El Rancho, but our meat loaf specials arrived, and Blake and I hurried to eat dinner. Then I walked him to my new ride so he could follow me back to the hotel. "What's this?" He touched the fender.

"I like old cars. After my rental car got busted up, I won some cash playing craps." He didn't say anything. "You know, Blake, it doesn't take a lot of money to buy cars like this. It mostly takes nerve and a Triple A card."

"Why are they called 'suicide doors'?"

"I don't know. Maybe they were dangerous since both doors open from the middle. As a style, it was soon discontinued."

"I guess that made it easier to get into the backseat. Like it did for the Kennedys."

"Why are you going back to Oklahoma? Aren't you still the police chief of Gallup, New Mexico, in the United States of America?"

"If I don't go see Claudia, you'll sneak away and go yourself. I know you're safe here."

8

Wally Furman's rich voice complemented his silvery hair. He now wore sweats and running shoes, and, if he hadn't displayed a gun in a shoulder holster, I might have thought he was an ordinary guest. "You're going to be staying in the Lana Turner room," he said.

"Fine with me. I've been there before. *Imitation of Life* is one of my favorite movies. How long have you known Blake?"

"Since the Academy."

I tried to get him to say more, but he'd seen all those movies in which agents are handsome and taciturn.

We walked up the stairs to the Lana Turner. "We chose this room," he said quietly, "because it's in the open, not down a hallway, and the ones on either side are empty. We'll keep them that way." He showed me where microphones were embedded under the table lamp and above the bathroom door, and he programmed my cell phone to reach him by punching #1, Blake #2, and 911 on #3.

"Listen, I don't agree with you that I'm in any danger. I just got rattled by Dabley showing up. If Magnus wanted to hurt me, he would have done it when he had the chance, and these people with Claudia seem like freelancers. Are there more reasons to be frightened that you're not telling me?"

"We think there might be other loose cannons around. There's a grapevine out there, and, like your reporter friend, you are not popular. It would be much better if you skipped this trip to the prison tomorrow, but we'll be right behind you."

"And, of course, you want me to find my brother for you. Also, Joe Magnus."

"Magnus has already been picked up and is in custody. But we think your brother may try to contact you again. We want to protect you, and, yes, we do hope to find him."

"Magnus is in custody. How remarkable that they found him so suddenly, don't you think? Has it occurred to you, Wally, that there might be people in BATF or even the FBI who already know where my brother is too? And who knew that they'd have to pick up Magnus now?"

"I hope you won't be offended by this, Miss Burns, but you do seem paranoid about the government. It's understandable in your situation, but not realistic."

"Paranoia seems like a pretty sensible response. The FBI had a file on me. Have you talked to Ed Blake about this mess?"

"Blake and I don't agree on many things, but if there were problems in either agency before—and I'm not saying there were—they have been cleaned up long since."

"I'm glad you believe that, Special Agent Furman. Have you ever heard of the Cassandra myth? She could see the future, but nobody would ever believe her. I feel a lot like Cassandra."

He waited for me to say more, as if he were a shrink with a client.

"Okay, you're a lot brighter than Special Agent Mintern was," I said. "But come down to the lobby with me, and let's work that old player piano. I love that thing. Also, I want to tell you a story."

The cavernous lobby of the El Rancho was dominated by its large winding staircase. The dark wood stairs and floors were carpeted with Navaho rugs. The chandeliers and sconces cast an amber glow, and next to the antique player piano was a four-foot-tall amethyst geode on a stand. Black-and-white photographs of movie stars lined many walls.

"Think of this story as a parable," I said, while Patsy Cline sang to us. "It's about a key. When I first got sober, I was not trustworthy, but my mother still let me keep a key to her condo. Then somehow I lost it. You have to understand that my mother's key was serious business. We were staying at her beach house, a little cottage on a lake north of town. She wasn't scared at the beach house, but in Charleston, in her condo, she lived in fear, behind walls and gates with a guardhouse. The lake was very big, eleven miles across. It was nighttime when I realized the key was gone. I walked out onto the dock. There were lights at the end of the dock that shined down into the water, and sometimes I saw big fish down there. That night I saw a largemouth bass swimming slowly around one of the poles. I prayed, although I didn't know how to pray, and I didn't understand yet that praying for specific outcomes is a mistake. I mean, of course you can pray for specific things, like 'Please, God, don't let my sister die horribly' or 'God, give me a parking space,' but that kind of prayer is spiritually problematic. So, I'm out there on the dock saying, 'God, God, God, let me find the key. She'll hate me for this, and it will scare her so much she'll have to change the lock, and I've hurt her so much already. Please let me find the key.' Then I went into the house to confess, but first I had an overwhelming desire to eat sugar. So, I go to the kitchen cabinet and drag down this big bag of hard candies. I'm digging way down because I want a cinnamon piece and they're the scarcest ones, and then, at the very bottom of the bag, what do I find but the key to my mother's condo? The lost key. So, was that a coincidence or was it the result of my prayer?"

He didn't answer, just gave me that quiet attention, so I continued. "I think this is probably the explanation. I must have reached into that bag before, although I had no memory of doing so, and I must have had the key in my hand when I reached in, and I must have dropped it there. So, after I prayed and went to eat sugar, my hand knew where the key was. My hand knew, not me. That's why I'll be able to find my brother now.

Something will pull me toward him, or pull him toward me. I just have to wait and trust."

"That's certainly an interesting way to think," Wally Furman said.

"Nah," I said, "it's loony, but it'll work, you'll see."

9

The next morning Furman followed me to the 8:00 A.M. meeting on Persimmon Street. Several months ago, when I'd first gone to this meeting, an elderly Native American woman named Nilda had given me her phone number, and last night I'd called her from the Lana Turner room. I offered to come to where she was, but she said she would rather join me at the morning meeting.

When I arrived a few minutes late (I still wasn't used to parking the Lincoln), I saw that she'd saved a place beside her in the chairs along the wall. I sat next to her for the rest of the meeting and studied her hands. Her fingers were short, her palms wide, her amber skin hairless and dry. She rested her hands quietly in the lap of her skirt, and I wanted to touch them. She was a heavy woman who did not fidget. On both of her wrists were turquoise and silver Navaho bracelets that fit as if they'd been made for her.

I listened vaguely to the meeting. My first sponsor had taught me always to listen for one useful phrase or idea, and, if I found that one thing, I had spent my hour well. A young woman said, "I can always ask a better question. The better question always is 'What might be good about this situation?' Sometimes I have to ask that over and over. What might be good about this situation?"

After the meeting, Nilda and I walked across the road and sat on a sunny wooden bench near the train station. I'm sure Furman remained unhappily close by, but this was the spot Nilda chose. First, we exchanged basics: She had eleven years sobriety, I had eighteen. I was five years older—she was only forty-nine—which surprised me.

"I know a little about your niece," she said. "After you were here before, I tried to pay more attention to the news. Your niece killed her children, and she is going to receive a life sentence, yes?" When I nodded, she said, "How can I help you? Are you having trouble with your sobriety?"

"Not with my physical sobriety. With my emotional sobriety. I'm high-strung anyway, and I keep feeling like there's something more I should be doing about Ruby and her children and my brother. I keep thinking I am in some way responsible for what has happened, but I don't even know why I think that."

"Perhaps that is your ego. Your ego wants you to matter more, yes?"

"Maybe. But these are my blood relatives."

She stroked one of her bracelets. "Powerlessness over water is our greatest difficulty here. We can irrigate and choose crops that don't require much water, but we cannot refill the aquifer."

I let this advice, if it was advice, settle in. "You're Navaho?"

"No, Zuni and Nogalu."

I wanted to touch her arm, but instead I touched the other bracelet.

"I love the Navaho designs," she said. "My first husband was Navaho."

"This is my real question, Nilda. Am I my brother's keeper?"

She smiled, her teeth white against her bronze skin. "You imagine you will accept my view, yes?"

"I just want your opinion. Your sober, human opinion."

Her laughter grew loud and astounded. "This is my sober, human opinion: I don't know."

Before I left for the prison, I dropped the top on the Lincoln, striped my cheekbones and nose with zinc oxide, and pulled my Charleston cap down to shade my eyes. I was wearing cut-offs and sandals and an ARMY shirt with the sleeves torn out, and I carried the trout bag, into which I had stuffed underwear and a toothbrush.

The car following me wasn't Furman's, so I punched #1 on my phone to make sure I was okay. Furman said the man in the car was Special Agent Brownell. Then I pulled onto the side of the highway again to call Blake. The unknown car pulled over ahead of me, and I watched the back of this stranger's head while Blake and I talked. Blake said that Claudia was going to be all right but would stay in the hospital for a few days of observation. "She seems pretty excited by what happened, your protégée."

"How did they find her?"

"My guess is she stopped in one too many places asking for help to find the Elohim City compound. Somebody gave her bad directions and put the word out that she was poking around. Hatred of Jews is very big with these Christian Identity folks. Maybe there aren't enough Natives or black people around here to hate."

"Are you doing okay? You sound like you aren't."

"I'll be glad when this is over. Claudia gave excellent descriptions. These were young, inexperienced people, and we'll get them. The man punched Claudia once, and she went right down. We think the woman did the carving because it was so hesitant. Claudia didn't even need stitches. I think she was hoping for scars."

At the prison, Sister Irene sat erect in her metal chair behind the metal desk in her small, windowless office. She wore her dowdy blue habit, and her hair was flat and severe. Only her eyes signaled the quality that drew so many toward her. I told her what had happened to Claudia, and she said, "You like this young woman very much, don't you?"

"Yes, I like her, but not like that. I'm just the fairy godmother of her writing career."

"And you are playing that role because?"

"I don't know, because people helped me. Because I wouldn't even be alive without all the help I've had."

Her cover broke. "Ha," she said. "Ha ha ha!" Then her laughter became real and gay.

"What's going on, Sister? You seem different."

"We'll talk tonight. Ruby is the one who is different."

•

Ruby's gaze was open, peaceful, shining. "I am so grateful that you came to see me again." We were sitting in the general visiting area of the prison, a low-ceilinged room with a scuffed, clean linoleum floor. Regular hours wouldn't begin for another ten minutes, so the room was unoccupied, except for a guard at the locked door. There was a single window, high and dark, where another guard could observe the room.

"Ruby, I'm still so angry with you," I said. "I can't figure out how to forgive you. I thought I knew how, but I don't."

"Please don't carry anger like that in your heart," she said. "It will harm you, Aunt Ellen, and I'm not worth it." She reached one hand tentatively across the gray metal table, but I didn't take it. Her nails were bitten to the quick, her thumbnail distorted and dark with dried blood.

"And I'll never be able to forgive my brother," I said. "Maybe I can put it behind me, but forgiveness isn't even part of the goal."

Her other hand held a Bible against her breast, this one bound in pebbly white leather that was worn and zippered shut. "I doubt my father has forgiven himself," she said, "so when you find him, you will have that in common."

"What's happened to you, Ruby?"

"Sister Irene has been helping me."

I studied her face, so much like mine. There seemed to be a faint radiance around her now, and I felt its warmth.

"This was Sister Irene's personal Bible, Aunt Ellen, from when she was a little girl. Let me show you." She unzipped the Bible, revealing thin, nearly translucent pages with tiny smudged print. In the back pages for recording births and deaths, someone had written, in a child's hand, *Callie died, Nov 7, 1955*. "Callie was Sister Irene's younger sister. She was eleven years old when she died of a brain tumor. Sister Irene wants me to live."

I put my index finger on the penciled words but didn't speak.

"Sister Irene says I can be of great use here at the prison," Ruby continued. "That I can be an inspiration for those who can't forgive themselves. So when you find my father, Aunt Ellen, please tell him to let go of all the bad things he has done. Let go of the broom handle and of me. Tell him that we are all born forgiven."

"I'm so glad you believe that, Ruby, and I wish I did. But let me understand something. Are you thinking that you are one of the bad things my brother has done? That you are like the broom handle?"

She spoke so quietly I barely heard her. "I understand that I am forgiven, Aunt Ellen, but I still don't want to live. Sister Irene says that will come too, if I just keep holding on."

I could not look at her. "Does your mother come to see you? Does anyone come besides me?"

"She came twice, but I've asked her not to come anymore. She's had enough pain."

I thought I might cry, but I didn't. The visiting room was as bleak as a hospital. I stood up and turned my back, nearly staggering, because something was happening to me. I felt light and heavy, warm and cold, and the motes of dust in the air were changing to gold flakes while I watched. When I turned to face her, what passed between us was as real as the table, the white pebbled Bible and the gold flakes, and my words seemed to come from somewhere else. "I forgive you too," I said.

10

I stumbled out to my car without speaking again to Sister Irene. The guard at the gate needed to take my pass, so I left the complex slowly, but once I found the highway I roared back toward Sister Irene's house with my FBI caretaker flying dutifully behind me.

In the yard, I waved him away and raced up the stairs to the apartment over the garage, where Jesus hung, half formed.

On the fragrant prayer bench, I dropped to my knees. "You fucker," I cried, "people are responsible for what they do. They have to be. Aren't we?"

But waves of what felt like release began to pour over me, and for the next several hours I seemed to be asleep yet conscious. Wordless puzzles were flying together, the pieces soldered so well that even the seams were fading. Not since my weekend with Rama had I felt so blessed, and again I saw the edges of the world, the large reddish sandstones on the rim of time, before something thick as honey began flowing through me and I fell deeply asleep.

An explosion woke me. It took several seconds to get oriented and realize I was face-to-face on the bed in the dark with the one-eyed cat named Sweetie. Sweetie had climbed the tree to the second-floor window and kamikaze-leapt straight into the glass. She was stinking and snarling and bleeding from several cuts. I picked up a pillow and tried to swat her with it, but she launched herself at me, latching on to my left forearm with her teeth. I hit her so hard with my other fist that she ran in circles several times on the bed, maybe from pain, maybe from the relief that someone had finally knocked some sense into her.

My arm hurt like hell and began to bleed from the bluish-white punctures. I rolled calmly off the bed, went to the door, and opened it. "Okay, Sweetie," I said. "Are we done now?"

With clumsy dignity, she walked out of the door and down the steps, and I followed.

My keeper had turned on the headlights of his car, and I stopped by his window as he rolled it down. He was young and stern and earnest. "I'll bet you thought being an FBI agent would be a lot more exciting than this. Here's the current situation: I've been bitten by a cat with a bad attitude. That's her sulking over there. I'm going into Sister Irene's house now to get my arm cleaned up, and I'll probably sleep over there too."

Sister Irene opened the door before I could even knock. She was wearing a bright yellow housecoat, and polka-dotted underpants were wrapped around her head. The cat and I were standing side by side. "My mother does her hair like that too," I said.

Sister Irene cleaned and disinfected my wound, and she explained to Sweetie that she would have to stay outside because of her unpleasant odor. Then she said to me, "I told you Sweetie was a reasonable cat, once she gets your attention. You'll need a tetanus shot if you haven't had one recently. Cat bites can develop into nasty infections, so take care of this." She rinsed the punctures once more, slathered them with antibiotic cream, and wrapped my arm with gauze. Then she got a blanket for me to sleep on her sofa.

"I've already been in bed all afternoon and evening," I told her. "I've been sleeping for hours."

"Well, I hope you can sleep some more, because I am dog-tired." She leaned over and kissed me on the cheek, and I smelled her face cream.

"I figured out what it is about your eyes," I said. "It's forgiveness."

My arm throbbed in the dark.

I wish I could say I had a premonition of what was to come next, but I did not.

11

Ruby ate her Bible. Lying silently on her cot, hidden under a blanket in the semi-dark cell, she tore off page after page, chewing and swallowing. The paper was so thin that she got all the way through Deuteronomy before her throat dried out enough to choke her. It must have been difficult to stay prone, because the body will fight for its own survival. That's why I could never reach terminal velocity in skydiving. My arm would not wait for fifteen seconds but kept pulling the cord by itself. That's why, when a drunk out in Sacramento tried to chop off his own head with an ax, he ducked at the last instant, losing part of his skull and frontal lobe. He died a few weeks later. He's a legend in California AA.

12

I did not find my brother, he found me.

I had gone into a Gallup grocery store for a twelve-pack of Cokes and more ice cream to stock the mini-fridge that had been moved to the Lana Turner room. Wally Furman's man waited outside near the front entrance while I parsed flavors, stooping down to inspect the bottom shelf, paying little attention to my surroundings.

"We heard about Ruby's death," Claude Dabley said from behind me.

I stood up, clutching a pint of vanilla Häagen-Dazs, and tried to recover my composure. "What are you, some kind of fucking ghost? Don't you realize an FBI agent is standing right outside the front door?"

He handed me a cheap phone. "We'll call you on this."

It was as simple as that. The phone dropped into my trout bag, and I decided not to tell Wally or Blake.

13

Blake returned quickly from Oklahoma, but Claudia stayed there to write. She was a minor news item herself now, so I texted this message: *Go to meetings, Claudia. Go every day. Keep that sobriety blooming.* When she tried to call me, I only texted: *I'm glad you're okay, but I need space right now.*

Ruby's suicide was mildly newsworthy, so the press badgered me briefly. Estelle protected herself and my mother, but Del Mead showed up in Gallup, standing right in the lobby of the El Rancho. I emerged from the Lana Turner room and stood at the top of the curved stairway, talking down to him. "Sorry, it's Claudia Friedman's story now. But there are lots of other sources for you."

Mead did write the first national piece about Giang's Albuquerque restaurant, because, unlike its decor, its cuisine was not at all ordinary. In the interview Giang talked to Mead in interlaced clichés, and Mead did not seem to grasp that he was being mocked. Santane had asked Del Mead for privacy, and, except for a picture of her walking into her salon, he left her alone. In the newspaper photo, she looked impassive, even tranquil, and she sounded that way when I called her once to discuss

Ruby's suicide. Ruby would be cremated, we decided, and I would take her ashes to South Carolina.

It took four days of AA meetings, the last one sitting beside Nilda, for me to decide what to do about Dabley's phone, which I had shut off as soon as he handed it to me.

I reached out and touched Nilda's turquoise bracelet, whispering. Could she arrange for a letter to be sent to me via her address? I promised I wouldn't get her in any trouble, but I didn't want the FBI folks who were following me to find out. I knew she'd seen them hanging around.

Nilda gave me a long, appraising look with her calm eyes.

I whispered, "I am my brother's keeper."

Wordlessly she wrote down her last name and a box number right here in town.

Deceiving Wally and Blake about Dabley, the cell phone still hidden in my trout bag, was surprisingly satisfying. From the pay phone in the Persimmon Street Clubhouse, I called Bertie's Home for Funerals and spoke directly to Miss Manigault.

"Miss Manigault, this is Ellen Burns, Ruby Redstone's aunt and Estelle's friend. Do you remember burying my little grandniece? Yes, I thought you would. Listen, I hate to put you to this kind of bother, Miss Manigault, but I do have a kind of emergency. I'm still out here in New Mexico with Ruby's family, and I'm wondering if you could please call Estelle on her work number at the hospital and tell her that I need her to call me at a specific time on a certain number." I turned Dabley's phone on long enough to give her the number, then turned it back off. "Miss Manigault, I need for Estelle to call me at exactly ten tonight. It's really important. And could you please ask her to call me from a pay phone? That's kind of important too. Actually, it's crucial. No, ma'am, I will not get her into any trouble. I swear it. I give you my word."

At 9:45 that night I dialed Wally and said I was going down to Dairy Queen for some ice cream. He sounded sleepy, so I didn't know whether he'd have somebody follow me or not. Sitting in a booth with a chocolate ice cream Blizzard with pecans, caramel, Reese's Pieces and too thick to drink through a straw, I stayed visibly occupied until just before ten, then walked into the bathroom. The phone rang just as I locked the door.

"What is it?" Estelle said, her voice tight with alarm.

"I only have a minute or two. I'm sorry to put you in another difficult situation, Estelle, but I may be in some real trouble now."

"Are you in danger?"

"Listen, you don't know anything about this part of my life, but in the early seventies I was a federal fugitive for a while. My girlfriend, the one who shot herself, she was the real fugitive. I just hid out with her for a few months. Do you remember when I showed you the drawer where my mother keeps all of my memorabilia? My baby pictures and wedding pictures and her signed copy of Royce's novel?"

"What is it you want me to do, Ellen?"

"There's a big black envelope where she stores the stuff that she can't decide whether to keep. In that black envelope is, well . . . it's the paperwork from when she checked me out of a mental hospital in Dallas. She has the papers for my alias when I was underground. She has the birth certificate, an old driver's license, and a bunch of other stuff with that name."

"I hope you're kidding about this."

When I didn't answer she said, "What was your alias?"

"Evelyn Roach."

"Oh, my God, what am I supposed to say?"

"That you'll do it, please. That you'll overnight it to me care of Nilda Jamake, Box 540, Gallup. I don't know if this will work, Estelle, but I've got to give it a try."

When she didn't reply, I said, "How's Momma?"

"Not eating much. Getting frail. She's salty but frail."

"I swore to Miss Manigault you wouldn't get in any trouble, so you know that I mean it."

She wrote down the address, and we quickly got off the phone.

The next day, I went to see Santane while my escort waited for me, parked in the heat outside her shop with his air conditioner running. After some initial resistance, Santane provided me with a human hair wig, streaked blond and set in a French twist, that a breast cancer client had donated to the shop. "Santane, this is amusing for reasons I can't fully explain at the moment," I said as I tried it on. "But I had a wig like this in college. All the women in my family did. My sister called us 'The French Twist Gang.' Our wigs were dark, though, and they were matched to our real hair."

She did not smile. "You know he might be even more dangerous."

14

My disappearance was not all that difficult to manage. The FBI was trying to protect me and locate my brother, and the idea that I might simply vanish through my own agency was not anticipated. Within two days, I had accumulated several thousand dollars in wired cash, bought a used car that had been dropped off in the El Rancho parking lot with the keys hidden in the wheel well, and even managed to get a driver's license for Evelyn Roach with her birth certificate by claiming I needed to go to Bocca to speak with the priest at the church Ruby had attended. The priest wasn't around, but in Bocca I also bought a flowered dress, a bra, a flowery purse, cat-eye sunglasses, and women's sandals. When I left the El Rancho early the next morning carrying my mother's purple-flowered suitcase, I tried to walk more like a woman. My follower did not even recognize me.

My instinct to head north had been right. When I turned on the phone, it rang within ten minutes. A sweet-sounding woman who said her name was Mary directed me to a small town in eastern Idaho in the foothills of the Rockies. I stopped in Boise to have dinner at a Country Crock restaurant, and before I left, I changed back into my regular clothes in the bathroom. I kept the wig on so the waitress, a heavyset white woman, would still recognize me. "I've got to drive all night," I said by way of explaining the drastic change in my appearance. "I wanted to get more comfortable. Those bras, they just drive me crazy."

"Oh, honey, if I didn't wear one, my boobs would reach my knees. I love your glasses."

The cat sunglasses were hanging out of the pocket of my shirt. I handed them to her—"You take them"—and I was still smiling when I got back on the road and pulled off the wig.

The dealer's plates were still on the car, which worried me, but there was nothing to do about it now, so I traveled off the interstate highways as much as I could.

I was very tired when I reached the small town named Salvado, three hours east of Boise. It was after ten o'clock. As directed, I parked in the corner of a truck stop parking lot beside a yellow drop-off bin for clothes being donated to a local charity. My lights and motor were turned off, and the engine ticked while I twisted my neck and stretched my arms, trying to loosen them.

Within a few minutes someone tapped on my window, and the woman who had said her name was Mary asked me to step out of the car. "I'm so glad to meet you," she said, touching my hand. "But I'm afraid I'll have to drive now."

Considerably older than me, Mary looked like what my father would have called "good country people." She wore a flowered cotton skirt, a jean jacket, and work boots, and her gray hair had been pulled back into a neat bun. With a gap-toothed smile, she suggested I might want to grab "a few hours of shut-eye" because it was going to a long drive. Then she confiscated my phones and my trout bag and said she would have to go through my purple-flowered suitcase later.

I knew nothing about where I would meet Royce, but Mary's manner was so reassuring that, after thirty minutes of back roads during which neither of us spoke, my long day caught up with me and I dozed.

I awoke as dawn began lighting orderly fields of wheat on my right. We were on a dirt road. Mary thrust a thermos of lukewarm coffee toward me. "It's good that you slept," she said. "I've had plenty of this, so the rest is yours." We drove wordlessly on for another half hour while I sipped black coffee and the sun rose. The gold fields were lovely in the early light, and the dark green forest to our left glistened.

"Who owns all this land, Mary?"

"I don't know," she said.

"Do you know who I am?"

"You're his sister, aren't you?"

"And you know who he is?"

She didn't reply, and I studied her rough knuckles on the steering wheel. "All of this seems so ordinary," I said. "I thought I would be much more scared."

At the end of the planted fields we crossed a small stream and passed by a group of trailers arranged in a rough horseshoe around what looked like a half-buried entrance to a bunker.

"What's that?"

"A bomb shelter," Mary said. "The original owner sold shares in it, but that was over twenty years ago. It can hold more than a hundred people. Lots of smaller shelters were built in this area around the same time."

"Who owns them now? What are the trailers for?"

Again, she didn't answer.

"Are we still in Montana? Are those the bomb shelters that the crazy preacher Billy Valentine built?"

All she said was, "We're not in Montana."

Soon we passed through some white gates that looked a lot like the ones at Blacklock, and I wondered if that was a deliberate gesture on Royce's part. About thirty yards of driveway in, we arrived at a gray, low-slung bungalow, and in front of it stood Claude Dabley, whom I'd begun to think of as "The Narrow Man." Everything about Dabley was lean and sharp, as if he had been elongated in a circus mirror. He wore khaki pants and a dark tailored shirt that seemed vaguely military, but maybe that impression was a result of the pistol he had holstered on his hip. Dabley did not seem happy to see me, although he stepped forward and nodded.

When he opened the door of the bungalow, I heard Mary drive away with my car, my suitcase, my phones, and my trout bag.

Across an expanse of Navaho rug, Royce sat in a wheelchair behind a gray metal desk. The right side of his face was the color of ground beef and twisted by a web of scars. The cheek drooped and his eyelid hung down, so he was probably blind in that eye, but the good eye was unmistakable, and the rest of my brother's face was familiar too, though deeply scratched by age and pain. His right hand was hidden by a throw that looked like mink covering his lower body.

"So, it's really you," I said.

"Yes," he said. "And it's really you." He gestured toward the oak armchair on the other side of his desk. "Sit down, Ellen. You look very good. Better than me."

"I had a face-lift," I said, "a few years after Momma's. She paid for it."

"Can we get you something? Coffee? Breakfast? I don't think a face-lift will work for me, do you?" His voice was disarmingly friendly. When he raised his left hand, I felt his odd charisma and slumped into the chair across from him.

"Don't cry, Ellen," he said. "It really doesn't hurt much anymore. I have a great deal of help. Also, many medications."

I wiped my face on the sleeve of my safari shirt, fumbled with one of my chest pockets, and pulled out the rattles, wrapped in white tissue. I tossed them onto the green blotter of his desktop, and the tissue slowly unfolded. There were four yellowish rattles attached to each other, graduated in size, the smallest no bigger than a pea. "I thought you'd want these back."

He glanced at the rattles without comment, then exposed his right hand so I could see the dark nubs of fingers, before he tucked them back into the fur blanket. "Because I heard Ruby wondered why I didn't write my own letters." As the left side of his face smiled ironically, the scars on the right pulled tight and squirmed.

"I need to know why you sent Ruby these rattles."

"My foot is also damaged," he said. "They tried to save it, but almost half had to be removed. The prosthetic is useless, and my knee is not strong. There are several scars over my body too, of course, and they itch a great deal."

"Thank you for that information, but I want to know why you got in touch with Ruby. If you wanted to see her, why didn't you do it last year, or five years ago, or ten?"

He sighed deeply, and I thought I heard a rattle in his breath. "When we located Santane, we merely monitored her occasionally. But then Ruby came to her. I thought it might be time to let my daughter know I was still alive."

"I liked this situation better when you were dead."

"I'm sure you did."

"We buried you. We buried something. Maybe it was rocks. What the FBI sent fit into a child-size coffin."

"I heard about that," he said.

"How do you hear all these things? Is there some kind of white terrorist Pony Express?"

"*Terrorism* is not the correct word, Ellen. We are freedom fighters, and there are many more of us than you understand. It started in the fifties. Segregation ending, the busing fiasco, how stupid was that? All people want to be with their own, and we are no different, just clearer on what must be done. The Brotherhood's actions and what McVeigh did were useful but premature."

"I really didn't think I would give a fuck about what happened to you in that fire." I wiped my nose with my hand because the only tissue available was the one beneath the rattles. "But it's hard to see you this hurt."

"Of course you care about me, Ellen. I'm your blood."

"I cared about Ruby and Lucia and River too, and they were my blood. I cared about them a great deal. And I cared about the children in the day care center in Oklahoma City, although I didn't know them. It's called humanism, I think."

Ruby and the children's names hung in the air, and he looked above me with his good eye as if he were trying to imagine them. "My sweet Ruby," he finally said. "Dabley brought me a Polaroid of her, but he could not acquire one of her offspring. I so regret being unable to meet them. I don't suppose you brought me any pictures?"

"No, I didn't bring you any fucking pictures of her 'offspring.' I buried Lucia Burns Godchild—in case you don't know her name—next to your supposed grave. Maybe you heard that River's father took custody of his son's remains but not of hers?"

"The personal aspects of this situation have been unfortunate in many ways," Royce said.

The wood-paneled room was too warm. A large fire burned in a stone fireplace, and Dabley stood rigidly before it, staring down at the flames. The Navaho rugs, which were probably authentic, covered much of the planked floor. Behind my brother was a counter with a computer and a printer atop it, along with a thick pile of printed pages. To the right was a liquor cabinet with an ice bucket and glasses. A large window looked out at the dark green woods, and there were geological maps on several walls.

"Why did you want to see Ruby?" I said. "And why did you let me find you? Why do you have geological maps?"

"We brought Coca-Colas for you," he said and gestured toward the liquor cabinet. "I understand you don't drink alcohol anymore, and I respect that. Claude, would you mind preparing us some breakfast? I'm sure my sister hasn't eaten in a while, and she's had a very long drive."

Dabley raised his head and stared balefully at me before he replaced the screen in front of the fire and left the room.

"Where are we, Royce? I know I'm somewhere in the Northwest. Are we still in the U.S.? For all I know, we're in Canada. Or maybe Mary was driving us in circles all night. Who owns this land? Why did the FBI notify us you were dead?"

"Easy," he said. "Too many questions all at once. First, how is our mother?"

I struggled against a conversation that would in any way seem normal. "You're a fucking monster, Royce. I've read your writings. I know what you did. Do you want me to believe you've changed?"

The right side of his face smiled, and I caught a glimpse of his false incisor. "I doubt you know as much about me as you think," he said. "In any case, perhaps I am merely someone you disagree with politically."

"Disagree with politically? Terrorism isn't political. Terrorism is war." I gestured toward his mouth. "Do you remember when the big horse threw you and that tooth got knocked out?"

"Yes, I was ten, and the dentist replanted it successfully, but Marie bumped into me and knocked it out again."

I gestured toward his raw, sagging face. "It looks like you lost more teeth in the fire at Whidbey Island."

He seemed amused that I named the location of the fire. "Yes, four permanent teeth are gone. I believe when we were children we called them the six- and twelve-year molars, but of course that is not their technical name. Do you really want to go down memory lane with me? I doubt that's why you're here."

"Momma is okay," I said. "Her mind is going, so she thinks you're a character on *The Young and the Restless.*"

The look in his good eye might have been sadness.

I stood up, walked over to the fireplace, and removed the screen. Taking my time, I selected a split from the wood box and arranged it on the fire. "Let me ask you this again," I said. "Why did you let me find you now? And why did you send Ruby the rattles?"

"Maybe the real question," he said from behind his desk, "is why did you want to find me, Ellen? You've been searching for me relentlessly. What is it that you want?"

When I didn't reply, he said, "You do realize you've made a great deal of trouble. There are factions, even among those of us who share the same goals. The publicity about Ruby created enough problems."

"Publicity? It's the publicity you care about?" I stood behind my wooden chair, locking my furious hands around the top edge. "Do you understand that three people are dead? That one of them was your 'beloved' Ruby? That she killed herself and murdered her children because of you?"

His one eye looked at me evenly. "I don't think that's a fair assessment of my role, but I do understand why you might see it that way."

"What about your kidnapping plan? Was that really your concoction? You used to have an elegant mind, Royce, but I guess you lost something when those black and diamond snakes crawled up your legs." He looked surprised, even alarmed by this reference. "Santane showed me the letter you left for her," I said. "Other papers too. That little story 'For Joey'— how touching. I saw Joe Magnus a few weeks ago. He's a racist monster like you."

"The plan I devised was quite simple," he said, "and it should have worked. My assistant Mary would pick up all three and bring them here, and soon it would appear they had been kidnapped. Obstacles arose that were unanticipated."

"Magnus said to tell you that if he finds you, he'll kill you."

"I doubt he'll find me. He's a known informant."

"Did those obstacles that arose have something to do with the men removing guns from the Catacombs the day before?"

"Joey was not such a bad man," Royce said. "He was confused, and he didn't have the opportunities we did. But then he became so full of hate, and he turned that on me too."

"I don't know what you could possibly mean. Joe Magnus was always full of hate. He's a racist, a terrorist, a member of the Brotherhood, and a killer. I just don't know if you've become a killer too."

"Ellen, why do you want to know more about these matters? It's not safe to know more about these things. And it wasn't safe for you to insist on finding me."

"Well, my best guess is that you don't have any intention of letting me leave here. I heard Mary driving away with my things and my car. So maybe you could just tell me this, are you still dangerous to anyone beside your own relatives? Why did Dabley propose bringing the children first? Were you planning to have them killed?"

"Do you really think I would be capable of doing such a thing?"

"I'm asking the question, aren't I?"

"Ruby was born into my hands, Ellen. I have missed her bitterly. Santane too, but that is another matter. Santane has made her own life now." The emotion in his damaged face seemed sincere.

"But what about Ruby's children? Why did you want them brought first? I know about what happened at Nod."

Either he was alarmed or I imagined it. "I see Ruby told you a great deal. Joey had arranged that without my consent. With a veterinarian. A barbaric, repugnant, insulting idea. If you know about that, then you know I put a stop to it."

"Yes, with a snake."

"A completely harmless king snake, but a big one. People are afraid of snakes. I learned a great deal from that event with Ruby. I began to understand how we might use the personal power of blood for our own purposes. Since I could not allow such a thing to happen to my own daughter, that proved to be a great lesson. We would have to find simpler, more scalable, more personally distant solutions to our problem of racial dilution."

"What exactly do you mean by 'our own purposes'?"

"I may be damaged, Ellen, but I remain a revolutionary. I am still a leader, and one of our current goals is to establish white communities, white neighborhoods, white towns."

"And how is that so different from what exists now?"

"Because we have an analysis, a plan, and what we are doing is not defensive, it's calculated."

"White neighborhoods aren't your only goal. What about those bomb shelters we passed? What are those for?"

"We live in dangerous times. You must know that nuclear war is inevitable, sooner or later. The planet is increasingly overcrowded with the lesser races."

"You may still consider yourself a revolutionary, Royce, but you look like a pathetic, half-dead man stuck in a wheelchair, with a couple of lackeys to do your bidding."

"I'll bet you're familiar with this line, Ellen: 'One death is a tragedy; one million is a statistic.'"

"You're quoting Stalin to me? You're quoting fucking Stalin to me?"

"Well, he did summarize the problem nicely, didn't he? Should we consider the group or the individual? Let me explain better. Nuclear war is, as I said, inevitable. Overbreeding in the other races means more and more uncivilized people will have their fingers on nuclear triggers. We believe that only technology and weapons can save us. Eugenics will build us a glorious future, and that work is going on now. Unfortunately, I will probably not live long enough to see it."

"A glorious white future?"

"Yes, of course, a white future. Or an Aryan one, whatever you choose to call it. White culture and civilization. We must begin breeding with the best of our human stock and get rid of the damaged and the weak. Once you accept that reality, solutions become more and more obvious."

"So, are you building bombs? Making ricin? I know you learned to make ricin."

"Do I look like I could accomplish those things?"

"And this remains my real question: why did you want to see Ruby? Maybe you're planning something big, and you've decided to keep your own blood safe, no matter how polluted it is."

"Then you understand why you're here."

I turned around, realizing I had walked into a trap, but not the trap I'd expected. "What's going to happen, Royce?"

"By the time you know, it will be over."

Dabley was standing in the doorway to the kitchen, listening to us. "I've made breakfast," he said.

Royce slid open his desk drawer and removed a hypodermic needle. "Don't be alarmed," he said. "This is not intended for you. I take many medications on a daily basis. Could you assist me, Claude?"

Dabley wore cowboy boots with metal toes, and they clicked on the floor three times before he reached the rug. He was carrying a small medicine vial and a piece of rubber tubing.

"It's only morphine," Royce said. "To make inhabiting my body more bearable. Along with other medicines, of course. We will talk more later."

"I never liked morphine that much," I said, as if this were a reasonable remark. I scanned the room, trying to figure out what to do. "Shooting coke—now, that was another matter."

"There's no one else in my circle," Royce said, "who would recognize a line from Stalin."

"I'm not in your circle."

Dabley had tied off Royce's arm above the elbow and tapped the crook for a vein. As he injected the morphine, Royce said, "Ah, the circle of life," and started to giggle. This was a terrible sound, a high, crazy giggle that hung in the air until his head dropped forward. Dabley reclined the wheelchair enough that he could tilt Royce back. He put several small pillows around his neck to steady his head. "He'll be out for about an hour," Dabley said. "He's fine. He needs these respites. When he wakes up, he'll have no more pain for several hours."

"And who the fuck are you, really?" I said. "What's your real role here?"

"Come into the kitchen," Dabley said. "My role is simple. Your brother is a great man, and I am honored to serve his plans."

In the kitchen was a gas stove, a double sink, a sideboard, and a long table surrounded by eight ladder-back chairs. Dabley lifted the lid on a skillet and pulled several hot biscuits from a toaster oven. He had already laid out two plates with silverware. There was a can of Coke beside one and a glass of milk with the other. "I don't drink coffee myself," he said, "but we bought lots of Cokes."

"How many Cokes?" I said, thinking I might get some sense of how long they intended to keep me.

"A couple dozen."

"I don't plan to be here long enough to finish them."

He slid hot scrambled eggs onto the plates and invited me to sit down.

Up close, Dabley was even more remarkable-looking. The narrow face and nose, the narrow mouth with its small, white teeth, were offset by light green eyes set wide under thick black brows. "Is your whole family skinny like you?"

"The eggs are fresh," he said. "We have a chicken coop outside. I don't have any family."

"Lucky you."

We ate in silence. The eggs and biscuits were warm, and the Coke glistened with cold as I popped off the top. "I guess I really was hungry. So, Dabley, I know you don't want me here, but why?"

"Your brother's texts are studied in many quarters, and he has written much more that will be published later. And there are other things that will happen. I am happy to serve him, but he is not always reasonable."

"You mean there was too much risk with Ruby and the kids, and now with me?"

His nod was like a wince.

"But surely someone within the feds knows he's here? Surely he's being protected."

"Then you must grasp why your presence here complicates that."

"What has he been writing?"

He studied me for a second before saying, "A novel about a man who sacrifices his mixed-race children for the greater good."

I started laughing, a strangely inappropriate response, and when I glanced down at my hand, my fingers had turned into thick brown vines wrapping around the fork. I threw the fork onto the floor, but the floor began to ripple around me. When I looked back at my hand, it flicked strobe-like between itself and the vines. "Have you drugged me?"

I tried to stand up but could barely move my legs. My feet began sinking into the floor.

"You've fucking drugged me." Dabley's face was melting into orange rivulets, and when he smiled, his teeth grew large and bulky. He made a thick rumbling noise.

"It's LSD. Oh, no, how much did you give me?" but my words sounded like Dabley's as I tried to say, "He wanted you to do this, but he couldn't watch it? Fuck him."

The fibers of the Navaho rug turned spongy when I tried to crawl. The geometric patterns rose, and red threads were untangling, striping my arms with blood. The dark diamonds tried to pull me down and bury me, but now I have been hit—no, not hit, it is only the edge of his desk, my brother's, and The Narrow Man is behind me. He cracks the seal on the Absolut and hands it to me. I am on my feet, and I don't know whether I am trying to save my brother or kill him. My body won't obey me and the wheelchair won't move, but he is on the floor, my brother, his damages uncovered, the mink throw beside him. He is not conscious while I am at the fireplace pouring alcohol into the flames. The flames flash blue and run back up to my hand. I drop the bottle, but my hand blooms fire, flames licking from each finger. The sound of Dabley's gun is just a small *pop*.

15

For more than a year now, I have tried to remember what else happened that night, or even if it was the same night, because I learned later that I stayed missing for two days. A hypnotist has tried to help me, I've studied meditation, and I've taken many long walks on the Isle of Palms, but no matter how I've struggled, too much time is gone, eliminated like jump cuts in a movie. I remember crawling across the rug in front of the fire, I remember my chest ballooning with rage, I remember Royce on the floor and the flames streaking from my hand while Dabley dragged me through the doorway. The vestibule caught on my waist when I bumped over it. I will never know why Dabley saved me and went back into the bungalow, or why, when he tried to shoot me, he missed.

But here is a vivid memory I know isn't true: I am walking down a long yellow hallway with a little boy who says his name is Royce One, and that his brothers are named Royce Two, Royce Three, and Royce Four. He is showing me an underground greenhouse where castor beans are growing tall and darkly green. *Oh, he's making ricin*, I say, and the boy says, *Yes, it's magic.*

•

When I awoke, I was in a hospital and my wrists were tied down. My right hand was wrapped loosely in gauze, and Ed Blake and Wally Furman stared down at me. "You're okay," Blake said. "You've had another stroke. Your hand is scorched, but it's not badly damaged. Last night an old woman in a pickup truck dropped you off at a regional hospital in northwest Washington and then disappeared. We had you flown here to Albuquerque for treatment. Your car was found in a parking lot in a little town named Salvado."

I struggled to free my left wrist.

"You kept trying to pull the tube out of your mouth."

I made a scribbling motion with my fingers, and he untied my right hand.

"You should have told me about the first stroke," he said.

Wally Furman, visibly angry and unhappy, stood next to Blake. "What you did was foolhardy and dangerous," he said in his stern movie-star voice. "You put us in an awkward position. Don't you understand it wasn't just your brother I was trying to protect you from?"

"I thought you might want this," Blake said, holding a yellow pad near my hand and giving me a pen.

I wrote, in clumsy block letters, *RICIN. EXTERMINATE THE BRUTE.*

"Your brother is already dead," Blake said. "They've found his remains in northern Washington in another fire. A second male body too. A terrorist action of some type was in the works, but it's been shut down. Or we think it has. Explosives and guns and survival gear were found in a bomb shelter nearby, but they might be part of a larger enterprise. There's a widespread search going on. Ellen, were you in that fire? Did you see your brother? What happened?"

I wrote, *I DON'T KNOW.*

After the tube was removed from my throat, Blake and Wally kept attempting to debrief me, but I pretended that my speech and thinking and memory were too damaged to reply. Whenever they tried to hand me notepads, I just shook my head.

After another few days, I was transferred to a rehabilitation center in Santa Fe. Unable to read or to attend AA meetings, I listened each night to tapes of the stories in the Big Book, these tales of redemption, because I was looking for hope. My mind had cleared enough to know I was responsible for my brother's death.

When Sister Irene first appeared at my bedside, I said slowly and thickly, "Can you help me?"

Sister Irene's gaze was untroubled. I could not grasp how she had moved past Ruby's death and the loss of her childhood Bible so easily. "I think so."

I did not tell her any of what I remembered. All I said was, "Your eyes aren't enough."

She picked up my hand, and a calm energy ran from her palm into me. "Everything is all right, Ellen. Everything is profoundly all right."

I shook my head and pulled my arm away.

"You are forgiven. For whatever it is you did, or think you did."

"And my brother?"

She hesitated. "Some people think repentance is necessary."

The second time Sister Irene appeared by my bed, I had been asleep. When I opened my eyes, two people were sitting beside me. One was a tiny African American woman wearing the dark blue shirt and trousers that the trusties at the prison wore. She was nearly bald, but wisps of crinkly gray hair clung to her scalp. Her eyes were covered with a white film. Although she looked blind, she was staring right into me.

Sister Irene was dressed in her dowdy habit, but her hair had been gelled straight up, and she held up a foot to display a red shoe decorated with rhinestones. "I keep these in the car," she said. "This is Lila Ames, Ellen. I've told you some things about her. She talked with Ruby a number of times, and she knows your story as well. She's my real confessor, my confidante. Do you remember how I told you she had moved to New York from Georgia when she was still in her teens? That she grew up on one of the Sea Islands where they still speak Gullah? She insisted on coming to see you today. I think she is too weak to be going anywhere in a car, but she is very stubborn."

Lila Ames leaned forward and said, "Mus tek cyear a de root fa heal de tree." This was an expression I knew: *You must take care of the root to heal the tree.*

"Please don't do this," I said.

But Lila Ames began to speak a torrent of Gullah, and she punctuated the rising and falling, the cadence of what she was saying with *uh-huh, uh-huh,* while tapping her leg lightly. Then she began to sing, or maybe she was praying, slapping both of her knees lightly in rhythm. "Heah I be, lawd, heah I be, heah I be, lawd," while Sister Irene hummed harmony.

Here I be, lord.

My hand healed nicely, but the stroke left me with a permanent limp. My speech improved although I continued to speak very slowly, which was a relief. When I had recovered sufficiently to leave the rehab center for an afternoon, I took a taxi to a town named Socorro, to the Bratton Skydiving Center. Socorro did not appear to have a reason for existing. I saw no industry, only a small school, a diner, a post office, and a main street that was mostly boarded up. The only new building was a highway patrol station. All signs leading to the airport were handmade, and when I reached the center, I realized that the town's main business might be skydiving. There were two small Cessnas and one larger plane for group jumps, but it was midday on a Monday, and the only people at the center were a pilot and an instructor. I tried not to limp or stand awkwardly, but I don't think they would have cared since I would be strapped to the front of the instructor like a baby.

Later I tried to tell Sister Irene.

After the jumpmaster and I rolled out of the plane's door, after I finally achieved terminal velocity, the air turned cold and hard and thundering. We fell facedown, arched belly-first toward the earth, and again I saw the reddish sandstones of my dreams. The red deserts and mesas of New Mexico had probably been the source of my visions. My unconscious was once again demonstrating its brilliant sense of humor.

"What's so funny?" shouted the jumpmaster, to whom I was securely fastened.

I might have shouted back, "In my most transcendent moments, did I have visions of the end of time, or did I merely retrieve a picture of a desert I had seen as a child, an image that touched me deeply and later reemerged as revelations?" Instead I yelled, "I don't know!" Because really, who cares? The connections in my brain have always been tenuous and punny. Once, when I couldn't stop eating melons, I kept repeating, "Oh, I'm just so melancholy."

My mother stopped recognizing me soon after I returned to Charleston. She babbled a lot but remained strangely happy. I envied her. She didn't seem to mind the diaper that was now necessary, but maybe she didn't even know what it was. Convincing her to eat became increasingly difficult, even bologna sandwiches with the crusts cut off. I gave her all the medicines intended to help her appetite and mind, but nothing halted her body's ruthless clock, which caused her to shrink and wither. I began to see the bones in her face. After a while I stopped staying at her condo because she required nurses and aides twenty-four hours a day, and the spare bedroom was needed. Most nights, though, I still drove across the Cooper River Bridge to visit her, so we could watch *Wheel of Fortune* together.

CODA

Where any story begins is arbitrary, threads pulled and worried till a mat of events untangles (or does not), but the end of any story is fixed: and then he died, and then she died, and then they all died.

My own death will come in Greece, on the island of Naxos, where, in the waters on the west side, I have discovered a sunken ruin. This will happen in the summer of 2001, two months before the World Trade Center falls from the sky. My German shepherd rescue dog—I've named her Sweetie—will stay with Estelle while I rent a cottage on Naxos for the month of July. Each day on Naxos, I put on fins and a mask and stumble across a rocky beach to stare down in wonderment at an expanse of paving stones fitted tightly together more than two thousand years ago. The sea is scattered with ruins like this—shoes and ships and sealing wax—but this lost pavement, this fragment of what was once a town square, enthralls me.

I discovered Naxos near the end of my relationship with Meg. When we first arrived on the ferry, the sight of the enormous stone lintel set atop tall marble columns at the entrance to the harbor transfixed my attention. The building it would have belonged to was never completed, so all that remained was an empty frame. After Meg left me, I kept returning to Naxos because the sight of the empty frame comforted me.

I don't know whether individual stories can still matter, but I do know that if Ruby had not appeared on television claiming that her children had been kidnapped, if I had not recognized her immediately and thrown myself headlong into her life, if I had not searched for my brother and found him, I would never have attempted to write this account. Words that matter must be fitted hard against each other like these stones, made into a surface that can hold weight and power, and the result cannot simply be an empty frame. I hope this frame is not empty. I hope the story of what happened in my family matters, because, after my death, the rise and organization of the white supremacists will continue.

I still don't know whether my brother was evil or damaged or simply a twig floating on a river of historical events. But I do know that when he was a boy he killed a man in self-defense and did not know how to inherit that violence. And neither of us knew how to inherit our white skin after the civil rights movement made that whiteness visible. In this narrative, I have tried to claim my skin in a way that disavows its supremacy, but I cannot untangle every knot or illuminate all opacities, even in my own character. I know, however, that my brother died because of my actions and that I became, like him, someone who could spend the lives of others for my beliefs.

All stories may end the same, but before this one reaches its inevitable conclusions, other important things must happen.

Claudia must publish her book, God Loves the Children of Nod, in which she attacks me fiercely for arrogance and racism. Her book will be a financial and critical success, but Claudia will end up nearly a suicide like her mother, and another treatment center and a halfway house will be necessary before she can embrace her own survival. At first, I will blame myself for the loss of her sobriety, until someone in AA gently points out that once again my ego is trying to take responsibility for someone else's choices.

My mother will shrivel and die, and I will finally come to understand that she was neither her mind or her body, because the one she inhabited for eighty years shrank and emptied itself, yet I could still feel her presence. I will bury her husk next to Lucia's, because Lucia surely needed another mother, just as she needed a father who wanted her and a country that understood her value.

Giang's restaurant will become a destination prized by food critics who appreciate the irony involved in creating superbly original fare within consciously clichéd decor. I will never eat at Giang's restaurant. I will lose touch with him *and with Santane also, but not before she writes to tell me that Ed Blake now lives in his log house with a young woman named Olivia.*

Lila Ames will die before me, and for her funeral I will send Sister Irene a blue silk cloth embroidered with rhinestones to drape across her body. Afterward, my connection to Sister Irene will fade quickly too. I've always been a person who knows how to leave.

I will refuse to speak again with Blake or with any government representative, and, when I am forced to be deposed about the fire that killed my brother, I play dumb, a pose that becomes easier and easier.

I still attend AA meetings almost daily, and since I say so little, people begin to assume I am wise. I sponsor a number of women, but this sponsorship consists mostly of offering phrases like "Go to meetings," "Work the Steps," and "Pray, even if you don't understand what it is." People in the program seem to have trouble breaking away from my gaze. "It's your kindness," they say, or, "It's your eyes."

Sweetie will take daily walks with me on the beach, each of us favoring a damaged leg. Sweetie will never be leashed or confined like Ruby and Lila Ames, so the Isle of Palms Animal Control officers will return her and write out their tickets without much comment. Perhaps they have decided I am wise too. Or simply crazy.

Estelle and Dan Peters will marry, and they will found a clinic on Johns Island named for her family, the Manigault Center for Health and Prosperity. Estelle, past ordinary childbearing age, will, with the miracle of hormones, conceive twins who are born perfect, a boy and girl, a jackpot.

The night the millennium changes and the computerized world does not implode I will spend with Dan and Estelle and their families and friends. Estelle is not yet pregnant, but she is rambunctiously happy. There will be more than a hundred guests, many of them children, at the family's compound on Johns Island, and we will eat fried chicken and biscuits and grits, and there will be roasted oysters and even a barbecued pig that required some twenty hours of tending and swabbing with a mop soaked in Tabasco sauce. When night falls, giant speakers will blast Chuck Berry and Tina Turner into the yard, and I will discover that all South Carolinians, black or white, like the wicked dance we call the shag. After midnight, we cheer that the millennium has ended without dreadful incidents to mark it, and we will share many hugs and awkward kisses. Estelle offers me the opportunity to spend the night in her blue room, a cabin just large enough to contain a double bed, an armchair, and a desk. She lights a kerosene lamp and leaves me there, surrounded by indigo walls and a pale blue floor and ceiling. Even the window shades are blue. "I've never let anyone else sleep in here but Dan," she says. I doubt she ever tells Dan that we were once more intimate friends.

Not long after the New Millennium party, I will begin to pretend that I can't speak at all, and I will converse only with my dog, whose name I sometimes forget, and for the next year and a half I will live quietly in my hexagonal house on the Isle of Palms as I write out this account. I do not remodel my house, and I forget entirely about the alarm system, because I am no longer angry or afraid. I am, in fact, oddly happy, serene, at peace, which seems like God's final joke.

In the summer of 2001, I will return to Naxos, where I will be floating in salty water when the third stroke comes, staring down at the tightly fitted stones, and I will drift for several hours before anyone discovers I am gone.

ACKNOWLEDGMENTS

So many people have helped me focus and refocus (and refocus) this novel through its many drafts that I am afraid of forgetting someone, so please forgive me if I have. First, my colleagues at Connecticut College, Julie Rivkin, Liz Reich, James Downs, Candace Howes, Stuart Vyse, Suzuko Knott, Steven Shoemaker, Claudia Highbaugh, and John Gordon have all offered me crucial feedback, criticisms, and much-needed encouragement. Writer Sharon Thompson has been amazingly patient and generous, as was my former editor at *The Village Voice*, the inimitable M Mark, under whose mentorship I first found my authentic voice. My dear friend Elyse Cherry read every iteration, and seemingly able to hold them all in her head, talked with me for hours as I tried to work through the meaning of what I was writing. The dazzling young writer (and my former student) Jessica Soffer exchanged manuscripts with me, and we critiqued and supported each other as much as we could. Several other fine novelists—William Lychack, Harlan Greene, and Jesse Kornbluth—offered me detailed responses to ragged earlier versions, playwright Meryl Cohn spent endless hours on the phone with me discussing characters and actions, and Shannon Keating, Emily Becker, and Nat Rivkin—three more of my many distinguished former students—also have helped me a great deal. My previous editor Gary Fisketjon enabled me to see what was not yet working in several drafts, and over the last dozen years many students have sat through readings of various scenes and fragments. I am grateful to you all. My agent, Malaga Baldi, has been—and continues to be—a wonderful support, and it was she who led to me to my brilliant editor Dan Smetanka at Counterpoint, the first person who has ever actually convinced me to change a scene. And, of course, I am grateful to my family. First a shout-out to my mother-in-law, Sandra Hyman, whom I cherish more than she may know, and to my brother, Charlie McCrary, a very nice guy, who is being a good sport since he's nothing like the brother in this novel. But most importantly, let me try to express what feels unspeakable: my abiding love and appreciation for my wife Leslie Hyman, and for our twins, Julia and James Hyman. I could not have lived into this century without you.

BLANCHE McCRARY BOYD has taught at Connecticut College since 1982. She has written four novels—*Terminal Velocity*, *The Revolution of Little Girls*, *Mourning the Death of Magic*, and *Nerves*—as well as a collection of essays, *The Redneck Way of Knowledge*. Among the awards Boyd has won are a Guggenheim Fellowship, a National Endowment for the Arts Fiction Fellowship, a Creative Writing Fellowship from the South Carolina Arts Commission, and a Wallace Stegner Fellowship in Creative Writing from Stanford University.

4-11-19
978-19-11-4-21
7   8 (CM)